The Murder Mystery Book Club

C.A. Larmer is a journalist, editor, teacher and author of four crime series, two stand-alone novels, and a non-fiction book about pioneering surveyors in Papua New Guinea. Christina grew up in that country, was educated in Australia, and spent many years working in London, Los Angeles and New York. She now lives with her musician husband, two sons and their cheeky Bluey on the east coast of Australia.

Sign up for news, views and giveaways:
calarmer.com

ALSO BY C.A. LARMER

The Murder Mystery Book Club series:
Danger on the SS Orient (Book 2)
Death Under the Stars (Book 3)
When There Were 9 (Book 4)
The Widow on the Honeymoon Cruise (Book 5)
Gone Guest (Book 6)
Peril on the Indian Pacific (Book 7)
The Mysterious Affair at Styled Magazine (Book 8)

The Ghostwriter Mystery series:
Killer Twist (Book 1)
A Plot to Die For (Book 2)
Last Writes (Book 3)
Dying Words (Book 4)
Words Can Kill (Book 5)
A Note Before Dying (Book 6)
Without a Word (Book 7)

The Posthumous Mystery series:
Do Not Go Gentle
Do Not Go Alone

The Sleuths of Last Resort:
Blind Men Don't Dial Zero (Book 1)
Smart Girls Don't Trust Strangers (Book 2)
Good Girls Don't Drink Vodka (Book 3)

PLUS:
After the Ferry: A Gripping Psychological Novel

An Island Lost

C.A. LARMER

The
Murder Mystery
Book Club

(Book 1)

LARMER MEDIA

Published by Larmer Media
Northern NSW, Australia
calarmer.com
Edited by Annie at The Editing Pen
& Elaine Rivers (with thanks)
Cover design by Stu Eadie & Nimo Pyle

ISBN: 978-0-6488009-9-6

For Agatha Christie fans,
everywhere

A NOTE FROM THE AUTHOR

This book was originally published under the title *The Agatha Christie Book Club*. To avoid confusion and broaden future storylines, I have now renamed the entire series.

The content, however, remains largely unchanged, so too my beloved characters and twist-laden plot.

Happy sleuthing, fellow mystery lovers…

PART 1

Everything was ready. The table was set, the flowers arranged, the English Breakfast tea was brewing in a delicate china teapot and there was a plate of cucumber and crème fraîche sandwiches beside it (crusts cut off, of course). It was the perfect backdrop for the inaugural meeting of the Murder Mystery Book Club.

And it was the perfect place to set a murder in motion.

As the seven members of the new book club nursed cups of tea and waved around battered copies of the first book selection, *Evil Under the Sun*, one member was scrutinising the group. This person didn't really care about the story, didn't give a jot about *whodunits* if truth be told, had just feigned interest to gain entry to this club, and to get the devious plan rolling.

And it *was* a good plan. There was no point in false modesty now. It had taken a lot of time and a lot of effort, but it would all be worth it in the end. If it worked—*and how could it not?*—it had the potential to destroy one life, wreak havoc on another, and leave this bunch of pretenders for dead.

They would never know what hit them.

The book club member sniggered. Hell, even the great Agatha Christie would be left scratching her head…

PART 2 CHAPTER 1

Three weeks earlier …

Alicia Finlay was in the wrong book club.

She hadn't realised it at first. Had come along, faithfully, every month for three months, the latest Pulitzer Prize-winning novel wedged under her arm, a strained smile on her lips, and pretended to be having fun. But there was no fun to be had. Finally, on the fourth Monday night, it dawned on her.

You could blame the bottle of red.

Alicia had been sitting quietly enough, half listening to a monologue about the central themes of this novel—something to do with British Imperialism and 'inevitability', apparently—when a 2007 Margaret River Cabernet Sauvignon caught her eye. It looked delicious. So, too, did the plate of hors d'oeuvres that had been placed, along with the bottle and eight crystal wine glasses, just out of reach on a side table. Alicia spotted miniature crepes topped with salmon and goats cheese; asparagus sticks rolled in thin slices of prosciutto; and something that looked vaguely like pâté.

But she knew how these things went. It would all have to wait until the serious chatter was over. Alicia glanced furtively at her watch. Forty minutes to go. Her mouth salivated and she turned to the man on her right but he was deeply engrossed in something the woman to her left was saying.

"The glass church is, I think, a potent symbol of Oscar's vanity and, er, the vulnerability of his misguided belief system," the woman, Verity, a jittery, primary school teacher, explained. "It's, well, you know… both strong and fragile at the same time. Don't you agree, Alicia?"

Alicia darted her eyes from the side table where they'd strayed again to the grey haired woman talking and smiled awkwardly.

"Oh, um, I…" She paused. Chuckled a little. "Actually, sorry, I wasn't really paying attention. Thought I might help myself to a glass of red."

"Red?"

"You know, red wine." She stood up. "Does anyone else want me to get them a glass while we're chatting? Something to eat?"

The book club's hostess, Kirsten, sat forward with a start. As always, she was immaculately dressed, this time in a beige cotton top, black linen pants and chunky red, resin beads that looked like they'd been plucked straight out of an up-market magazine fashion spread. Her black hair had been yanked into a stiff straight bob around her neck, no doubt in line with the current fashion but, coupled with sharp cheekbones and porcelain skin, left her looking a little like a witch. All that was missing was the pointy hat.

"Ahh, sorry, Alicia," said Kirsten, "but it's not really time for wine, we're still in discussion mode." She tapped her thin, gold wristwatch twice.

"Oh," said Alicia, dropping back into her seat. "We can't discuss and drink at the same time?"

Kirsten smiled politely, exchanged glances with another club member—they had exchanged that kind of glance before—and shook her head, no. Her black bob did not budge.

"Why not?" Alicia persisted, and Kirsten looked slightly taken aback.

"It's just not what we do… *here*." She fumbled for her sheet of questions. "Okay then, if we can return to the subject at hand. Where were we exactly? I think we were up to question four? Yes, style of writing. Have you got anything to say about that, Wilfred?"

She stared pointedly at a large man with a shaggy beard and gold-rimmed glasses who was slouched in an armchair across from Alicia. He pushed the glasses back into position and then slid one hand down to his beard and began caressing it lovingly. He'd been waiting for this.

"Right. Well, I have to say I've never been a big fan of Carey. I think he tries very hard but I'm not quite sure he's pulling it off. His writing, well, it leaves a lot to be desired don't you think?"

A few murmurs of consensus broke out around the lounge room where the meeting was being held and, encouraged, he launched into his trademark sermon on the fallibilities of the modern author. There wasn't a decent writer left in the world, apparently; not since Hemingway and Salinger had a good book been published. Alicia couldn't help wondering what a microbiologist would know about that but pushed the thought away and let out a long, soft sigh instead.

Why hadn't she noticed it earlier? Why had it taken four sessions and a forbidden bottle of wine to make her see what was probably blatantly obvious to everyone else in the room from day one?

She just didn't fit in here.

The truth is, Alicia Finlay couldn't care less about literature. She just *wished* she did, the same way a woman who guiltily watches soap operas on TV wishes she could find the strength to switch over to that really important current affairs program on the public broadcaster. She just didn't care enough.

Alicia's mind wandered now to her own bookshelf in the cluttered, semi-detached terrace house she shared with her sister, Lynette, and their black Labrador, Max. The shelf was huge, took up an entire wall and tipped ever so precariously to the right. It was bursting with well-thumbed paperbacks, mostly crime novels, and mostly by traditional British authors. Alicia smiled. What really woke her up in the morning and saw her drift off to sleep at night was an old-fashioned *whodunit*. And if it happened to be penned by the likes of Agatha Christie or P.D. James, all the better.

She suppressed a giggle. Imagine if she suggested *Murder on the Orient Express* for the next book club. Wilfred would have a fit. Kirsten would choke on her chamomile tea. And I'd be in book heaven, she thought.

That's it. Enough's enough.

Alicia stood up. She walked across to the side table. She picked up the bottle of red and poured herself half a glass. As she did so, the room fell silent behind her and she could feel their eyes boring into her back. She wondered if Kirsten would tackle her to the ground and wrench the glass out of her hands screaming, "But it's not drink time yet!"

She turned around slowly and tried for her bravest smile. Kirsten's eyes were abnormally wide. Verity looked nervous, glancing between Alicia and Kirsten. And Wilfred had stopped stroking his beard.

"What are you doing, Alicia?" Kirsten asked.

"Just helping myself, before I head off," she replied.

She finished the drink in one large gulp, placed the glass down and reached for her handbag.

"But... but where are you going?"

Alicia took a deep breath. "Look, I'm really sorry, guys, I gave it a go, but this club is clearly not right for me."

They all looked stunned, as if it hadn't even dawned on them, and Alicia realised then that it probably hadn't. They were so self-absorbed they hadn't noticed the elephant in the room. A wistful look crossed Verity's face and for a moment Alicia thought she might leap to her feet and follow her out.

"But… but what about your book?" Kirsten demanded, grabbing Alicia's pristine copy of *Oscar and Lucinda* from the antique coffee table and thrusting it towards her.

"Oh, no thanks, Kirsten, you're welcome to it. I've got much better things to read at home."

And with that Alicia Finlay walked out on the Monday Night Book Club, their suffocating rules and their tediously dull literature, and she returned to her inner city home where her sister was just starting work on a crispy duck stir-fry, her dog was wagging his tail maniacally, and her latest crime novel, a well-thumbed copy of Ann Cleeves's first Vera mystery was waiting, temptingly, by her bedside.

CHAPTER 2

"You should start a book club," Lynette announced between mouthfuls of dripping duck and broccoli.

Alicia scoffed and Max pricked up his ears hoping the conversation had something to do with food and his mouth.

"Um, I don't think you've been listening to me, Lynny, I *hated* the book club. I'm never going back. Why would I subject myself to a whole new one? It's masochistic."

"No, not that kind of book club, silly. Start your own. One totally devoted to what you like."

"Well, that would be crime fiction and last time I looked, you don't have book clubs about that."

She scooped a chunk of duck from her bowl and dropped it into Max's waiting mouth. He slunk back under the table, satisfied.

Lynette frowned at her but let it pass. "Why not?" she said instead.

Alicia sat back and stared at her sister. Of the two, Lynette had always been the fearless one, ready to dive head first into life, never considering the consequences or looking back. Alicia, on the other hand, over-thought everything.

In fact, her imagination was so ripe it would often throw in an axe-wielding psychopath and a tsunami for good measure.

It surprised no one, therefore, when Alicia chose to study journalism at university with a major in creative writing. Now 30 and a magazine editor, she was four years older than her sister but a good deal shorter with shaggy blond hair, a petite build and wide, brown eyes. Like her imagination, her job was all-consuming and she was almost always late home from work, especially during deadlines when she could be found at her desk, slumped over copy until the wee hours of the morning.

Lynette, on the other hand, was usually home well before dark, her long legs tucked under a stool at the kitchen bench, her flowing blonde locks swept up into an impromptu bun, and her emerald green eyes scanning the many cookbooks she had collected like artefacts over the years. She was a budding chef who worked most days waiting tables at Mario's restaurant on busy Oxford Street in Paddington, and most nights honing her culinary skills in their small but surprisingly well-equipped kitchen. This suited Alicia (who hated to cook) and Max (who loved to eat) just fine. Lyn's creations were usually delicious but occasionally there was a catastrophe—an overly salted broth, a too-tart dessert— that would see Lynette swearing like Gordon Ramsay and Max happily gulping down the remains. Alicia was always ready with a comforting hug and a few steely words of advice, most of which Lynette ignored.

"You could do that cooking course I spotted in the paper the other day," Alicia suggested recently but Lynette shook her head emphatically. She was Generation Y. That meant bottomless aspirations and the patience of a toddler.

"I've decided to apply for *MasterChef Australia*," she declared instead, and Alicia tried not to frown.

"The TV reality show? That's a rather roundabout way of getting into the industry. You'd have more luck knocking on restaurant doors."

"Thanks for your positive vibes, Lis'."

"Sorry, but you know how hard it is."

"Hell, if a pimply faced kid can win it, I can't see why I'm not in the running."

Alicia had let it drop. Looking through to the kitchen now at the smudged cookbooks and endless scraps of paper with her sister's latest creations scribbled down, she wondered if Lynette would ever crack the big time. Or was she destined to a lifetime of experimenting on her grateful family?

She shrugged the thought away and considered Lyn's question. She was right, of course. *Why couldn't you start a book club devoted to crime?*

"Seems to me," Lynette continued, "that plenty of other people love crime fiction, too. You're hardly alone."

"Hell, more people read crime fiction than snooty prize-winning tomes of trite. Just look at the *Millennium* trilogy or *Gone Girl.*"

"Exactly. So, it won't be hard to get a group together. Just ask around. Or get on Twitter. You'll be inundated. But if you're not, I'm happy to plump up the numbers. I've always had a soft spot for Miss Marple, you know that."

In fact both sisters had been Agatha Christie devotees since childhood, a legacy passed down from their mother, Amelia, who possessed almost every book in existence and read and re-read them regularly. Their father, Tom, and brother, Monty (named after Agatha's own brother no less), were less enamoured of the Queen of Crime and preferred a modern thriller complete with rogue CIA agents and at least one missing nuclear bomb.

Alicia put her fork down. She could hear her heart beating suddenly, as though it had only just come to life.

"I'm not sure how it'd work," continued Lynette but Alicia was way ahead of her now.

"I know how it'd work. Oh, it'd be great. We'd all choose our favourite crime novel and focus on a different one each month... no, fortnight. They don't take long to read, why wait a whole month? I'd start with *Evil Under the Sun* and then…" She stopped, darted her eyes from left to right. "No, no, forget that. We could all choose our favourite crime *author*, and focus on that author's books for a few months, then switch to a new one. Sort of like a degustation of their work. Obviously, I would choose Agatha Christie, but we could call it the Murder Mystery Book Club."

Lynette looked impressed. "And I would select Ann Cleeves. How are you enjoying *The Crow Trap* by the way?"

"Loving it," said Alicia. "Vera's like a British version of Columbo, or a modern-day Miss Marple. And I *love* this idea of yours, too. I think it's the best you ever had."

"I thought my duck creation—I'm calling it Lucky Duck by the way—was the best idea I ever had."

"Nah, that comes a distant second. Good name by the way."

Alicia began to contemplate the club and her heartbeat continued to accelerate. She hadn't been so excited by anything in such a long time, not since Ginny, the receptionist at work, had convinced her to take over her seat at the Monday Night Book Club.

Her heart skipped a beat. She knew how that had turned out. She slumped over her bowl. "You really think it'll work?"

Her sister winked. "'Course it will. You just have to get the right people together this time. Set up a Facebook account or start tweeting every one you know."

"And you don't think it's a little, well, macabre?"

"What do you mean?"

Alicia shifted in her seat. "You know, devoting a book club to crime and death and that kind've stuff?"

Lynette laughed. "For you, not at all. But don't forget, Alicia, it's just make-believe. *Fiction*, remember? It's not like you're dealing with real-life murder, after all."

Alicia laughed and crunched down on a snow pea. "You're right, Lynette. It's an innocent book club, what could possibly go wrong?"

CHAPTER 3

A week later Alicia's excitement about her new club had turned to bitter disappointment. Not a soul had been in touch. Despite Lynette's digital suggestions, Alicia had decided to advertise for members the old-fashioned way, the way Agatha Christie or Dorothy L. Sayers would have done it, and placed an advertisement in the classifieds section of her local newspaper.

It read: *"Mystery lovers unite. If you want to join Sydney's inaugural Murder Mystery Book Club, send me an email listing your favourite crime writer and the reason you love them so much. To meet every second Sunday from 2pm."*

For the sake of expediency, Alicia had placed the ad online so that it could make the following day's edition, and was about to hurl it off into cyberspace when she paused, then quickly changed the word 'email' to 'letter' and added her name and home address. She paused again.

What if some crazed nutter tracked her down? What if he started stalking her? Broke into her house and rummaged through her lingerie drawer… Or worse—what if the only respondents were into nail-biting thrillers, complete with torture chambers and psycho serial killers? After all, not all mysteries were alike. Perhaps Alicia should be more selective, requesting only fans of "police procedural" and "cozy" mysteries…

Alicia had shaken the thoughts away and paid the requisite fee, but now wondered why she had bothered. She'd settle for a Harlan Coben thriller over this silence any day.

Were book clubs a relic of the past? Was there anyone outside of her family who actually sat still and read a decent crime novel anymore? Had they really all moved on to Netflix and blogs?

Finally, on the eighth day she got her answer.

It was late Friday evening after a gruelling day at work. Alicia's thoughts were far from cosy as she made the final, exhausting stretch towards her home in the low-lying former docklands area of Woolloomooloo. Tacked on to Sydney Harbour, Woolloomooloo is an eclectic suburb merging boisterous pubs and low-rent council flats with luxurious warehouse apartments and five-star restaurants frequented by celebrities and billionaires alike. Alicia lived on the low-rent side so always walked with a quick in her step.

Despite being the proud owner of a bone-coloured 1972 Holden Torana, she rarely drove to work, instead preferring to catch the bus. It was easier than stressing through the traffic, gave her a chance to catch up on her reading and, because the relevant bus stop was a good kilometre from her house, provided an excellent opportunity for some daily exercise.

This evening, however, she was not in the mood. As she walked, Alicia's mind began playing its usual tricks on her. She envisaged the van that was driving perfectly normally down the road suddenly swerve for no good reason— perhaps the driver had a heart attack or was just plain mad— then alight the footpath and take her out. She shrugged the image away and kept walking. A crunching noise caught her attention and she glanced to the side to see an elderly man placing garbage in his bin. He looked at her, smiled then looked away. What was behind that smile, she wondered? *What if he decided to creep up behind her, knock her over the head and toss her in the bin?* No one would ever know. She quickly crossed the road, and continued walking.

A few meters from her gate something in the letterbox caught Alicia's eye. She picked up her pace and threw herself upon it, screeching it open to reveal a bundle of letters clumped together with a thick, red elastic band. The top one read in smudged blue scrawl: *The Murder Mystery Book Club.*

Offering a little jubilant fist pump, Alicia thrust the bundle under one arm, foraged through her handbag for her house keys and let herself in. Max was already slouched on the sofa and didn't bother more than a pathetic tail wag to greet her home. He had clearly already been fed.

"Hello to you, too, Maxy," Alicia called out to him and then strode through to the kitchen where, sure enough, Lynette was hard at it.

"Prawn and vermicelli salad in a chilli ginger sauce," Lynette announced, holding up a half-shelled crustacean.

Alicia held up her own bounty: "A bunch of letters, all addressed to The Murder Mystery Book Club."

Lynette whooped with delight. "Okay then, you win. What do they say?"

"Dunno, haven't opened them yet. You didn't notice them in the letterbox on your way in?"

"Letterbox?"

"You know, rusty white thing on one side of the gate. Designed to put written correspondence in."

"Oh, is that what that thing's for?" Lynette smiled. "Come on, then, crack 'em open, let's see what you've got."

"No, no, I need a glass of something for this."

She crossed to the cupboard, pulled out two red and gold Moroccan tumblers and reached for the bottle of merlot beside the microwave. Lynette intercepted her.

"Back away from the red. It's seafood tonight. You need the chilled Chablis in the fridge."

"Oh, right, sure."

She placed the red back, retrieved the white from the fridge and poured them both a glass. Then she settled herself on a kitchen stool and turned her attention to the mail, wondering as she did so why her generation had been so eager to forfeit snail mail for email and texts. There could be no substitution for the sheer joy you received when spotting a genuine, thick, woody smelling envelope in the letterbox, when holding it in your hands, trying to decipher the writing, wondering who could it be from. Then turning it over, getting your first clue, ripping it open, unfolding the pages…

"Oh get on with it," Lynette said rolling her eyes as Alicia held the first letter to her nose.

She ignored her sister, grabbed a knife from a drawer and carefully sliced the crushed envelope open. Inside was a piece of lined paper that had clearly been ripped straight out of an exercise book. It was folded several times, so she straightened it out and began to read aloud:

Dear Book Clubber. Way 2 go! I luv all crime, especially if I don't get caught (lol). I'd love to crash your group. Got nothing else going on right now and the last group I belonged to kicked me out (fwits)! Can't do Sundays but anytime during the week works for me. Just after midday. Do we BYO or you gonna supply?

Taneal

PS: Got an email address?

Alicia dropped the letter on the bench and stared at her sister, stunned, before they both burst into laughter.

"Not the most promising start," Alicia said.

She took a large swig of her wine, pulled out the next letter and studied it. The handwriting seemed normal enough and was done with a neat, black ink, but she hesitated before reading it quickly to herself.

Hello. I'd love to join your group. My all time favourite author is Jane Austen. That Darcy, eh? Most smouldering hero ever!

The letter then launched into a long essay on the sexual tension between Darcy and Elizabeth, and was eventually signed Jane (not Miss Bennett) Zantilopous.

Alicia groaned, then scrunched it up and threw it across the kitchen.

"Not another loser, surely?" Lynette said, looking up from the sink.

"Don't ask," Alicia replied, reluctantly returning to the pile.

The next few letters were fans of modern crime writers like Lee Child and James Patterson, and managed to get most of their facts straight. But they were lacking in genuine passion and Alicia's own passion was beginning to wane, until she pulled out the fifth and final letter.

This one brought the smile back to her lips.

It was written in an elegant hand, the envelope decorated with bluebells and the sweet scent of freesia emanating from inside. She unfolded the crisp paper, also adorned with bluebells, crossed her fingers and began to read aloud:

Dear Alicia,

You cannot imagine my delight at seeing your advertisement yesterday. A Murder Mystery Book Club! All my dreams have come true. I adore all things mystery but especially Agatha Christie, and if pressed I'd have to say Evil Under the Sun *is my favourite. The suspense! The drama! The red herrings! I think she could teach some modern writers a thing or two. I especially love the lack of gore and the glamorous frocks.*

Would love to find out more about your club. I run a vintage clothing store on Victoria Street so feel free to drop in and say hello. Otherwise my details are enclosed.

Thanking you in advance (and high anticipation),

Claire Hargreaves

PS: Sunday afternoons work beautifully for me. High tea anyone?

Alicia beamed from ear to ear. "She's perfect," she said. "Just perfect. Now we just need five more…"

CHAPTER 4

By the following Thursday, Alicia had received 16 letters—some hilarious, some slightly nutty, and some just plain boring. But there were four that held real promise. Apart from the vintage clothing storekeeper Claire, there was an intriguing letter from a doctor who confessed to enjoying any crime writers who utilised poisons in their books.

"I have a little knowledge on the subject myself," he wrote, "so am always ready to catch authors out on the facts, although one author never gets it wrong—Ms Christie. My favourite book, then, has to be *Sparkling Cyanide*. Surely this poison has become synonymous with Christie herself?"

It was signed Dr Anders Bright and went straight to the Yes pile.

The third letter was stranger still but in a very different way. It was from a woman called Barbara Parlour, a self-proclaimed "boring, middle-aged housewife" who wrote that murder mysteries kept her sane during "life's many sad and tragic moments".

What sad and tragic moments? Alicia wondered, wanting to know more. Lynette was less convinced.

"She sounds a bit pathetic to me," she said. "Is she going to sob the whole time?"

"Sounds like she needs a lift, that's all. The club could be good for her."

"But would she be good for the club? It's not a suicide prevention centre."

"Now you're being melodramatic, Lynette, the woman is probably just talking generally."

"Hey, she started it, not me."

In the end, Alicia found Barbara's words too intriguing to ignore and added her to the yes pile. She wanted to know more about this sad woman who clearly turned to Agatha Christie for respite.

The final letter was actually a black and white postcard with the silhouette of a hangman's noose on the front. On the back, incredibly neat handwriting declared:

Agatha is the Queen of Crime. I am the Queen of Surry Hills— not quite as famous, I know, but equally as enthralling I can assure you. Give me any book featuring Hercule Poirot, and I will show you crime perfection. Call me. Pretty please. Perry. xo

Alicia laughed out loud. This guy sounded like fun and the antithesis of Barbara. It would be an interesting mix. She ticked him off and then went through her list one more time. There were now six potential members, including Lynette and herself. Granted, they were almost all exclusively fans of Agatha Christie, but that made it all the better as far as Alicia was concerned. And it was certainly enough to kick- start the club, so she sat down that night after dinner and compiled each one a brief, hand-written reply on her finest stationery. In each letter she thanked them for their interest and suggested they come along to an afternoon tea at her place the following Sunday to discuss how the club would work.

She had already decided on a few loose rules and placed a copy of these in each envelope. While she had hated the rigidity of the Monday Night Book Club, she wasn't so naïve as to think that a few basic parameters weren't necessary to make the group run smoothly. Without them, it only took one domineering character to start steering the club in the direction they chose. There would be no bossy Kirsten-types in this group.

Alicia read over the club guidelines and smiled:

#1: A maximum of eight members, male or female, all ages welcome. All have to be fans of murder mysteries. (Any more than eight, Alicia thought, and no one would get a word in.)

#2: Due to the obvious bias of the members, we will kick-start the club with a focus on Agatha Christie first. Each member will take turns choosing the Christie mystery to be read and hosting the event. (Never simultaneously. That would be too much like hard work.)

#3: The person who chooses the book should prepare questions or a few loose talking points to encourage discussion. They can choose their favourite AC or simply one they'd like to explore further.

#4: The person hosting the event will hold it at their house or a venue of their choosing, and is responsible for the refreshments. Members can bring their own drinks if they like. (Alcohol welcome!)

#5: Members of the club may eat and drink whenever they like during the discussion. No restrictions.

#6: Have fun! (And lots of it, she thought, reading over the guidelines one final time with a shiver of delight.)

The following morning, Alicia dropped the letters into the post-box on her corner then made a beeline to her nearest library. She knew this detour would mean getting into work late, but she couldn't help herself. While the Finlay sisters had a pretty good collection of Christie's books at home, there were plenty missing and Alicia wanted to see what treats the library held for future reference.

Alicia's local library was a grand old building with the elegant columns and intricate stonework of the early 1900s, yet updated with modern conveniences like automatic doors, air-conditioning and a rather complicated after-hours book-return chute on an external wall that required you to scan your library card in first, leaving most elderly patrons flustered. The library was just a few blocks from the house and while Lynette found the place antiquated, constantly arguing the case for eBooks, iPads and Amazon, Alicia cherished it. Nothing, she decided, would ever replace the old-fashioned paperback.

Despite this, she still wandered in feeling guilty. It had been many months since she'd found time to explore the library's hallowed halls and seemingly bottomless book collection. A little overwhelmed now, she headed straight for the front desk where a short, plump woman in her mid-20s with luridly bright copper hair into which black and white zebra printed spectacles had been wedged turned to greet her.

"Hello! Were you after something, possum?"

Alicia placed her handbag on the desk. "Yes, I want to look up everything you have on Agatha Christie."

The librarian giggled. "Got a month? We have a *huge* selection. She wrote more than 60 detective novels alone, but then you probably know that if you're a fan. Was there anything specific you were after?"

"I just want to see what you've got that I haven't read."

"Next question, then, darls, are you into her crime novels exclusively or open to other material? She wrote other fiction, too, you know, under the pen name Mary Westmacott? Most people don't know that. It's kind of romance, I suppose you could call it, and was reviewed better than her crime back in the old days. Her plays were also well received. Still nothing's ever sold as well as her *whodunits*." She paused, blinked, scrunched up her lips. "Or maybe you were after general reference? There's Agatha's autobiography, of course, a total gem, although not quite as revealing as Thompson's biography on the author. Biographies are often more interesting, aren't they? Probably because you can say stuff in there the author doesn't want you to know. Ha! We *love* those juicy details. Now that's a mammoth book but, oh, such a top read, simply riveting."

She paused again so Alicia quickly said, "All of it I guess."

The librarian giggled and pulled her glasses down onto her nose. "Fabulous. Follow me."

Shoving some books to one side, she opened a small trapdoor and squeezed out of it into the main room. She was wearing a bright, floral dress with a full skirt and a purple waistband, and on her feet were matching purple slippers with spangly silver beads. She dashed away, across the room to a section at the front filled with hanging newspapers and glossy magazines on one side, and oversized reference books on the other.

"Now, for general reference, this is *the* place to be. Just go to the 'biography' section and look up 'C'."

She waved one arm along a row of books, then turned abruptly and headed back across the room to the fiction section, Alicia close behind. She stopped at the letter C and tapped short black nails across the spines.

"We don't have every single Christie novel, obviously. And, of course, many of the ones we do have are out—which is to be expected, she's one of our most popular reads but then I don't have to tell *you* that."

She giggled again, her red curly hair flopping about her face as she did so. She brushed it away, pushed her glasses back into position and turned back to the shelves.

"You'll find lots to keep you entertained here, possum. To look up her romance, just make your way to 'W', it's right down the end."

"Thanks so much," Alicia said as the librarian waddled back to her desk.

As she began scanning the titles, Alicia had a thought. She stopped, turned back, and called out to the librarian, "Hey, just wondering—how do you feel about book clubs?"

The librarian turned around with a wide, girlish grin.

~~~~~~~~

Three days later, in a very different part of town, someone was reading through Alicia's rules carefully, thrilled to be accepted and prickling with excitement, too.

It had been so easy. Alicia had fallen for the pretence, and the other book club members would, too. Now the first step was in place.

Just two more steps to the ultimate revenge.
~~~~~~~~

CHAPTER 5

Sunday morning dawned bright and clear and, determined to get the club off to a good start, Alicia rose early, dressed in some old jeans and a T-shirt, and devoured some cereal quickly before pulling out the vacuum cleaner and giving the house a good going over. She wanted everything to be perfect.

As Lynette prepared cucumber and crème fraîche sandwiches and a batch of fresh scones with homemade strawberry jam and whipped cream, Alicia wiped down their rustic wooden dining table and covered it in a fresh checked tablecloth. Next, she pulled the dining chairs—all mismatched and brightly painted in blues and reds and yellows—to the side so the group could have easy access to Lynette's delicious spread, but the main action would happen in the adjoining living area and that's where she turned her attention now.

Their lounge room was what you'd call 'cosy bohemian', an accidental mishmash of colours, textures and styles. A battered chocolate-brown leather armchair, Alicia's favourite, sat in one corner with a lavender mohair throw across it, and a brown and white floral cushion wedged into the side. In the centre of the room was a deep-blue, three-seater sofa, bright cushions at random intervals and, in front of it, a metallic-blue sea chest that served as coffee table/foot rest/dumping ground for every magazine, book, journal, coffee cup and gadget they had used in the past week.

Scowling at it now, she began sorting through the debris, finding each object its proper home so there would be plenty of space for the guests to dump their own debris later that day. In the other corner of the room was a second armchair, this one recently upholstered in a rich, cerise cotton that might have looked gaudy in any other setting, but worked well to brighten this large dark space. On it, she placed a toffee-brown cushion, the same colour as the shaggy rug on the floor, and switched on the tall lamp behind the leather chair so the room was bathed in an amber glow.

Alicia even went to the trouble of straightening out the old wooden bookcase, dusting the shelves and rearranging the titles. Despite their passion for crime, the sisters read many other genres and she was careful to place biographies together on one shelf, classics on another, and, yes, even the occasional award-winning tome on the highest shelf, the one least likely to be used. She also took some time to select the background music. It couldn't be too lively or it would distract from the discussion, but she didn't want to send them into a coma, either. Eventually she settled on Nina Simone and pressed 'Play' as she dashed upstairs to change into tailored pants, a fresh white T-shirt and ballet slippers. She dabbed on a little lip-gloss and mascara, pulled on some hoop earrings and a dangly silver necklace, and was just returning downstairs when the doorbell rang.

Max barked furiously and Alicia glanced at the wooden clock at the top of the bookshelf then grabbed the dog and pulled him to the tiny outside terrace. The look of dejection that crossed his face was heart wrenching but he would have to remain there for now; she didn't want to scare off club members before they'd signed up. Then, inspecting her reflection quickly again in the hallway mirror, taming her shaggy hair with one hand, removing a stray spec of lip-gloss with the other, she opened the door.

Dr Anders Bright stood there with a meek smile on his face. He felt like a goofball, had almost not come, but he knew he had to go through with this if he was ever going to move on. The Murder Mystery Book Club would be the answer to all his problems, he was sure of it. For some reason, though, he wasn't expecting the Alicia woman to be quite so young, and quite so attractive, and what little confidence he had managed to cling on to evaporated immediately, along with his ability to talk. He gulped hard. Felt like an adolescent boy suddenly.

"Dr Bright?" she said, sweeping her eyes across his denim jeans and long-sleeved blue shirt.

"Anders," was all he could manage.

"Anders, great, come on in. You're the first."

She opened the door wider and he had to lower his six-foot-two frame a little to duck through. As he followed her into the lounge room he gave himself a stern talking to.

Christ, man, you're acting like a child. You're a reputable doctor for goodness' sake, pull yourself together!

When he faced her again, his smile was a little more assured, revealing perfect white teeth that hinted at years of tortuous braces. His eyes were a warm, honey brown, his eyebrows thick and dark like his hair, which flopped down across his face, overgrown and messier than most of his medico mates. And while he was certainly thin, even a little lanky, he had surprisingly broad shoulders that also revealed a childhood spent swimming up and down a pool. He'd hated squad training but it certainly improved his physique and put an end to angst-riddled years of bullying.

"You're early," Alicia said, and he grimaced, knowing the club didn't officially start for another ten minutes.

"Sorry, it's a bad habit of mine. Can't seem to help myself."

"Not a bad habit, surely? Better than turning up late."

His wife would beg to differ, he thought, and nearly said as much before he caught himself and just smiled.

Alicia beamed back at him, thinking, 'What a lovely smile. And those shoulders. Mmm-mmm.'

She said: "Pick a seat, any seat," then watched as he strode over to her favourite armchair and dropped down into it, looking as though it's the only place he belonged. Her heart beat triple time and she hoped he couldn't hear it through her shirt.

"I'll just be a sec'," she stammered. "We're, er, just getting the food sorted."

"Pretend I'm not here."

Not bloody likely, Alicia thought as she ducked into the kitchen where Lynette was pouring boiling water into a coffee plunger. She had also found time to change and was now clad in a tiny green dress and short stiletto boots that were more 'nightclub' than 'book club', but Alicia wasn't about to say so. Lynette, like all her friends, believed that the shorter the outfit and the higher the heels, the better. Comfort could take a flying leap.

"Well?" Lynette said. "Two heads, as you expected? An escapee from the loony bin?"

"It's the doctor, Anders Bright."

"Ah, the poison expert. Old and crusty?"

She lowered her voice. "Young and crumpety, actually. Quite delicious looking. Mid-30s I'd say."

"And he's into AC? Oh well, we won't let that put us off." Lynette placed the lid on the coffee pot. "I'll go introduce myself."

Alicia's heart flagged. Dr Bright would take one look at her prettier, younger sister and that would be the end of it. It always was with men; they fell for Lynette hard. She had the blonder hair, the longer legs, the superior self-confidence. Alicia was used to it. It rarely bothered her if truth be told, but there was something about this guy, about his awkward shyness that left her intrigued. She gave herself a small shake.

It's a book club, Alicia, not a blind date.

Laughter flowed from the lounge room and she sighed, reaching for a jug of minted iced water. Just then the doorbell rang again and Max began to bark like a rabid dog.

"I'll get it," called Lynette, then, "Shut it Max!"

The next person to show up was Claire Hargreaves, the vintage clothing store-owner who was dressed exactly as you'd expect a vintage clothing store-owner to dress. Her 1940s-style red, cropped jacket had broad, padded shoulders, glossy black buttons and was cinched at the waist. Under it was a grey, pencil-thin skirt with matching grey platform pumps. Her glossy black hair had been styled into elaborate curls and pinned back behind a small black hat with a large black bow. She was wearing matte-red lipstick, lashings of mascara and, if Alicia was not mistaken, long, fake eyelashes over catlike eyes. Above them two pencilled eyebrows rose thin and perfectly plucked. She smiled brightly as she shook both sisters' hands, then the doctor's, then glanced around the room. Spotting the teapot and scones she clapped her white gloves together with delight.

"It's just as I'd hoped," cooed the 30-something, thrusting her gloves into a faux lizard-skin purse. "And Nina Simone to boot. Shall I sit anywhere?"

"Please do," Alicia said as the doorbell chimed again.

Lynette returned to the kitchen to fetch the coffee while Alicia opened the door. This time it was the chirpy librarian, Missy Corner, who giggled then threw her arms around Alicia like they were old friends.

"Helllooo. Bet you didn't think I'd show?"

"Well, I—"

"Just try to stop me!" She paused when she heard the barking. "You have a pooch? I *love* pooches."

"Yep, that's Max the hungry beast."

"Max? Really? After Mr Mallowan?"

Alicia looked at her, stunned. "You really are an Agatha expert. Yes, we did name him after Agatha Christie's second husband, Max Mallowan. I don't think anyone has ever picked that up. Ever."

"How hilarious," Missy said. "But hang on, why didn't you call him Peter? That was the name of Agatha's mutt, wasn't it? Oh yes, she adored that dog. Now what kind of dog was it? Um, no, no, don't tell me, I can remember this." She placed two fingers to her brow, her eyes squinting. "I should know this, I read her bio not so long ago. Oh that's right…" She dropped the fingers, smiled victoriously. "A terrier. A 'wire-haired terrier' they called it, whatever the hell that means. Maybe we should get a picture of it? What does your mutt look like?"

"Oh, he's a black Labrador. Harmless but zealous, so we've banished him to the back terrace so he won't scare anyone off."

"Oh, unlikely to scare me, I *adore* dogs. My family used to have the *cutest* King Charles Spaniel you ever saw. Her name was Poncy." She stopped. "Oops, sorry, I'm rambling now. Do shut me up when I start rambling too much, it's such a bad habit of mine."

Alicia laughed. "Oh you'll be fine, come on through and meet the others."

She turned back to shut the front door when she spotted a short, well-dressed man racing up the footpath. He was waving a hand in the air frantically.

"Apologies," he sang out. "Didn't mean to make a grand entrance, just having one of those days."

Alicia smiled. "Perry Gordon I presume?"

He twirled around and did a fake curtsey, a flash of hot-pink lining showing beneath a black, tailored jacket. Like Anders, he, too, was wearing jeans, but his were black and skinny fitting, and he had a chiselled goatee and one earring. He dressed like a 20-year-old but was into his 40s.

"That'd be me. You must be our hostess with the mostess, Alicia Finlay?"

She nodded. He air-kissed her on both cheeks.

"Well done you for making this happen. I just love the sound of a Murder Mystery Book Club. Brilliant idea. Can't believe I didn't think of it myself. Shall I?"

He indicated the house and she opened the door wider so he could strut through.

In the lounge room, Missy was already slathering jam and cream on a steamy scone and stopped when she spotted Alicia.

"Oops, sorry, don't mind do you? I know it's cheeky of me to start ploughing in but I'm famished."

Alicia laughed. "Not at all. In fact that's exactly what I want. Please, everyone help yourselves and get as comfortable as possible. There's tea, sandwiches, scones. If you'd like coffee or water, we've also got that. We're just waiting on one more person then we can get started."

As the small group settled in, Lynette pulled Alicia back into the kitchen.

"That Claire's a style merchant. Did you see her hat?"

"Yes, beautiful," said Alicia. "She does own a frock shop of course."

"And she's a walking advertisement for it. So who's left?"

"As far as I know, just Barbara Parlour." Lynette looked blank. "The 'miserable housewife'."

"That's right, this should be interesting."

"So glad I'm entertaining you, Lynny."

She laughed. "Oh it's going to be great. Come on, I'll help keep the conversation flowing."

As it turned out, she didn't need to bother. With both Missy and Perry in the room, there was no shortage of lively repartee. Both were a bundle of energy, Missy giggling and sharing tales of her adventures in the library—apparently book sharing is more eventful than you'd expect—and Perry outdoing her with stories of his 'naughty housemate and his noisy lovemaking'.

"Honestly, the man is an *animal*," he declared, a hand held against his heart, feigning horror. And so it was the group barely noticed the ten minutes it took for the final guest to arrive.

Barbara Parlour knocked so gently on the door that it was only Max's frantic barking that alerted them to her presence. She was well into her 50s and wearing a simple blue dress with a single strand of pearls around her neck, and ash-blond hair tied in a modest ponytail behind her head.

She smiled shyly as Alicia led her through and said, "Everyone this is Barbara Parlour."

A sudden quiet descended upon the group. Claire's catlike eyes turned positively feline, narrowing into two thin, curious lines, a frown across her perfect forehead. Dr Anders looked uncomfortable, shifting in his seat, unable to meet her eyes, and Missy beamed from ear to ear.

"Oh, *hello*. I know you," she said.

Barbara blushed crimson red. "I don't think so..." she began.

"Oh yes, I've definitely seen you somewhere," Missy persisted. "Have you been to the local library lately?"

"No, no, I never use libraries," Barbara said, looking away and towards the table. "It all looks simply beautiful, Alicia."

"Thank you," she said, wondering at the mixed reaction Barbara had received. "Can I get you some tea?"

"Oh I'll get it," Barbara said, stepping towards the dining table and helping herself to a cup. As she poured the murky brew Alicia couldn't help noticing that the older woman's hands were trembling slightly.

"Come, take a seat," she said, indicating the sofa where Claire and Missy were sitting. Claire shifted over a little to allow space and gave the older woman a warm smile.

"Come on, you can be the rose between two thorns, as my fiancé Charlie would say," Claire said and Missy gave her a teasing scowl.

"Speak for yourself, I'm no thorn."

Alicia laughed and glanced towards Perry who was seated across from the sofa, a cup of tea on his lap. A tiny shudder raced down her spine. Perry was staring, open-mouthed towards the sofa where Barbara was settling in beside Claire, and looked as though he had just seen a ghost.

Alicia's shudder intensified.

What was going on? Did Perry also know Barbara? Did Anders and Claire? Before she could give it any more thought, Lynette was tapping her gently on the knee.

"You okay, Alicia?" she said, giving her a pointed *get-your-act-together* look.

Alicia coughed. "Sorry, yes, all good. Okay, so let's get started shall we?" She took a deep breath. "Hello everyone and welcome to our first-ever Murder Mystery Book Club."

Missy gave a boisterous cheer, which seemed to lighten the mood instantly and Alicia felt herself relax a little.

"I know I sent you all a list of 'guidelines' but please keep in mind that I want this group to be as chilled out as possible, so they're just loose rules to get us started, nothing more than that."

"I reckon they're great," Anders said. They all turned to look at him. "It's just that, well, you do need a little structure, don't you? To get started."

"Yes you do," agreed Perry, who had regained his composure and was now offering the doctor a leering smile.

Alicia frowned. It looked like she had stiff competition for the dashing doctor. She coughed again and pressed on.

"I guess the main reason for today's meeting is to get to know each other a little better, and discuss what Christie books we'd like to read first and then what other authors we can focus on after that. Once we've sorted that out, I can send you all a schedule and we can have our first proper book club. Before that, though, why don't we introduce ourselves again, maybe say a little bit about who we are and why we've come along." There was an awkward silence. "I'll start shall I?"

She took another deep breath. "As you know, I'm Alicia Finlay, this is the house I share with my younger sister Lynette and that annoyingly loud creature outside called Max."

As if on cue, the dog barked and everyone laughed.

"Shut it, Max!" roared Lynette.

"Thank you, Lynette. What else? Um, I edit magazines for a living, but my great passion is reading crime novels, and I especially love Agatha Christie, which shouldn't come as any surprise to anyone here."

"What made you decide to start the club?"

This was Claire, seated forward with her back straight and her hands together in her lap.

"Lynette suggested it, actually. It's a long story, but suffice to say I'd had a dismal experience with a previous book club and decided to get more like-minded people together. Anyway, that's enough about me. Lynny?"

She turned to her sister who had just stuffed half a sandwich into her mouth.

"While she's scoffing her face, may I?" said Perry with a wink, and Alicia nodded.

"Okay then, I'm Perry, 46, single, although hopefully not for long…" He slapped Anders with another of those looks that left the poor man blushing uncomfortably. "And I, too, have been in plenty of dismal book clubs, thank you very much. I mean, just because you like books, doesn't mean you have to be boring. I also love a good murder mystery, but have to earn a living, *darlinks*, so I work at the Sydney Museum, in the Palaeontology department—that just means anything old and fossilised."

Missy gasped. "How appropriate. Agatha Christie adored poking around with fossils. She'd be most impressed. Spent many of her happiest times on digs in the Middle East would you believe? Of course that was with the second husband, Max…"

"Yes, well, I must confess, Aggie did fuel my love for all things old and dusty. It does get a little dull in there, though, but my social life makes up for it in spades. I own a fabulous pad in Surry Hills, which, as I've told some of you, I share with an equally fabulous but extremely randy flatmate who, when he's not bonking his beautiful boyfriend senseless, helps pay the bills. He's a budding author, about to get his first big—"

He stopped suddenly and something flashed across his eyes. Alicia noticed a look of guilt or shame but before she could give it more thought it had disappeared.

"Anyway, I'm getting *waaay* off track here," he said. "Over to you, little sis."

He waved a hand at Lynette who was just brushing the last of the crumbs from her fingers. She flicked her blonde locks over her shoulder, crossed her legs, and smiled.

"Thanks, Perry and hello all. As I think we've clearly established by now, I'm the little sister around here, 26, also single—there are just not enough fabulous men out there I tell you."

"I'm with you, girl," said Perry, winking again.

"Like the rest of you, I love a good murder mystery but love to cook even more, and you can thank me for the scones later. In between cooking, I wait tables down at Mario's in Paddington."

"Wait tables? Really? You should be cooking for them," said Claire, indicating the half-eaten scone in her hand.

"Wouldn't that be nice," Lynette said wistfully, her smile dropping slightly.

"Mario's a moron," Alicia explained. "He's been promising her a switch to the kitchen for years but Lynette's problem is she's also a fabulous waitress. You should see her weekly tips. Me? I can barely open a wine bottle without breaking the cork."

"Yeah, me too," laughed Anders. "Got a medical degree but it still doesn't prepare you for a corkscrew. Thank god for twist-tops, that's all I've got to say."

"Well, while you're talking, how about telling us more?" said Alicia and he blushed slightly, clearing his throat.

"Alright then, um, what can I say… I'm Anders Bright, and I have to admit I feel a bit out of my league here. I like all styles of crime fiction but haven't read a huge amount of Christie if I'm being honest. What I have read, though, I've really enjoyed. As I said in my letter to Alicia, I particularly admire her passion for poisons. Of course in Christie's day every good house had plenty in the pantry, things like arsenic and rat poison, that kind of stuff. Today the Therapeutic Goods Administration has banned so many of them which makes it much harder to quietly do away with that unfaithful hubby or irritating daughter."

A china teacup clunked onto its saucer and Alicia looked up to see Barbara mopping up the mess it had left behind on the tea chest.

"Are you okay?" she asked as Barbara swiped at the spilt tea with a paper napkin.

"Oh, just clumsy, that's all. Silly of me. Please, Anders, go on."

He glanced tentatively at Barbara then glanced away. "Right, yes, um… Let's see, what else was I going to say? Oh yes, I also have never been in a book club before. But I'm willing to give it a go." He brushed a stray lock of hair from his eyes. "I'm a city GP, by the way, work not too far from here, and I am sure my fellow medicos would laugh heartily if they knew I was signing up."

"Well. We'll try not to take offence at that," Perry declared, mocking outrage and Anders looked flummoxed.

"Sorry, I didn't mean it like that, it's just… well, it's not really their thing—"

Perry slapped him on one broad shoulder. "Just messing with you, darl." He laughed. "So, you haven't told us your marital status."

He gave Anders a cheeky sideways look and again Anders seemed flustered.

"Oh, er…," he hesitated then said very softly, "I'm single, I guess."

Alicia felt a tingle of joy. *Here was some good news after all.* Perry was a tremendous tease, she could tell already that Anders was no match for him, but she was happy he'd asked nonetheless. Knowing her form, it would take Alicia two years to find out what he'd managed to discover in about two minutes flat.

"So, who's next?" she asked trying to sound nonchalant.

Missy thrust a hand in the air so Alicia gave her the nod. She told the group in some considerable detail about her chance meeting with Alicia.

"So she implored me to join and I thought, why the hell not?" She giggled. "I mean, what else have I got to do on a Sunday arvo, besides sitting at home feeding Fudge and Pudge? Oh, they're my goldfish by the way, not nicknames for my thighs."

She squealed with laughter at this, her zebra-print glasses almost flying off, then repositioned them and continued. "I, too, am single." She stopped. "Seems to be a pre-requisite to this club, eh?"

"That's because if we had partners we'd have better things to do with our time than read murder mysteries," suggested Perry and she giggled again before continuing.

"Like all of you, it seems, I read lots of crime but *adore* everything about Agatha Christie, although if anyone's read her autobiography or any biographies on her for that matter, she was certainly no saint. I think that makes me adore her even more."

"Yes, guys, we're very lucky to have Missy here. She is *the* expert on all things Christie," said Alicia and Missy shooed her away with one hand.

"What's it like working in a library?" asked Barbara and Missy smiled widely.

"Love it. I mean who wouldn't? I have an entire office full of books. What more could a bookworm ask for?"

"Decent pay and conditions?" Barbara persisted, an eyebrow raised.

Alicia wondered if she was fishing for a job.

"Oh, you get paid just enough to survive," said Missy. "But yes, they do let you out for lunch occasionally, usually around noon if anyone wants to meet me for a coffee. I'm just down the road from here. A hop, skip and a jump. We could meet for a sanger, or a kebab, there's this great little... Sorry, there I go, rabbiting on again."

She giggled nervously and looked up at the ceiling.

Claire spoke next, her crisp, soft tone denoting a slight English accent. "I'm Claire Hargreaves, 35, and I'm afraid this is where I break the mould. I've been engaged for the past four years to a lovely man who works in the book publishing business."

Missy giggled again, then flung a hand to her lips. "Sorry," she said, looking mortified. "It's just that, well, four years seems an awfully long time to be engaged, that's all."

"I agree," said Perry. "What's the hold up?"

Claire's shapely eyebrows drew together tightly. She smoothed her skirt down with one hand, adjusting the hem and then tucking a stray thread under with the other. "There's no holdup, *per se.* We're just waiting for the right time, that's all."

A dark cloud crept across her face and before Missy and Perry could do any more damage, Alicia quickly changed the subject.

"So tell us about your shop," she said. "You mentioned it in your letter."

"Oh, yes, my lovely little boutique." The cloud lifted. "It's called the Timeless Vintage Clothing Store and it's down on Victoria Street in Potts Point."

"Oh I know it. I love it!" squealed Missy, clearly trying to make amends. "Got some fab '50s frocks from there last summer."

"Yes, well, I'm sure a few of you have probably been in there at some point, it's been around for a while." Her eyes strayed across to Barbara. "We have every era you could possibly desire. But I also have a tiny café at the back of the shop so, like Missy, I implore you to come and join me for a coffee any time you like. First latté's on the house. Let me also just add, in case you're wondering, that, yes, I'm British born, hence the accent, but my mother is Hong Kong Chinese and now lives in Paris—which is where I get a lot of the fabulous frocks for my shop. So I really am quite an eclectic mix."

"I'll say," said Missy, thinking how wonderful it must be to come from such a deliciously exotic background. She was born and bred in Oatley, Sydney, and felt about as exotic as an Ugg boot.

"Thanks, Claire," said Alicia. "So who's left? Oh, Barbara, your turn now."

They all turned to face the older woman who placed her teacup to the side with a slight rattle.

"Hello everyone. Yes, I'm Barbara Parlour. I'm not much good at public speaking I'm afraid."

"Well, what do you do for a living?" prompted Alicia.

"Oh, I'm just a housewife."

"Home technician, please," said Perry with a wink.

"No, just a housewife," she replied dryly. "Or at least, that's what my husband says. He's in the banking industry, you see, but is hoping to get into politics soon."

"Politics? Really?" said Anders, sounding slightly alarmed.

"Yes, he is running for pre-selection later in the year for the state's conservative party."

She smiled but it was strained, a little like the smile her husband would no doubt master as a politician, not quite reaching the eyes.

"Um, what else can I tell you? Honestly, my life is extremely boring. Oh I do have a daughter. She's 16 going on 26." She shot the doctor a quick look and laughed nervously. "Never listens to a thing I say, but then neither does her father. She's got his foul temper, too..."

Barbara stopped and looked down at her lap as the room turned deadly quiet. Someone coughed. She shook herself a little and continued. "Anyway, that's neither here nor there." Another nervous laugh. "Um, like Dr Anders, I too don't really belong to any clubs, so saw the advertisement and thought I'd give it a whirl. Maybe cheer myself up a bit."

She smiled fleetingly and then looked back down at her hands, which had been fidgeting the whole time.

"Goodo," said Alicia, trying to lift the mood. "Okay, then, let's move on to the book selection shall we? Does anyone have any strong ideas about which books they'd like to focus on first?"

And so the conversation turned to all things Agatha Christie and the mood did indeed begin to lighten up. Within the hour they had the first six books lined up, starting the following Sunday with *Evil Under the Sun*—Claire's choice but a favourite of every single person in the room. They had agreed to meet every fortnight, no one keen to drag it out for a full month, and also concurred with all of Alicia's suggested guidelines.

"I'll host the first one, if you like," said Perry, twiddling with his earring.

"No," said Barbara suddenly. "I'd really like to hold the first one at my house. If you don't mind?"

He stopped twiddling and shrugged.

"Are you absolutely sure?" asked Anders. "I'm also very happy to do it—"

"No, I insist. Best to get it over and done with, then I can relax for the next few months."

That made sense to Alicia. "Fine. Is everyone okay with that?"

They all nodded and so it was agreed, they would meet at 2:00 p.m. the following Sunday at Barbara's east Sydney address. She would provide the afternoon tea and Claire would bring along some questions. They then exchanged contact details, and began to say their farewells.

Barbara left first, glancing at her watch worriedly, followed soon after by Dr Anders and Claire. That left Missy and Perry who helped the sisters clear the cups and clean up.

"She's an odd one," Perry said as he rinsed some crockery in the sink.

"Who? 'Just a housewife'?" asked Lynette and Perry nodded.

"Seems really sad and lonely to me," said Missy, taking a saucer from him and wiping it with a fresh tea towel.

"Well, hopefully this club might give her the boost she needs," said Alicia, not keen to start bitching about members so early in the game.

"And what do we know about Ms Claire Hargreaves?" asked Perry, one eyebrow raised.

"Not much, apart from what she's already told us," replied Alicia. "Why?"

"Oh, nothing." He hesitated, was about to say something then clamped his lips shut.

Alicia grabbed the tea towel from Missy's hands. "Come on you two, Lyn and I can finish up here."

She saw them out then turned back to her sister.

"He's right, though, isn't he? About Barbara. She is a bit odd."

"I thought you were cool with that," said Lynette.

"Yes, but, I don't know, there's something kind of *worrying* about her."

Lynette shrugged and pulled off her boots, massaging her weary ankles. "Come on, she'll be fine. They can't all be fabulous and fun like Perry and Missy. Besides, it's a smart idea to have the first one at her house; you'll see, she'll feel more comfortable there. It'll be great."

<p style="text-align:center">~~~~~~~</p>

Later that evening, as Barbara returned home, she was feeling anything but comfortable. There was someone in the group she had not expected to see, someone she recognised from *before*. A slight shiver raced down her spine.

She wondered, suddenly, if she was safe, then shook the thought away. She was letting her imagination run away with her again. It would all be okay, this group would be good for her, they all seemed like such lovely people, such good, honest, *caring* people. There was nothing to worry about. It would all work out perfectly fine.

As she picked up the book on her nightstand and flipped it open to the bookmark, Barbara couldn't help feeling a twinge of apprehension that just wouldn't go away…

CHAPTER 6

Missy Corner was famished and bored in equal measure, two states of being that did not suit her flighty temperament one bit. She glanced at the clock. Ten minutes until lunchtime, and it couldn't go fast enough. She loved her job at the library, she really did, but sometimes things got a little, well, *dull*. Especially if it was a quiet day with only the usual suspects loitering by the shelves, milling over their favourite titles and suggesting authors to each other furtively, as if passing on state secrets. Occasionally things spiced up— a hunky Swedish backpacker strolled in, keen to use a computer, or a long-awaited bestseller arrived and she got to record it in the hard drive, laminate it carefully and place it proudly on the shelf for the usual suspects to squabble over.

Or, as happened a few weeks ago, a woman strolls in off the street and invites you to join her book club. Now what were the chances of that?

Missy's mood lightened. The Murder Mystery Book Club was the most exciting thing that had happened to her in months. She glanced at the chipped black nail polish on her gnarled nails and then placed one to her teeth and kept chipping away at it. Hell, it was probably the only exciting thing that had happened since she'd scored this job, 18 months ago. Before that, she'd been idling through life, taking the odd bar job, redecorating her bedroom at home, a weekend up the coast now and then with old school chums. Nothing special.

Now, suddenly, she had something very special happening in her life, and every two weeks at that. It gave her renewed focus, renewed direction. She looked forward to the next book club, the first official meeting this Sunday, and had already read the book several times so she had plenty to offer. She just had to learn to shut her big mouth more often or they'd grow weary of her as her friends often did.

She couldn't remember the last time they'd invited her on one of their weekends away.

Missy felt a lump in her throat, and tried to swallow it down. Sometimes she wished she could just be like everybody else. She wished she knew where the off button was and how to use it occasionally as her father often suggested. She sniffed, determined not to let the Big Blue take over again. It had been many months since she'd been low and she was damned if she was going to drop down there again.

She had the Murder Mystery Book Club now. No need for that.

Missy glanced at the clock. Midday. Yippee. She grabbed her gold-coloured backpack and turned to her boss who was busy at a terminal, checking in books from the book drop.

"Off to lunch, lovely," she said, swooping down to give the older woman's shoulders a squeeze.

"Have fun," Geraldine murmured her eyes firmly on the screen. She liked Missy, but she liked it even better when she had the place—and her ears—to herself. The young woman could really talk, not exactly an ideal trait in a librarian.

Pity she hadn't been so chatty in the interview, Geraldine thought, *she might never have given her the job.* She sighed and continued tapping.

Missy stepped out into the sunlight and grappled through her backpack for her prescription sunglasses, swapping them for the spectacles in a matter of seconds, then made a beeline for the kebab stall up the street. She had her heart set on a beef gyros today, was already imagining the tzatziki sauce dripping through the onions and tomato, and perhaps that's why she never noticed the sudden roar of an engine behind her, or the yelp of a passerby to 'Watch out!' as a car made its own beeline straight towards her.

Within seconds Missy was lying, twisted and lifeless in an open doorway.

The passer-by, an elderly gentleman with thick white hair and stunned wide eyes, would later tell police that the car accelerated, deliberately steered off the road and up onto the footpath towards the unsuspecting librarian.

Missy, who came to soon after with a raging headache and aching arm, would beg to differ. She was just in the wrong place at the wrong time she told the cops, that was all. What is indisputable is that she was one very lucky woman. After glancing behind herself a split second before impact, Missy had spotted the looming bonnet and flung her body towards the shop door, landing hard on her left wrist and giving the manager of the convenience store, a tiny Korean man who spoke broken English, the shock of his life.

Meanwhile, the offending vehicle, a dark blue or black BMW—depending on who you asked—corrected itself, returned to the road and sped off, never stopping to see if Missy was alive or to render aid.

A classic hit and run.

Missy was shaken but not stirred. "It was all just a stupid accident," she told the police who had arrived soon after, followed by an ambulance.

"No, no, no!" cried the Korean shopkeeper. "Driver out to get you."

"I have to agree," said the elderly man. "He seemed very determined."

"He?" asked the police officer, a stocky, middle-aged man who looked about as excited to be there as Missy was.

"Well, I didn't get a good look at the young man, the car windows were dark—"

"Dark?" said the second officer, a young woman with bleached blonde hair and slightly more spark in her eyes.

"Tinted I think you call it," said the elderly man. "But it's always young men, isn't it? P-platers who cause all the trouble on our roads these days."

"So it had a P-plate?" the female cop asked excitedly.

The man stared at her mutely for a few moments. "Er, well, no, I can't say that for sure either."

"No, no, no P-plate!" said the Korean. "This person mad killer. Try to kill this woman. Gangster maybe? Mafia? Black car always Mafia."

Now it was the police officers turn to be speechless, and Missy, whose wrist was being bandaged into place by a kindly paramedic, had to speak up.

"This is all extremely silly," she said, giggling despite the pain. "Why would the Mafia, or anyone for that matter, want to run me over? I'm just a boring librarian."

The police were inclined to believe her and, after taking the witnesses' details, promptly excused them. Maybe it made their job easier to believe it was an accident, maybe they agreed with Missy that boring librarians were rarely targeted by lunatic Mafioso drivers. In any case, they assured her that she was most likely the innocent target of a drunken driver who had fled the scene to avoid being caught.

"Wouldn't be the first time," the stocky officer sighed, tucking his notepad back into his jacket pocket and giving her a weary look that suggested he'd seen it all before.

By the time Missy returned to the library, a good two hours and one bandaged wrist later, she had stopped shaking and begun remembering how hungry she was. The only angst she now felt for the crazed driver was on behalf of her neglected stomach.

"I'll run out and get you something, dear," said Geraldine, herself feeling guilty for the mean thoughts she'd had earlier about her fellow librarian. "You just sit here and relax. Once I get back you might want to take an early mark and head home. You've had quite a shock my dear."

"Oh I'll be okay, Geraldine," Missy said, settling on the stool by the computer terminal. "Luckily it's my left arm, so I can still do a little typing. I'll leave the heavy lifting to you."

As Geraldine left to fetch some belated lunch, and Missy began tapping away at the screen with her one working hand, she couldn't help going over the accident detail by detail—the flash of a dark car, the crashing of her body against the doorway, the wide-eyed hysteria of the eyewitnesses. She couldn't remember, now, exactly what was said but one sentence remained etched in her brain: "This person mad killer. Try to kill you!"

It was a truly ridiculous statement, she'd already decided that, so why was she still feeling so jittery?

CHAPTER 7

Barbara's 'house' was actually a luxurious monstrosity wedged between two other McMansions on a leafy Woollahra avenue. It took Alicia and Lynette quite by surprise. They stared at the address in their hands again and then up at the sprawling two-storey structure with its sandstone pillars and gaudy mermaid waterfall out the front. Around it was a short, pebbled driveway lined with meticulously trimmed hedges.

"Not much to be depressed about," Lynette said, unlatching the gate at the front.

They were gathering for the first official book club and Alicia had parked her Torana a block back, not expecting to get a close park, and she was frowning now as she spotted one right beside the house. Within seconds, a shiny silver Saab was reverse parking into it, Dr Anders stepping out and locking his car electronically with his key soon after.

"No one home?" he asked, sounding upbeat.

"Just about to go in," said Alicia, pushing the gate open and leading the way across the driveway, past the three-car garage with an olive green Jaguar, gleaming silver Mercedes and a motley collection of bicycles, old golf bags, and packing boxes, to the enormous front door. There was an intercom on one side and she pressed it once then waited a few seconds before a lively voice crackled back at them.

"Yo! Who is it?"

Unless Barbara had had a personality transplant this had to be the daughter thought Alicia. She introduced herself.

"We're here for the book club," she said.

"The *what?*"

"The book club. Is Barbara there?"

There was silence for a moment and then a beeping sound indicated that the door was being unlocked.

"Shall we?" said Lynette and she pushed it forward just as Barbara began to pull it open on the other side.

"Hello, welcome," she said, waving one arm for them to come in.

Barbara was dressed today in black trousers and a plain white shirt, with a thick, lilac coloured scarf twisted several times around her neck. It was a warm day, they were almost into summer after all, so Alicia couldn't help wondering whether the house was air-conditioned or if Barbara simply didn't feel the heat. Alicia had deliberately chosen a pair of loose khaki trousers and a flowing cotton shirt, and already felt sweaty.

"You've got a lovely house here, Barbara," Anders was saying, looking around quickly, and she smiled.

"Thank you. Come through, I'll show you around while we wait for the others."

"Really, there's no need," he said but she ignored him and led them through to a plush lounge room with white shuttered windows, thick, creamy carpet and pearly white furnishings.

It was way too pristine for Alicia's tastes. Max would make mincemeat of the vintage Persian rug and she would spend the whole time stressed out about paw prints on the white suede leather lounge suite. This room was decorated lavishly with giant art works, framed photographs, enormous vases wedged full of Oriental Lilies, red roses and Singapore Orchids, and a gleaming black, grand piano in one corner.

Above the piano, a large, framed photo caught Alicia's eye and she couldn't help grinning. It was a particularly gaudy looking portrait of the Parlour family, all decked out in their Sunday best. It was the usual story: the whole family—at the beckoning of the mother, no doubt—had clearly dressed up in clothes they didn't normally wear to get photographed by someone they didn't actually know to hang on a wall and loathe for the next five years until Mother insisted on an update. In this one Barbara looked a few years younger, a good deal blonder, and a whole lot more glamorous in a sparkling red and gold top, and dripping with gold jewellery. The smile on her face was wide and determined. She had changed considerably since then.

Barbara's daughter was wearing a blue polka dot dress and a wide matching headband. She looked about 12 but adolescent surliness had already crept into her eyes. She was also smiling, but only just. The husband's smile, too, was strained, and he had that dapper *1980s Dynasty* look about him—suit, tie, suspenders, the works. This was supposed to be a happy family portrait, but it left Alicia cold. When she glanced at Anders she noticed that he, too, looked uneasy.

Below the portrait, on a tall, white side table, were a bunch of medals and trophies, and Alicia noted at least two for Barbara, including a large tennis trophy with the words 'Most Improved' engraved onto the front.

Before she could study them further, Barbara was dragging them through the opulent dining room with its glittering chandelier and varnished timber table that could easily seat 12, to the most enormous home kitchen she'd ever seen. Lynette's eyes widened.

Barbara had every gadget a budding chef could want—a wide, commercial-sized oven, a monstrous two-door fridge with ice dispenser on the front, an espresso machine wedged into one wall, and a mammoth Microwave oven. Barbara could fit an entire roast and its accompanying vegetables in there with room to move.

"I would kill for this kitchen," Lynette told the older woman who looked around as though only just noticing it. "It's totally loaded."

"Oh, thank you," she said. "I must confess I don't do a lot of the cooking. That's what Rosa's for."

"Rosa?"

"My housekeeper." She smiled a little sheepishly, and quickly added, "She only comes in a few hours a day, just after midday to cook the family meal, tidy up a bit. Nothing too dramatic. Usually out of here by 3:00 p.m. She's a gem. Makes a mean coq au vin, Arthur's favourite. That's my husband. The only time I'm in here is when I'm on the phone."

She indicated the silver hands-free telephone sitting in its cradle on one end of the marble bench top. Beside it hung a large whiteboard with several numbers scrawled onto it in blue marker pen, as well as a bunch of messages, including one for 'Holly' to call 'the Coach'.

The doorbell buzzed, startling Barbara who grabbed hold of her neck and padded her scarf down. "That must be the others, please come through to the patio, we'll sit out there today."

She led them though French doors to a sun-dappled garden with an elegantly welded metal table and matching cushioned chairs. The area was paved with terracotta tiles and planted out with tree ferns, pink cordyline, bright yellow mimosa and white scented jasmine. Beyond it, through the hedges, you could just catch sight of a glistening swimming pool and what looked like a Balinese-style pergola. As they took their seats, Barbara returned inside to welcome the other guests. Within minutes they were joined by Missy and Perry, who had arrived together in his red Mazda sports car, followed by Claire in a spotless, baby blue vintage VW Beetle.

Missy was still nursing her injury, her left arm wrapped in bandage and held tight to her chest in a sling that reached down across her neck and back.

"Hey, what happened to you?" asked Anders getting up to help her to a seat.

"Oh, I sprained my silly wrist," she said, still managing to offer them a grin. "Well, I didn't. Some maniac tried to take me out."

They all stared at her aghast, and Missy giggled a little. "Oh, it's okay, I'm exaggerating!"

Missy explained how, earlier that week, she'd been heading off for her lunch break when a 'madman' veered onto the pavement and sent her flying. "I put my hand out to catch my fall and landed firmly on my poor little wrist. Just lucky I'm so well padded, I could have done a lot more damage." She giggled again as she eased herself into the chair.

Alicia felt a surge of vindication. *See, it did happen!* Her imagination wasn't so outlandish after all. Missy's accident was the sort of thing she, herself, had imagined hundreds of times before, while walking home from work, to and from the shops, heading out to a movie…

"You sure it was an accident?" she asked and Lynette scowled at her. "I'm just wondering, that's all."

"Oh it has to be, honeykins," said Missy. "They didn't stop so they may not know they hit me."

"Did you get the number plate?" Alicia persisted. "Catch a look at the driver?"

"Oh it was a blur, really. All I could see was an old dark-coloured BMW. You know those ones with the dark tinted windows? Mum calls them Drug Dealer Windows, and she's not wrong. You gotta wonder who needs to hide as they drive around. Honestly, if you want to look guilty, get dark windows installed!"

"But should you be here?" asked Claire, also looking concerned. "It might be a little stressful after what happened. Maybe you need to be resting, take some time off—"

Dr Anders was less sympathetic. "It's just a sprained wrist, Claire, there'll be some damage to the ligaments but she hasn't even got it in a cast so it can't be too bad. I'm sure Missy can handle it. You're on anti-inflammatory painkillers, right?"

She nodded.

"She was run over, Anders," Barbara said. "That can be very upsetting."

"No, Anders is right," interrupted Missy. "My doc tells me I'll be good as new in a few weeks. Besides, I'm not taking it personally, despite everyone's attempts to make me."

"Everyone?" asked Alicia, an eyebrow raised.

"Oh, well, there were a couple of witnesses who had some elaborate theory that someone was out to get me."

"Really?" said Claire. "Could they be right? Do you think you were targeted deliberately?"

Missy giggled again. "My goodness me, there are conspiracy theorists everywhere. I'm fine, people, *fine*. Honestly."

They all looked at her as if they didn't quite believe her, except Anders, who'd seen this kind of accident before, and Perry who'd already had this conversation on the drive over and was well and truly fed up with the subject.

"In that case, shall we get on to even juicier crimes?" he suggested, holding up his copy of *Evil Under The Sun*.

They all nodded agreement and began settling in, choosing their chairs and dragging their own copies out of handbags, backpacks and, in Anders' case, a large pocket hidden inside his jacket. Alicia wondered what else he had in there and whether there was room for two.

She gave herself an invisible slap across the face and looked around to see Barbara disappear inside the house again, so she jumped up and followed her in. The older woman was in the kitchen, wrestling with a packet of wafer thin crackers and swearing quietly to herself, so Alicia took them off her and opened them.

"Everything okay?" she asked and Barbara nodded primly. "It's really good of you to go first."

"Happy to," she said, offering Alicia a strained smile. It reminded her of the portrait in the lounge room.

Barbara indicated a large white platter where a mixture of cheeses, pâté and olives had been placed and Alicia added the crackers and a clump of grapes that Barbara was now handing her. As Barbara fetched a cheese knife and some plates, Alicia strolled around the spacious kitchen admiring it. You didn't have to be a budding chef to know it was beautifully designed.

"So is your husband around today or did you banish him?"

Barbara looked at her a little alarmed. "Oh, I wouldn't dare banish him from his own house! But I did mention that he might want to make himself scarce."

"And your daughter?"

"What about me?" came an indignant tone from the other side of the kitchen.

Alicia turned around to see a tall, slightly overweight teenager with pimply skin, shiny dark hair, a piercing in her nose and a scowl across her forehead. Adolescent surliness had clearly caught up with Barbara's daughter now.

"Oh, Holly darling, you gave me a fright! I thought you were going to be out today."

"Well, obviously, I'm not," she said, giving her mother a 'duh' look.

"Then come in and meet Alicia, she's the head of the new book club I was telling you about."

"Yeah, whatever," she said, heading for the fridge instead. "Dammit, all the juice is gone."

"Not to worry dear, we'll get Rosa to fetch some more when she comes in tomorrow."

"Rosa? Why can't you do it? It's not like you've got anything else on your plate." She glanced at Alicia.

"Oh, that's right, you're too busy with your precious new book club."

As she skulked out she rolled her eyes, and Barbara turned to Alicia, mortified.

"I'm so sorry, she's not normally that rude." She stopped, a half smile fluttering on her lips. "Well, actually, yes she is, but I was hoping you wouldn't have to see it for yourself. Come let's get this food out before the club wonders where we've got to—"

Suddenly Holly reappeared, her face drained of all colour. "What the *hell* is going on?" she screamed, catching Alicia by surprise.

"What… what are you talking about, darling?" asked Barbara, dropping the platter to the bench top with a thud.

"Don't act all ignorant on me, mother! You know exactly what I'm talking about. Out there, on the deck…" Holly flashed Alicia a quick glance then turned her piercing eyes back onto her mother who visibly shrank under the angry glare.

"You mean my book club?"

"I mean *him*. What is he doing here?"

"Holly, darling, I'm sorry, I didn't know—"

"Bollocks, Mum! Of course you friggin' knew. You know everything that goes on around here. You set the whole thing up, didn't you? *Didn't you?*"

Alicia stepped forward, eager to defend Barbara but she had no idea what Holly was screaming about. Could she really be this upset over a few friends of her mother's taking over the patio?

"This is supposed to be my safe place, how could you do this to me?" Holly was screaming.

"Holly, please—"

Before she could say anything more, Holly had stormed back through the kitchen and into the bowels of the house, leaving two stunned faces behind her.

"I'm so sorry," Barbara said again, barely able to meet Alicia's eyes.

"Don't worry about it," Alicia said soothingly. "I hear teenage girls can make mountains out of molehills. Come on, we'll go join the others."

Alicia helped Barbara gather the platters and take them out to the deck where the group were chatting amongst themselves. She glanced at Barbara, who looked lost in her own thoughts, arranging the food on the table and handing out napkins.

"Oh, drat, I forgot the homemade lemonade," she said, snapping out of it. "Alicia, do you mind grabbing it from the kitchen while I run to the bathroom? It's just inside the fridge, in a jug. We'll need glasses, too."

Heading back to the lion's den wasn't exactly enticing so Alicia gave her sister a quick look, nodding her head towards the kitchen.

Lynette stared at her confused for a few seconds, then jumped up. "I'll give you hand shall I?"

"That'd be great, thanks, Lynny," she said leading the way inside.

Back in the kitchen, Alicia glanced around to make sure Holly was nowhere to be found, then exhaled.

"Everything okay?" Lynette asked.

"I'll tell you about it later," she whispered. "Let's just get back out there as fast as we can. Now, where are those glasses…"

While Lynette fetched the jug from the fridge, Alicia searched through a few cupboards until she found a pearly pink set of eight matching glasses, and placed seven of them on a tray that was leaning against the microwave. As Lynette shut the fridge door she laughed. There were a bunch of photos attached with magnets, including several of Barbara with a tennis racquet in hand land Arthur at the golf course, a family photo on a large white yacht, and several of Holly as a young child, one licking a bright pink ice-cream, another blowing a kiss to the photographer.

"She's a cutie," Lynette said and Alicia stepped over to take a look.

"About as cute as a brown snake," she hissed. "I just met her, she's now twice the size and a major brat. Barely acknowledged me, and bit her poor mother's head off. God knows why."

Beside the photos was the usual fridge paraphernalia—a school newsletter, a few magnetised ads, one for a local plumber, one for a luxury spa, and a phone bill that went for many pages.

"Whoa, somebody's been doing a lot of yakking."

As if on cue, the kitchen phone began to ring. Alicia stared at it, then at Lynette and back at the phone.

"Should we answer that?"

Lynette shrugged. "It's not our house. Surely some—"

"I'll get it!" called Barbara from inside the house and she came rushing into the kitchen, scooped up the phone and said, breathlessly, "Hello, Barbara Parlour speaking."

There was a pause and then she said again, "Hello? Hello? Anyone there?"

Alicia and Lynette exchanged another glance as Barbara continued to stare blankly at the phone. Eventually, the older woman hung up with a frown.

"Wrong number?" said Alicia.

"Hmmm, not sure. Just a quiet breathing on the other end, then nothing. That's the fourth time that's happened this week. I don't understand it at all."

Out of the side door a large man burst through. He had neatly trimmed grey hair, and was wearing a light pink Polo shirt, pleated bone trousers and boat shoes.

"Who was that on the phone?" he barked, then stopped short when he spotted the sisters. His tone lightened considerably. "Oh, hello, didn't see you there."

He swept his eyes over both sisters, settling at last on Lynette, or at least, on the fleshy bit below her neck. She wasn't exactly well endowed but this didn't seem to put him off.

Barbara started fidgeting and grabbed her throat again.

"Oh, Arthur, um, well, I don't know who that was. It… it just hung up. Another crank call I believe."

He dragged his eyes back to his wife and frowned. "Another? Have we been getting others?"

"You know we have, darling. Anyway, where are my manners?" She waved a shaky hand at the sisters. "Arthur, this is Alicia and Lynette, two members of my new book club."

"Book club?"

"You know, I told you about it yesterday." She gave him a slightly worried look.

"The Murder Mystery Book Club," Alicia announced, stepping forward to shake his hand. She was determined to get on the good side of at least one member of Barbara's family. "You've got a beautiful house here, thanks for letting us invade."

A wide grin broke out across Arthur's well-shaven face. "The Murder Mystery Book Club?" They nodded and his grin turned a little snide. "That's right, Barbs told me about her latest little project. I didn't even know she was into crime fiction. I thought biographies were more her style. In any case, can we really call this one a book club?"

He had the patronising tone of an English Professor and while Alicia tried to laugh him off, Lynette was not so accommodating.

"I don't see why not," she said crisply.

He sniggered a little. "No offence, girls, but you won't exactly have much to discuss. It's hardly what I'd call literature."

"That's exactly why we love it," Lynette replied. "It's for people who aren't so far up themselves they wouldn't know a good story if it smacked them over the head."

Barbara gasped and looked like her eyes were going to explode, and Alicia felt deep sympathy for the woman. Her family was horrendous. No wonder she turned to Agatha Christie for solace.

"Right, well, okay then," Barbara stammered, clearly trying to regain control. "We'd better get back out."

She steered them past the frowning husband and out to the deck.

When they were almost at the table she turned around to face them. Once again, the humiliation on her face was heartbreaking.

"I am so sorry about my husband, he can be a little, well, *cynical* about anything I'm interested in. You mustn't take offence."

"It doesn't aggravate you?" asked Lynette.

"Well, yes, I suppose it does sometimes. But that's okay, I'm used to it. I've got a good life, really I do."

Alicia wondered who she was trying to convince more, the sisters or herself.

"Apologies everyone," Barbara was now saying to the other members who were quietly waiting for the show to begin. "Let's kick off, shall we?"

The rest of the afternoon was relatively peaceful. Claire produced a neatly typed sheet of 'talking points' regarding *Evil Under the Sun* and they each took turns to discuss a wide range of issues, from the setting to the plot.

"I love this line from the book," said Claire, turning to a page she had marked with a yellow post-it note. "As you know the good detective Hercule Poirot has found himself stuck on a remote island at a boutique hotel with a cast of suspicious characters. One of them, the 'tough, athletic Emily Brewster' is going on about the fact that the place is way too beautiful and peaceful for bad things to happen. But Poirot begs to differ." Claire began reading Poirot's words from the book. "*…But you forget, Miss Brewster, there is evil everywhere under the sun'.*"

She looked up at them. "I just wonder, do we really believe that? Is evil lurking everywhere?"

Lynette scoffed. "No, that's just for dramatic effect. Agatha does that kind of thing in all her novels. It's to build suspense."

"I agree, it's just a literary device," said Anders.

Alicia noted he was looking especially handsome today in black jeans and a deep grey, well-fitting T-shirt, which, now that the jacket was removed, accentuated his broad, muscular shoulders. He caught her eye and she blushed as she glanced away.

"I believe it," said Barbara suddenly, vehemently, and they all turned to stare at her.

"Really?" said Missy, glancing down at her bandaged wrist and up again. "You really think there's evil everywhere? Even here, in your beautiful house?"

"Especially here," she said softly, so softly in fact that only those closest to her—Alicia on one side and Anders on the other—could hear it. They exchanged another glance, this one more apprehensive.

"I've got another quote," said Perry, grabbing his own well-worn copy of the book. He flipped to a page he'd marked with pencil. "This is a line from Reverend Stephen Lane—don't you love the way there's always a shifty looking 'man of the cloth' loitering about?"

"Well, I don't know about shifty, but there always were clergymen in those small English villages," said Claire. "Probably still are; and they were the often the centre of the village. Sort of like the moral compass."

"Yes, but they aren't in a small village in this book," said Missy. "They're at a boutique resort, remember? Bit of an odd place for this bloke to show up. But anyway, what's the quote, Perry?"

"Right, well, the Reverend is talking to Poirot about this whole idea of evil under the sun. He says…" Perry paused, deepening his voice and putting on his best plumy accent. *"But M. Poirot, evil is real! It is a fact! I believe in Evil like I believe in Good…"*

As he spoke, Perry's voice became louder and louder, and he raised one fist for dramatic effect. At the end of the quote the group laughed and clapped.

All except for Barbara.

She sat staring at Perry, her eyes wide, her head nodding vigorously as though she couldn't agree more.

~~~~~~~~

Later that night, as Alicia settled into bed with her latest book, she recalled Barbara's look, her words, and that feeling of nervousness that seemed to permeate everything she did that day. It was almost like there was something evil lurking in her Woollahra house, something that clearly had Barbara on edge.

Yet Alicia couldn't work out what. Her family were horrible, sure, but were they *evil?*

She looked down at the second Vera mystery in her hands and gave herself a little scolding.

"You need a break from crime fiction, young lady," she said as she relaxed into the pillow and, ignoring her own advice, resumed where she'd left off.
~~~~~~~~

CHAPTER 8

The next book club, a fortnight later, had been scheduled at Dr Anders' house and Alicia was really looking forward to it, and not just because she had a minor crush on the scheduled host. Today they were going to study *The Mysterious Affair at Styles*, the first book in which Hercule Poirot makes an appearance, and she already had a bunch of comments pencilled in her copy, ready to dazzle them all with her supreme insight. This book was Barbara's choice. She had insisted, rightly enough, that they go 'back to the beginning', and Alicia was keen to see just how the older woman had interpreted it. Sadly, she never got the chance.

Barbara Parlour did not show up.

For 20 minutes the rest of the group sat in Anders' living room making small talk and a quick meal of the cheese and crackers he had presented rather clumsily on a dinner plate. It wasn't at all what Alicia had been expecting; at least the house wasn't. This was no bachelor pad. There were bright paintings, ethnic statues and colourful, Indonesian *ikat* rugs at various spots, and Alicia wondered as she glanced around whether he had a sister to help him decorate, then chastised herself for being so sexist.

Unlike Barbara's place, however, there was no personal paraphernalia on display, which she also found odd. No happy snaps of cute nieces or pictures of sporting triumphs (Anders holding an oversized fish or looking dapper in ski gear and goggles). There was, however, a stunning upright Steinway piano in one corner, as well as a large bookshelf crammed to overflowing. Most of the books looked like classics—*Catcher in the Rye*, *Moby Dick*, that kind of thing—and there were plenty of hard covers amongst them. She suspected he was a collector. Anders, too, had chosen music for the day, but he was playing some moody blues, and this surprised her, too. She would have picked him for a jazz nut, or a classical kind of guy.

She clearly had a lot to learn about Anders Bright.

"How's your wrist?" Anders asked Missy, noticing the sling had gone.

"Oh, still a tad tender, thanks darls, but all good." She smiled wickedly as she added, "And in case anyone's wondering, no, there have been no more attempts on my life. Touch wood!" She tapped her head and burst into peals of laughter.

Alicia laughed along until she spotted a clock on the wall. It was 2:20 p.m. Her smile deflated and she reached for her notebook, took out the contact details she had typed up for each of them, and tapped Barbara's mobile number into her phone then waited as it rang. She assumed that the woman was running late or desperately lost. It went straight to her voice mail.

"Any luck?" Lynette asked and she shook her head no.

"Well, bugger Barbara," said Perry. "Let's just start without her."

"She's bringing the questions, remember?" said Missy and he scowled.

They continued making small talk for another ten minutes before Alicia turned back to her contact list.

"I do have her home number, I suppose I could call there."

"She would've left by now, surely," said Anders.

"She could be sick in bed, or have forgotten?" suggested Claire.

Lynette nodded. "Or maybe that horrible husband of hers has some idea where she is. Give her house a call, sis, see where she's at."

Alicia reached for her notebook again and looked up Barbara's home number then placed the call. This time it rang and rang and rang. She was just about to give up when a flustered female voice answered.

"Yes?"

"Oh, hello, sorry to bother you. I'm looking for Barbara."

"Who this?"

Alicia wondered the same of her. It didn't sound like either Barbara or her daughter. There was a strong accent.

"It's Alicia Finlay, from book club." The woman said nothing, so she quickly added, "It's just that Barbara hasn't shown and we're wondering if she's been held up."

There was another pause. "One minute, okay?"

The phone was dropped and Alicia could hear footsteps moving away, then, eventually, heavier footsteps returning.

"Hello, is this Alissa?"

"Alicia, actually, from Book Club. Is that Arthur?"

"Yes it is. Is Barbara with you?"

"Sorry?"

"Barbara." He sounded impatient. "My wife, is she with you?"

"No, that's why I'm calling. We've been waiting for her to show. Is she not around?"

"Not at the moment, no." His voice turned hushed. "You don't happen to know where she is do you?"

"Er, no, sorry. Can I—"

"Never mind, she's probably caught up somewhere. Thank you."

He went to hang up so she called out, "Just a second, sorry, are you saying she's missing?" There was a pause. "Arthur, where is Barbara?"

"I'm not sure."

"How long has she been missing?"

A slight scoff. "She's not *missing*. She's just, well, *out*, that's all."

Alicia changed tack. "How long has she been 'out' then?"

"Since last night but it's nothing for you to concern yourself with. I'll let her know you called when she gets back."

He hung up then and she stared into the phone, confused. Every eye was upon her.

"Well?" said Perry. "Misery Guts on her way?"

Alicia shook her head. "She's missing."

"Huh?"

Alicia relayed the conversation she'd just had with Barbara's husband and they all mulled it over for a while.

"Very odd," said Claire eventually, pinning a stray curl back under the small pillbox hat she was wearing that matched her bright purple '50s style dress. "The poor husband must be frantic. If my fiancé went missing overnight, I would be."

"Really?" said Perry. "Your fiancé never goes missing overnight?"

Claire flashed him an inscrutable look, her eyes squinting slightly. "Not lately, no."

Lynette and Alicia exchanged a glance then Alicia said, "It doesn't really matter, Claire. We didn't get a great vibe from Arthur last time did we Lyn? He was super patronising, a bit of a bully. I got the distinct feeling Barbara was scared of him."

"That might be stretching things a bit far," said Lynette. "But, no, he wasn't exactly your warm and fuzzy type."

"Oh, possums, she'll show," said Missy flippantly. "If what you say about the hubby is correct, they probably just had a tiff and she's skulked off to her mother's place to teach him a lesson. He sounds like a brute."

"Maybe even an unfaithful brute," added Alicia. "Remember that odd phone call in her kitchen, Lyn?

Barbara answered and there was just quiet breathing on the other end. Sounded like a hang-up to me. Could be the mistress hoping to get Arthur."

"You don't know that, Alicia. Honestly, you're such a drama queen," said Lynette, aghast. "I'm sure she'll show up eventually. She's probably busy somewhere or has just forgotten. She is getting on a bit, you know."

"She's in her 50s, Lynette," snapped Perry, the oldest in the room. "Not a candidate for dementia just yet."

"Either way, I'm sure if you call her later tonight, Alicia, she'll be there, super embarrassed and apologetic and all that."

"You're probably right," she said, putting her phone away and turning to her copy of today's book. "Okay then, let's get on with it. I don't think any of us need Barbara's questions to start chatting about this particular treasure. Anders, why don't you tell us all what you loved most about *The Mysterious Affair at Styles?*"

Two hours, two cups of tea, six cheese biscuits and a gin and tonic later, Alicia called an end to the club for the day and they all bid each other farewell.

"So you're going to call Barbara later?" asked Claire, and Alicia nodded.

"I'll text you all as soon as I speak to her and let you know she's okay. Lyn's probably right, she's probably just tied up somewhere."

"Hopefully, not in someone's dungeon," said Perry sending Missy into whoops of laughter again.

Alicia rolled her eyes at him then turned to Anders. "Thank you so much for a great club, and we'll all meet again next fortnight. Who's hosting, I've forgotten?"

"I am at last," said Perry. "You've all got my address but call if you get hideously lost."

He air kissed them all and they made their way out.

Once back at Woolloomooloo, with Max sufficiently walked and fed, and Lynette busily preparing a light supper in the kitchen, Alicia picked up the phone and keyed in Barbara's mobile number. Once again it rang until the voice mail clicked on. She left another message, trying to sound light and breezy but actually sounding more like a panicked stalker.

"Phone the ogre husband again!" called Lyn from the kitchen. "She has to be home by now."

Alicia took a deep breath and placed the call. This time the daughter picked up.

"Mum?" She sounded more angry than concerned.

"Er, no, Holly, it's your mum's book club friend Alicia. She hasn't shown yet?"

"No she has not." Again, the anger was palpable.

"Any idea where she is?"

"Nope."

"Can I speak to your dad?"

There was a pause. "He's not here."

"Oh, right, is he out looking for her?"

"Why would he be doing that?"

"Well, I thought if she's missing."

"She's not missing. Oh my God! She's just, like, staying away so she can avoid Dad and me. She hates us, and she can get F-ed!"

The phone promptly hung up and Alicia sat back with a start.

"Any luck?" called Lynette, about to place several homemade pizzas into the oven.

Alicia put the phone back and joined her in the kitchen, reaching for a glass of water.

"No, the daughter reckons she's just avoiding them, whatever the hell that means. And the husband is nowhere to be found."

"He's probably out searching for her."

"Yeah, probably. Hopefully."

Lynette reached for a stray chunk of goats cheese on the bread board and popped it in her mouth. "You sound worried."

"I am. I mean, I'm trying not to be, but, well, so soon after Missy, I can't help myself."

Lynette pulled up a stool and sat down. "Missy? What's she got to do with it?"

"She was run over, remember, by some unknown lunatic. And now another book club member has disappeared. It's suspicious, don't you think?"

Lynette stared at her sister like she'd just spoken gobbledygook. "Are you saying someone is targeting book club members? Is trying to kill us?"

Alicia blushed. Now that she put it like that she could see how absurd it sounded. "No, no, of course I'm not saying that. It just seems a little odd that's all."

"It's a little *coincidence*, Alicia. And completely unrelated. You heard what Missy said, hers was a stupid accident, some rev-head lost control. Barbara has simply gone AWOL, and we don't even know why. She might be perfectly fine."

"No, you're right. I know that. I just can't help thinking the worst. I got such a strange vibe last time we saw Barbara. She was so nervous and weird."

"Maybe she's always like that. We hardly know the woman."

"I know, I know…"

"What is it?"

Alicia scrunched her lips to one side. "What if Arthur's done something to her?"

"Sorry?"

"You know, chopped her up into little pieces and buried her in the garden or something."

Lynette looked at her sister pitifully. "Sounds like an Alfred Hitchcock plot to me. And why would he do that, pray tell?"

"I don't know. But they're not exactly the Brady Bunch over there. I reckon he knows more than he's letting on."

"There you go again."

"Yeah, yeah, my imagination is a killer, I know. But how strange is it for someone to just disappear and their husband and child to have no clue where they are? For 24 hours. It's just very suspicious."

"What would we know? Maybe it's normal practice for miserable married types to go walkabout." Lynette bent down and checked the pizzas. Stood up again. "But either way you've got to stop trying to relate this to Missy's accident. It's a totally separate matter." Alicia nodded, her sister was right. "So what are you going to do now?"

"I know what I'm *not* going to do," said Alicia.

"Oh?"

"I'm not going to give up on Barbara until I know she's safe and sound. And I won't apologise for that."

Even as she said the words, Alicia had that sinking feeling again. Despite what Lynette said, she felt a sense of doom sweep over her and wondered how safe any of them really were.

CHAPTER 9

"Of *course* she's safe," snapped Arthur at the front door of his house.

It was 8:00 a.m., the morning after book club, and Barbara's husband did not look happy to find Alicia on his doorstep so early asking what he called 'impertinent questions'. He was obviously dressed for the office, a grey suit on and a tie hanging loosely around his thick neck.

"How do you know that?" she persisted.

"Because, dear, my wife is a drama queen of the highest order. But of course you wouldn't know that. You've known her for, what, five minutes?"

"A few weeks actually."

He scoffed and began fiddling with the tie. "Let me fill you in on barmy Barbara shall I? This is not the first time she's walked out on me and probably won't be the last. No doubt she's somewhere right now having a good chuckle."

"Like where?"

He gave up on the tie. "I don't know. Um, like a friend's place or something."

"What friend?"

He paused. "I don't know, maybe she's at, um, Wanda's place. Bitching about me as we speak."

Alicia frowned at him. "And what if she's not? What if she's in danger or, I don't know, suicidal or something."

His jaw dropped. "Suicidal? Now you are getting carried away. If Barbara wanted to kill herself, she wouldn't slink away quietly, she'd do it right here in some dramatic fashion for all the world to see. Not to mention my future constituents."

"Well, the police might have other ideas about that. What are they saying about it all?" He looked at her blankly. "You have called them, haven't you? It's been two days now. You need to report her missing."

Arthur sighed heavily and looked at his gleaming gold watch. "I haven't got time for this rubbish. I have to get to work, somebody's got to pay for all her bloody designer clothes."

What designer clothes? Thought Alicia. Both times she'd seen Barbara, she was modestly dressed, fashion didn't seem of any interest at all.

"Look," he was saying, half shutting the door on her. "I'll call back at lunch time. If she's not in, I'll get in touch with the local police. Happy?"

"For now," she said as the door slammed in her face.

Alicia made her way to her office but couldn't help wondering why she seemed to be the only one who cared about Barbara's whereabouts and safety. By the time she parked her car and hurried in, however, she realised she was not alone. Every single member of the Book Club had contacted her mobile, enquiring about Barbara.

Alicia waved a quick hello to Ginny, the receptionist, who was pretending to shoot herself with two fingers as she listened to someone on the other end of the phone, and headed straight for her desk, dropping her stuff down and then preparing a group text on her mobile phone:

Hi Murder Mystery Book Club (MMBC). No word yet on B. Hub calling cops. Will check in after that. Fings crossed! xo AF

She sent it off and then tried hard to focus on her work, but failed miserably.

"You alright, sweet pea?" said Ginny over the espresso machine in the tearoom later that morning.

Alicia was frothing some milk for her coffee and Ginny had just placed a bowl of noodles in the microwave.

"Yeah, I'm fine," said Alicia. "You?"

"Urgh, just the usual irate subscribers, missing magazines, that sort of stuff. Really, they just need to build a bridge and get over it." She raised an eyebrow. "So how's your new book club going?"

The tilt of that eyebrow and the sarcasm in her tone indicated that she expected the answer to be negative, and Alicia didn't have the heart to tell her about Barbara. Ginny had thought the whole book club idea a ludicrous one when Alicia first broached it a few weeks earlier, scoffing at the suggestion that she might like to sign up.

"I'd rather pull my fingernails out then sit around discussing some ancient English broad," she'd said. "Besides, I don't know anyone who would. You have to face facts, Alicia. There's just not that many readers anymore. It'll probably take Kirsten three months to replace you in the Monday Night Book Club, if she does at all. People just do not read books. Period. These days they're all glued to YouTube watching some dumbarse guy tossing his baby about. Good luck finding eight people who not just read books, but like crime and, more specifically, Agatha 'Yawn' Christie."

Alicia had not been convinced. "She is the bestselling crime writer of all time you know."

"Irrelevant," said Ginny. "People don't *admit* to liking her for God's sake."

"They don't?"

"Christ no, how positively *provincial*. Besides, she was big in, what, the 1800s?"

"She didn't even start writing until the 1920s, actually, but what's a century between friends?"

"Same diff'. Does anyone even read her anymore?"

"Well, obviously I do. Lynette does."

"My point exactly."

Then, as if to emphasise that point, Ginny had swept her smudged black eyes down Alicia's outfit, to the flowing peasant top she was wearing over fitted blue jeans and back up to her face, shrugging her shoulders as if she'd just rested her case.

Luckily, Ginny's words had not been prophetic and she had found six people who adored Agatha Christie as much as she did. Perhaps that was why she was so worried about losing one of them.

As she frothed away, Alicia couldn't help feeling renewed anxiety.

Had something terrible happened to Barbara Parlour?

"Come on, what's eating at you?" Ginny asked again, impatiently eyeing her noodles in the microwave, and Alicia sighed and proceeded to tell her about the missing book club member.

Much to her surprise, Ginny just laughed it off. "She's done a runner. That's all it is."

"What do you mean?"

The microwave pinged and Ginny grabbed an oven mitt and pulled the steaming bowl out. "She's been to one meeting, right? She obviously loathed it and hasn't got the guts to tell you, so she's a no-show for the next one."

"But her husband says she hasn't come home…"

She snorted. "The husband's probably just pulling your chain. They're too embarrassed to tell you your little club is a *loser* one." She made the letter L with her fingers and placed it on her forehead.

"Very mature," Alicia said drolly, spooning some froth into her cup and giving Ginny's suggestion some thought.

"I really don't think that's it. Barbara seems way too polite—and grown up—to just slink away without saying anything. Now you I would believe that of."

"Hey!" Ginny retorted. "I did not slink away from the Monday Night Book Club. I just didn't get a chance to tell Kirsten that I wasn't coming back, and then you said you'd take my place and all was right with the world." She paused. "Until *you* deserted, too. I can not believe you walked out on them. What did Wilfred the Whinger say?"

"Not a lot as it happens," Alicia said. "He just kind of looked constipated."

"Oh he always looks constipated. But still, swigging their vino—and *before* official drinkies time. You anarchist."

Alicia took a sip of her cappuccino. "Anyway, that's all beside the point, I'm worried about Barbara."

"Yeah, well, stop worrying, it's not going to get you anywhere." Ginny took a slurp of her noodles and yelped. "Damn that's hot. So, what're you working on this month? More bumper Sudoku books? A Justin Bieber pull-out poster mag?"

Alicia scrunched up her face. "You won't believe it."

"Try me."

"Kittens. An entire magazine devoted to the glory of kittens."

Ginny burst into laughter again, her ruby red lips wide, her smudged eyes delighted. "Honestly, you get all the crazy jobs. Don't get me wrong, kittens are cute, but I'm not sure I'd want to create a whole magazine about them. No wonder you love murder mysteries. I'd be looking to kill someone when I left work each day, too. Speaking of which…"

She glanced at the doorway where a middle-aged man with shaven grey hair, baggy jeans and a black hoodie was standing. It was Hamish Keener, the editor of a raunchy men's magazine down the hallway. He had a thick cockney accent, a breathtaking beer gut and an ego the size of Uluru.

"Oh what a bloody surprise, Ginny's gasbagging in the tea room." He glanced at Alicia and smiled. "How are your pussies going?"

She shook her head sadly. "You're really quite revolting Hamish, you know that, don't you?"

He winked. "That's why I get paid the big bickies." He glanced back at Ginny. "Hate to break up your party, sweetheart, but the freakin' phones don't pick themselves up. D'ya think you can find five seconds in your clearly busy schedule to actually do your job?"

Ginny sneered back at him. "Up yours, Hamish."

"No thanks, sweetheart, we've been there, done that."

He promptly disappeared leaving a gasping Ginny behind him. She raced to the doorway and screamed after him, "Yeah and it was the biggest disappointment of my life!"

She turned back to Alicia and smiled, clearly unruffled by the exchange.

"I suppose I'd better get back to it before Hamish dobs me into Head Office." She picked up her bowl. "I got five bucks on your missing book club member reappearing by close of day."

If only, Alicia thought, returning to the overcrowded office she shared with a motley collection of other one-off editors and part-time sub-editors who couldn't quite fit in with their respective publications. This was the Sydney headquarters for international magazine publishing group Arial and, apart from Hamish's lads title *Lout*, there were 14 others in the three-story building, including women's lifestyle, teen and computer magazines, as well as random one-offs like the *Kitten Quarterly* that Alicia was currently editing. She worked alongside a graphic designer who helped her put these editions together in a matter of weeks, sometimes days. This one, however, was proving more laborious than usual, probably because she didn't really have an affinity for cats, as cute as they were. Now, a magazine about dogs, that would write itself…

Alicia slumped across her desk, worried and, now thanks to Ginny, confused. Was the receptionist right? Was Barbara just trying to wimp out? It seemed a rather odd way of going about it, but then she had seemed a rather odd person.

Alicia sat up. There was only one way to find out. She glanced around knowing she should be focusing on *20 Purr-fect Games for Playful Kits*, grabbed her handbag and headed out. She was determined to get back to Barbara's house and see if Arthur had made good on his promise. The feeling of dread that had been building up inside her for almost 24 hours had now reached a crescendo, and she'd already decided that if Arthur hadn't called the police by now, she would.

With her brightest smile in place, Alicia pressed the buzzer outside the Woollahra mansion where Barbara Parlour lived. This time, a small Filipino woman of indeterminate age opened the door. She was wearing a simple floral summer dress, with an apron over it and her long, black hair had been dyed a lurid shade of orange down one side. Probably a bleach job gone wrong, Alicia thought. Her make-up, too, was shockingly applied—garish red blush, thick pink lip-gloss and startled black lines where her eyebrows once sat. She looked almost comical but her frown was anything but. She was madly chewing some gum and there was an iPod Touch hanging around her neck and connected to one ear.

"Yes, what you want?" she asked impatiently, waving the other earpiece at Alicia who could hear something very loud and very tinny coming from it.

"Hello, you must be Rosa. We spoke briefly yesterday on the phone. I'm Alicia. A good friend of Barbara's."

While it was stretching the truth slightly, she did feel a definite bond with the sad housewife and, at this point, felt like one of the few friends Barbara had. The housekeeper looked surprised, gave Alicia the once-over and continued chewing.

"So, has Barbara returned?"

Rosa stopped chewing, squinted her claggy eyes together and said, "Uh-uh. I can leave message?"

Alicia shook her head. "Is Arthur here?"

"He busy."

"Right. Um, do you know if he's called the police?"

She looked startled by the suggestion and was about to say something when Arthur's voice came booming from deep within the house.

"Oi, Rosa baby! Where's that whisky got to?"

Alicia glanced inside and then back at the housekeeper whose eyes squinted again. She closed the door slightly, as if blocking him out.

"Mr Parlour he busy—"

Alicia put her foot in the doorway. "Doesn't sound real busy to me, Rosa. Come on, I want to speak to him, and I want to speak to him *now*."

The housekeeper contemplated this for a second before frowning again.

"You wait."

She closed the door and left Alicia standing outside for several minutes before it swung back open and Arthur appeared, a stiff smile on his face.

"Ahh, it's Alissa again."

"*Alicia.*"

"Right, Alicia, that's what I said. I can see we're not going to get rid of you so easily."

"I'm sorry to keep intruding," she said, "but I just have to ask one question and then you need never see me again."

He stared at her, waiting and she felt a little foolish.

"This is awkward but, um, is Barbara really missing?"

"Excuse me?"

"I mean, could she, well, just be avoiding me… that is, the book club?"

Arthur frowned. "No, I told you, she hasn't been home since Saturday afternoon."

Alicia's stomach tightened. "Right. Well, that really is a worry then and quite frankly I'm surprised you're not more concerned. It's Monday, she's been missing two whole days now."

His frown deepened. "Don't get your knickers in a knot, sweetheart, I have phoned the police and they are on their way over. Happy?"

"I'm not happy about any of this, Arthur. I realise I haven't known your wife long but when a woman—any woman—goes missing, I hear alarm bells. It should be looked into."

"And that is exactly what I am doing." He spat each word out slowly, as if dealing with an imbecile and Alicia was about to let rip when a police patrol car turned into the driveway.

She watched as two uniformed officers got out slowly and strolled up to the house. Arthur gave her an *I-told-you-so* smirk and then thrust one hand out for the police to shake.

"Thanks for coming officers, I'm Arthur Parlour. Please come inside."

"And you are?" one of the officers asked Alicia.

"Oh she's just a friend of Barbara's," Arthur said dismissively.

Alicia smiled at the young male officer and held out her own hand.

"A very concerned friend, actually. I'm Alicia Finlay. Barbara was supposed to be at my book club yesterday at 2:00 p.m. and never showed. We're really worried."

Arthur sighed loudly beside her but she ignored him and grappled for a business card in her handbag.

"Here are my details if you need to get in touch."

"And why would they need to do that?" Arthur said.

"You never know."

Alicia waved them goodbye and headed back to her car. Once inside, she scooped up her phone and placed another group text: *"Dear MMBC: Still no sign of B but cops now in the loop. If anyone wants 2 discuss, meet @ mine, 6:00 p.m. xo AF"*

CHAPTER 10

Not only did all the remaining members of the Murder Mystery Book Club want to discuss Barbara's whereabouts, they each came loaded with their own outlandish theories.

"It's the daughter," announced Perry as he pulled off his black and white, pinstriped jacket and began rolling up the sleeves of a white business shirt. He'd obviously just come from work. "She's definitely dodgy."

"Why on earth would you say that?" demanded Anders who was also in his work suit and was just dropping down onto the sofa, a large gym bag by his side.

"Well, during book club at her pad, while the rest of you were trying to outdo each other with your witty repartee, I scuttled around the side of the house for a ciggie, remember? And, yes, thank you Dr Anders, I know it will slice 15 years off my life, but boy it'll be one hell of a life."

Anders just scowled.

"Anyway, there's a tennis court round the back, no surprises there, and I spotted the young missy, tennis racquet in hand, snogging what looked like her instructor."

He stared at them all, looking very impressed with himself.

"So?" said Anders. "Having a fling with your tennis coach doesn't make you a killer."

"It does if Mommy dearest doesn't want you to hook up with an older man. He has to be at least 10 years her senior. A bloody great spunk, too, I might add. Maybe Barbs caught them at it and they hit her over the head too hard with a tennis racquet?"

"Oh for goodness' sake," said Claire, releasing her glossy black hair from a wide straw hat and brushing it down carefully with gloved hands.

"What, you think everybody is innocent, Claire?" said Perry rounding on her suddenly. "You think people don't pretend to be someone they're not?"

She looked at him, bewildered. "That's not what I was saying."

"Look, forget about the daughter," said Anders. "I've got a better idea. He produced a bottle of red wine from his bag.

"Ooh that is a good idea," announced Lynette jumping up to fetch glasses from the kitchen while they all settled in around the tea chest just as they had done that first book club meeting. He laughed.

"Getting drunk wasn't my idea," he said. "Although, it's a not a bad one in the circumstances. But, hey, listen, there was one thing I noticed when Barbara was showing Alicia, Lynette and myself through the house, that day we were there, and I don't think it's inappropriate of me to mention it… now that she's, well, disappeared." He paused. "There was a phone number scribbled quite large on the white board beside the kitchen phone."

"There were a bunch of phone numbers," said Lynette, returning with wine glasses. "So?"

"So, one of them was a toll-free number for a shelter."

"Shelter?"

"The Women's Harmony Centre—a battered wives shelter."

"I don't remember that," said Lynette.

"It was a bit cryptic. There were the initials WHC and the 1-800 phone number."

They all sat silently for a moment, the excitement of their little case edging away as harsh reality took over.

"Oh dear," said Alicia eventually. "You think she was being beaten up?"

Anders held his hands up, defensively. "I think nothing of the sort. I work on evidence alone and I didn't see any signs of bruising or broken limbs on the woman, but I did spot that number. It had been written quite large, so she certainly wasn't hiding it. But then, I guess if you didn't know what WHC meant…"

"So how *did* you know?" asked Lynette. "Maybe they're the initials for a hire car company or something?"

"It was definitely the Harmony Centre number. Sadly I know it off by heart because I've had to hand it out one too many times at the surgery. Never to Barbara, of course, please let me make that perfectly clear. *She* was not a patient of mine."

"So, let me get this straight," said Alicia. "Barbara had the number of the shelter but you don't think she was being beaten up?"

"I'm just saying, we don't know for sure but it does make you wonder."

"She *was* wearing a scarf around her neck that day," piped in Missy.

"Yes, I noticed that, too," said Alicia. "It was such a hot day, so it was a bit strange. You think she could have been hiding a bruise, perhaps?"

She raised her eyebrows to indicate yes.

"Listen, guys, I've seen elderly people come to my surgery in woollen coats mid-summer," said Anders. "I don't think we can read too much into a scarf." Then, to their disappointed faces he added, "I'm not saying she wasn't a battered wife, I'm just saying we need to tread carefully here. You don't want to start pointing the finger until you have some solid proof. Mud sticks. But the fact remains Barbara had the number of a battered wives shelter by her phone. We don't know why and for whom. Maybe it was for her. Maybe she was going to give it to a friend. Or maybe it's unrelated. One other thing: do you remember, Alicia, how she mentioned that there was evil at her house?"

Alicia considered this for just a second before it came flooding back. "Oh, that's right." She turned to the group to explain. "Claire had quoted from *Evil Under the Sun* and asked the question 'Is there evil lurking everywhere under the sun?' Most of us disagreed but Barbara was adamant that there was. Then you, Missy, pressed her on it."

"Oh, you're right, yes. I said, surely not somewhere like your beautiful house. I can't remember what she said after that."

"I know exactly what she said," interjected Anders. "I'll never forget it because it gave me the creeps. She said *'especially here'*." He looked at Alicia for backup and she nodded. "I can't say what she meant by that, no one can, but I think we should take note of it, and the battered wives number, too."

"That's a brilliant idea," said Alicia. "I'm going to take notes."

She jumped up to fetch her journal while Anders poured them each a glass of wine and Lynette returned to the kitchen to heat up last night's leftover pizza.

Ten minutes later the theories were running thick and fast. They all agreed something was amiss. Perhaps Barbara had had a fight with her housekeeper and been hit over the head with a rolling pin. Perhaps the housekeeper and the husband were in it together.

"*Lovers*," suggested Missy. "Out to rid themselves of the miserable fishwife. Oh I've read lots and lots of stories about this. It's very common, or at least it is in crime fiction. Agatha was a big fan of this scenario, too." She paused. "I wonder if she had any life insurance?"

"I still think the daughter was involved, I didn't like the look of her one bit," said Perry.

"She probably didn't like the look of you either," Anders said and Missy giggled. "Listen, what are we doing here?" he asked suddenly and they stopped their chatter.

"We're investigating, aren't we?" said Perry.

"Just as Agatha would do," added Alicia and they all nodded their heads.

"Do you think we should?" Claire asked now. "I mean, is that the right thing to do? To poke our noses in? Isn't that why we have a police force?"

"Yes, but it can't hurt for us to mull it over as well," said Alicia. "We're in the unique position in that we're detached from it all and can give the case some perspective."

"And you really believe we have a case here?"

Alicia didn't hesitate. "Yes, Anders, I really do. It looks to me like Barbara Parlour has vanished from the face of the earth. Her husband, daughter and housekeeper—not your usual frumpy housekeeper I might add—all seem very relaxed about it. Way too relaxed. I wonder now whether Barbara joined our group for a reason."

"How do you mean?" asked Lynette, refilling her glass.

"I mean, did she suspect that her life was in danger? Did she maybe hope that we would look out for her?"

"Now that really is stretching it," scoffed Lynette but Perry was nodding his head vigorously, stroking his black goatee at the same time.

"I think Alicia's on to something. Think about it. She was so *determined* that we have the first club at her house. Remember? I offered first—mine would have been fabulous, *darlinks*, you're going to adore my place—but she insisted we go to her pretentious hovel. Why? I thought she was just showing off but maybe she knew that bullyboy husband was going to do away with her and hoped we'd find a few clues while we were there. Then of course there's yesterday's book choice, which she also insisted on."

When they all looked at him blankly, he added, "Come on, gorgeous people, keep up with me. *The Mysterious Affair at Styles*. Get it?"

"Perry, Perry, Perry," said Lynette laughing. "You are as over-the-top as Alicia. Barbara chose that book because it was the first time Poirot appears. Pretty logical."

"Or was she trying to tell us something about her hideous husband and/or dreadful daughter?" He raised his eyebrows up and down.

Anders held up a cautionary hand. "We mustn't convict the family members too soon, people."

"Why?" demanded Perry. "Why do you keep sticking up for that lot?"

"No, no, Anders is right," said Missy. "It's almost always not the first people you suspect."

"Actually, that's not what I meant at all," Anders laughed. "I meant, we have to get solid evidence first. And besides, she could still show up. It is early days. Didn't you say, Alicia, that her husband thinks she's with a friend?"

"Yes, now what was the name… Wendy I think. No, Wanda. That's it."

"Right, so why don't we just check there first? Maybe Wanda can clear this whole mess up."

They all agreed it was a good idea.

"But how will I get her number? I'll have to annoy Arthur again. He won't be happy."

"Do it now," urged Perry and Alicia checked her watch.

It was not yet 7:00 p.m; hopefully Arthur wasn't sitting down to dinner. She grabbed the phone and put the call through. Rosa answered, her tone turning surly again when Alicia identified herself.

"Okay, he here," she said after a long pause, "but he no happy with you."

"Too bad Rosa, I need to speak to him. Can you put him on please? It's important."

After an interminably long time, Arthur appeared on the phone and, as predicted, was extremely unhappy to hear from the meddling book club member. The good news was, he also clearly didn't want to keep her on the line for long, and within seconds had offered up Barbara's girlfriend's full name—Wanda Birchin—and her home number.

"Now leave me the hell alone," he growled, hanging up.

"Didn't take him long to find the number," said Claire curiously.

"He was just desperate to get rid of me," Alicia replied, keying Wanda's number into the phone and pressing 'dial'.

"Halo, Wanda Birchin speaking," came the faux English accent Alicia had come to expect of wealthy, eastern suburbs matron types.

She introduced herself. "I'm looking for Barbara Parlour, actually, you don't happen to know where she is?"

"Barbara? No, of course not, have you tried the house? Asked Arthur?"

"Yes, she hasn't been seen for two days."

"Oh, I see." The tone turned wary. "Who did you say this is again?"

"It's a friend from her new book club. She didn't show up yesterday and her husband seems to have no idea where she is. We wondered whether you might know."

"Why would I know?"

"It's just, well, we wondered whether she might be staying with you."

Alicia scrunched up her face, realising it was a stretch but hopeful nonetheless.

There was a long pause on the other end so Alicia quickly added, "Listen, I don't mean to impose but we're all really worried about her."

Wanda exhaled loudly. "Yes, yes, of course." Her voice softened a little. "Can you come and see me? Tomorrow? Here?"

"Sure."

Alicia retrieved her journal and pen while the club members stared wide-eyed at her. She jotted down the address and hung up, then turned to the group.

"Well?" said Perry. "Spit it out."

"The plot thickens," said Alicia. "I think Ms Wanda Birchin has something to tell us."

Claire gasped. "You don't think Barbara really is hanging out there?"

"I don't know, maybe, maybe not, but it's clear Wanda knows something. Wants to see me in person, so I'll go there in my lunch break tomorrow, see what she has to say."

"Search the place while you're there," suggested Perry.

"Yeah, I'm sure she'll let me rummage through her house, Perry," Alicia replied, eye rolling him.

"You should really have someone go with you," Anders added, frowning slightly. "Unfortunately I've got surgery."

"I'll come with," offered Claire. "I can always shut up shop for an hour or so."

"That'd be great, thank you. How about I pick you up around 1:15?"

"Fine." Claire grabbed her straw bag, which matched her hat perfectly, Alicia noticed, and produced a small card with the shop details on it.

"I'll be ready and waiting. But what if she's not there? What if she has no idea what's happened to Barbara?"

"Then we follow Miss Marple's meddling example and we investigate," said Alicia, and they all raised their glasses in a toast to that.

~~~~~~~~

Just as the group were clinking glasses and agreeing to investigate, the police were doing a little investigating of their own. They had just discovered Barbara Parlour's shiny silver Mercedes Benz parked near a train station on the upper North Shore. It had been locked and several personal items left behind for all to see.

There was no trace of the missing housewife.
~~~~~~~~

CHAPTER 11

Wanda Birchin was the antithesis of Barbara Parlour. Dressed in a flowing leopard-print designer kaftan, with sparkly Chanel thongs, her overly streaked hair piled high on her head, her thickly lined lips bee-stung by Botox, she ushered the two women into her house with hands that were dripping with gems and gold.

"We'll go out to the pool," she purred. "It's such a glorious day."

As they were led through the house—another over-sized Mansion, this one decorated in various hues of red, black and gold, and nestled right up beside an exclusive golf course—Alicia and Claire kept a keen eye out for any sign of Barbara, but each enormous room appeared void of life.

"I trust you've seen the papers?" Wanda said, indicating for them to take a seat on white wicker furniture in the shade of a polished timber gazebo.

Beyond them, the long lap pool stretched, its water sparkling above turquoise blue tiles. It looked extremely inviting and Alicia couldn't help feeling a pang of envy. Sometimes it was better not to glimpse how the other half lived.

She looked away and down at the wicker table where several local newspapers were open at articles on the missing woman, then nodded gloomily. Alicia had heard the news over the radio that morning and caught up on the details online at work. At this stage, the facts were still sketchy. Barbara's car had been found abandoned at Hornsby Railway Station, on Sydney's upper North Shore—miles from Barbara's house—and the police had made a public appeal for anyone with information on the car or its owner to contact them.

"They're obviously completely in the dark," Wanda was saying, glancing at the papers then back at Alicia. "I do hope the old duck's alright. So, tell me, how are you lot involved in all of this?"

Alicia filled Wanda in on the newly formed Murder Mystery Book Club. She told her how they had waited for Barbara to show up at their last meeting, to no avail, and then detailed her conversations with Arthur and their concerns for Barbara's safety.

"I guess we're wondering if you have any idea where she might be." She hesitated. "She's not here is she?"

"Here?" Wanda blinked several times. "You mentioned that before and no, she most certainly is not. I struggle to understand why you'd imagine she is."

"Well, we're just thinking that maybe she had a fight with her husband and ran here to hide out for a bit. That's what he suggested."

Wanda looked amused suddenly. "Arthur suggested that? Cheeky bugger."

"Well you are her best friend, right?"

"Best friend? Who, Barbara?" She blinked again. "Did Arthur say that as well?"

"Well, he indicated—"

"Then allow me to set the record straight. Barbara and I are certainly *not* best friends. I mean, sure we used to have a giggle once upon a time over champers at the club, but not recently. We'd, um, well, fallen out if you must know."

"What over?" asked Claire.

Wanda glanced at Claire as though only just noticing her presence and, clearly deciding she didn't like what she saw—a prettier, younger model was probably not welcome in these parts—glanced back at Alicia and said coldly, "That's no one's damn business."

"Fair enough," said Alicia quickly, trying to keep the peace. "Can you at least tell us a little bit about Arthur?"

Before she had a chance to reply, a large, flabby woman appeared. Squashed into a simple white dress and flat white shoes, she was in her 60s with short grey hair and 'tuck-shop arms', the kind that flop about when they move. She looked like a nurse but was clearly the maid—or whatever it was that rich people called poorer people who fetched them things at will.

Without introducing her, Wanda simply said, "Thank God you're here, Florrie, what would I do without you?   A G&T would be fabulous. What about you ladies? Can I interest you in a gin? Wine perhaps?"

Alicia resisted the urge to check her watch, it was only lunchtime after all, and asked for a soft drink instead. Claire repeated the request and Wanda looked disappointed.

"Spoil sports," she said, giving Florrie the nod. As the maid returned inside she asked, "So what do you want to know about Arthur?"

"Could he be involved in some way?" asked Alicia. "I don't want to sound alarmist but he just doesn't seem worried enough."

Wanda shrugged. "He's hardly the doting husband at the best of times. But I can tell you one thing, he's worried as all hell now."

"So he should be, especially now they've found Barbara's car," said Claire.

Wanda ignored this. "The police are starting to get extremely nosey. Even took him in for questioning this morning. That won't do his political aspirations any good at all."

"Really? The police have questioned him formally?" said Alicia.

"Don't get too excited, darling, they haven't locked him up just yet. But yes, they're asking all kinds of awkward questions. I've just come off the phone from him. He's furious. Blames you entirely."

"Me?" she said, stunned.

Wanda chuckled. As she did so, Alicia noticed that very little of her face actually moved, revealing that she'd meddled with more than just her lips.

"Oh yes, Arthur says—and let me see if I can get this quite right—he says you're a 'dreadful gossip monger' and 'a bloody nosy bitch who's stirring up the pot!'"

She laughed again and Alicia wanted to swipe the rigid smile from her gargantuan lips.

"I'm not going to apologise for looking out for Barbara, somebody's got to," she retorted.

"Don't take offence, sweetie, I think it's admirable of you, especially in the light of the latest news. If I know Barbara, there's no way she'd leave her precious Merc just sitting there for someone to pinch. And what was she doing up at Hornsby anyway? Not her usual stomping ground I'd say. Very suspicious if you ask me. Although, having said that, I also think Arthur has a point."

"About me?"

"No, about Barbara. She could be a pain in the proverbial when she wanted to be, and very flighty at times. He believes she's just taken off for a holiday."

"A *holiday*? So why was her car dumped at Hornsby? Besides, wouldn't she tell someone?"

"She did, apparently. Before she disappeared she mentioned something to the housekeeper, that tramp. I honestly don't know why Barbara employs these women. Baiting Arthur if you ask me."

"Hang on a minute," said Claire, "are you saying that Arthur really is having an affair with his housekeeper?"

Wanda glared at Claire then turned back to Alicia.

"You really have no clue about any of this do you?"

The younger women glanced at each other and back at Wanda.

"Fill us in," said Alicia.

"There's nothing much to say," sighed Wanda. "Arthur likes to play up a bit. Big deal."

"So he was 'playing up' with Rosa then?"

"I don't know that for sure, and she's hardly a spring chicken. No looker. Still, you wouldn't put it past Arthur. He always did have trashy taste. Honestly I don't know what Barbara was thinking, employing such a floozy. Me? I only ever hire fat old *frauen*. Much safer that way. Oh, speak of the devil…"

Florence reappeared, her arms wobbling like loose dough under a tray of drinks, which she placed down without a word, a neutral expression on her face. She had brought Alicia and Claire a lemon squash each, and had added sliced lemons on the side. They thanked her but she didn't respond, simply turned around and shuffled away. Wanda grabbed her gin and tonic, slurping down a good gulp as though her life depended on it, and then winked.

"Don't think I have too much to worry about there," she said, indicating the maid and Alicia felt sick to her stomach. Perhaps it was best not to know how the other half lived.

"Anyway," Alicia said, trying to steer the conversation back. "What did Barbara say to Rosa?"

"Hm?"

"You said she told the housekeeper something before she disappeared."

"Oh, yes, apparently—and this is third-hand from Arthur, so let's take it with a grain of salt shall we?— apparently she told Rosa she was off to Europe or something."

"Europe?"

"I *know*. Obviously the silly tramp's got it all wrong. As if she'd just head off to Paris or wherever without any notice. No, Arthur tells me the police don't believe a single word of it. And it's not like her car was found at the airport. No, no, they think something far more sinister has happened."

"What do you think?" asked Alicia.

Wanda swirled the ice around in her glass then scooped a small chunk out, chomping down on it as she gave this some thought. "I don't know what to think, but I can tell you one thing, Arthur's right, Barbara is very unpredictable. You never know what she's going to do next. She really could make such a fuss about the smallest of things."

"Like being beaten up?" Claire said, trying to contain her growing anger.

"Beaten up? By whom?"

"The husband, of course."

"Arthur? Beating up Barbara?" Wanda's long, black eyelashes blinked several times and then she laughed that frozen laugh again as if she'd never heard anything so ridiculous. Noticing the other women's frowns, she threw one bejewelled hand to her mouth.

"I'm sorry, ladies, but *please.* Arthur? More like the other way around. Barb could be scary when she set her mind to it."

This surprised them and they glanced at each other again, not sure where to go next. Both Wanda and Arthur seemed to be describing someone other than the woman they had met at two book clubs.

"So you really don't think he was harming her?" asked Claire.

"I doubt it sincerely. He barely laid a hand on her; that was part of the problem I would suggest. No, no, no, Arthur might be a philandering fool but he's not violent. Not at all."

"Well, we spotted a number for a battered wives shelter at her house," said Alicia, "and she seemed pretty jittery when we met her."

Wanda kept shaking her head, swirling her glass around and around. "I really find this line of enquiry just too sordid for words. No, I just can't believe it of Arthur. Now, the daughter, well, she's a piece of work. She'd probably smack her mother around if she got half a chance."

"*Really?*" exclaimed Claire again, nearly choking on her drink.

Wanda stopped swirling. "I'm exaggerating, darling. Where's your sense of humour?"

"It went missing around the same time Barbara disappeared," Claire snapped back and Wanda gave her the once-over then returned her gaze to Alicia.

"Listen, I know you're concerned, and I think that's just charming of you. But I'm sure she's perfectly fine."

"Even though her car's been dumped?"

She shrugged one shoulder, her kaftan falling down low across it, revealing leathery, sun-scorched skin.

"So any idea then what might have happened or where she might be now?" asked Alicia.

"None whatsoever, and I'll tell that to the police should they bother to call. I do know her parents are no longer around although I believe there's another sibling lurking somewhere in the shadows. Yes, a younger one, causing all sorts of headaches if I remember right."

"Headaches?"

"Money problems, that sort of thing." She stopped and considered this for a second. "Can't recall if it's a brother or sister to be honest."

"Any idea where we can find him or her?"

Wanda drained her glass dry and then looked around as if hoping Florence would materialise again. She glanced back at Alicia. "Sorry, can't help you there either. You'll have to ask Arthur. He'll be *thrilled* to see you again."

Then she chuckled without moving a muscle.

CHAPTER 12

Arthur didn't get a chance to be thrilled; he was nowhere to be seen when, 10 minutes later, Claire and Alicia knocked on his front door. Rosa, however, was there, this time in a stretchy black nylon dress that was low at the front and too high at the hem for a woman her age. Her apron was gone but the scowl across her face was firmly in place.

"I know nothing of family," she told them. "Arthur too busy for this now. They find car, you know? He very stressed."

"Of course he is," said Alicia, feigning sympathy. "Can you please just let him know we'll give him a call later."

The housekeeper flicked her lurid orange and black hair and closed the door in their face.

"How rude," said Claire. "It's not like she owns the place."

"Certainly acts like she does."

Just then they heard a loud cry coming from one side of the house and Alicia imagined Barbara, blood gushing from a wound in her heart, staggering, half dead towards her. *Why didn't you help me!* she was screaming. *What took you so long?*

She shuddered and followed Claire around to the side where, through the security fence, they could just make out the tennis court. There was no sign of Barbara but they could clearly see Holly, tennis racquet in hand, berating an older guy clad completely in white.

"Must be the flirtatious tennis coach," whispered Alicia but Claire was staring at Holly, mesmerised.

"I've seen her before," she said.

"Yes, last book club, she was home, remember?"

Claire shook her head. "No, I never saw her that day…"

They edged forward to get a better look, bending down behind a hedge just in front of the court.

"We *have* to tell him," Holly was saying through clenched teeth. "We can't keep this quiet!"

"You don't even know if it was me," he replied, barely audible.

"Of course it was bloody you!" she screamed, hitting the racquet against his shoulder while he winced.

Alicia turned to Claire. "Wanda's right, she is scary."

It was obviously too loud as Holly stopped suddenly and swung around.

"Who's there?" she called out.

The two women hesitated then looked at each other again, sighed, and straightened up as Holly came bounding towards them, the tennis coach close behind. She stopped when she reached the fence and stared, open-mouthed.

"Oh. My. God. It's the busybody book club bitches again!"

The girl could really pull off a tongue twister, Alicia thought, trying for a confident smile. "Hi, Holly. Sorry, didn't mean to disturb you, we're just wondering if your mum's back—"

"Yes you bloody did and no she's bloody not." Holly looked around "Who else is out there?" She squinted her eyes as if trying to see past them. "Is he with you? Is that why you're here?"

Alicia was confused. "He? Who do you mean? What are you talking about?"

Holly stared at her and for a brief moment a look of utter vulnerability passed across her face. She appeared as though she was about to cry and Alicia stepped towards her, reaching out a hand through the fence, but Holly shook herself out of it and turned the look to one of rage.

"Why can't you lot just bugger off and stop spying on me!" she screamed.

"Calm down, Hol'," the coach said, reaching her side. "They don't mean any harm—"

Holly turned back on him. "Then why do they keep poking their ugly noses in where they're not wanted?"

He ignored her and stepped forward, holding on to the fence and smiling widely. He had boyish good looks although Perry was right, he had to be at least 15 years older than his student, fine wrinkles just appearing below aqua blue eyes. His skin was deeply tanned, his brown hair streaked with blond tints, and he had the broad, muscular shoulders of an athlete. Only his nose, crooked from some schoolboy fight or rugby game perhaps, worked to sully the golden boy image he had going on. When he smiled—which he was doing now, and directing at Claire—his teeth gleamed as white as his tennis shirt.

"Afternoon ladies, I'm Jake Smith. Tennis coach."

He held Claire's eyes for a little longer than was necessary.

"Hi Jake, I'm Claire," she said awkwardly. "And this is Alicia. We're from Barbara's book club. We honestly don't mean to spy on Holly, we're just worried about her mother, that's all there is to it."

Holly's eyes scrunched together. "That's really why you're here? For Mum?" She looked as though she didn't believe them.

"Yes, Holly," said Alicia. "We're extremely worried about her. You must be very worried too, surely?"

"'Course I am." She sniffed loudly and wiped one hand across her nose. "Everybody thinks I hate my mother, but I'm sick as, man. It's been three days, and now they've found her car all by itself, which is, like, *super-weird*. She wouldn't just dump her Merc, no way, and she wouldn't take off for this long. Not without phoning me. I mean, where the hell is she?"

"That's a really good question, Holly, and we're trying to find out," said Alicia. "Does your dad have any ideas?"

"No he does not. And I don't know why everybody thinks he does. He has nothing to do with this. It's my bloody uncle you should be spying on."

"Oh?"

"Oh *yeah*. He's the one who's going to profit big time by Mum's death."

"You think she's dead?" asked Claire.

Holly stopped, looked flustered. "Oh, well, I don't know…" she stammered, "but the police do and they're asking Dad all sorts of stupid questions like he's guilty or something. But I already heard Dad talking to his lawyer, and I know for a fact that there's no point him killing Mum because she's left everything to her brother. Don't worry about me. All that matters is knucklehead Uncle Niles."

"You mean, in her will?" Alicia asked.

"Duh!" Holly glared at her as though she'd never spoken to anyone quite so stupid before. "It *all* goes to him. Can you believe that?"

"You don't happen to know where we can find him?" she asked.

She shrugged. "Nope, he can rot in hell. Come on, Jake, I wagged school for this, so let's just get on with it."

Holly began striding back towards the tennis court and the two women turned to leave when Jake called them back.

"Listen, I know where you can find Niles—Barbara's brother."

"Oh?"

"He owns a café down at Balmoral, somewhere near the water. Barb told me about it once. Called it the Money Hole."

"That's not the name of it surely?" asked Claire and he laughed, running a sun-tanned hand through his hair and giving her a lazy smile.

"Nah, something to do with sand or beach or something. Oh, that's right, *Just Beachy*—crap name, hey? Barb says he's constantly asking for loans to prop it up. Drives her nuts."

"Jake!" screeched Holly from the court and he turned to go.

"Thank you," said Alicia. "You've been a great help."

"Anytime." He gave Claire a last, lingering smile before jogging off in Holly's direction.

"Oooh someone's got the hots for you," Alicia teased as they made their way back to the car.

She scoffed. "I get the feeling Mr Tennis Ace flirts with all the ladies, especially those he thinks he can get something out of."

"Like Holly Parlour?"

"And maybe, just maybe, Barbara Parlour, too."

"You think?"

"Well he seemed to know an awful lot of her family business and did you catch the way he called her 'Barb'? Bit friendly for a coach, surely? Makes you wonder, that's all."

Alicia's eyes squinted slightly. "Maybe he was having an affair with the mother *and* daughter, and Holly found out and killed her mother in a fit of jealousy. We've already seen how violent she can get."

As they walked back to the car, Claire stopped and grabbed Alicia's arm. "*That's* where I've seen her before," she said.

"Who? Holly?"

She shook her head. "No, well, yes. Listen, I recognised Barbara when we first met at your house and I couldn't for the life of me work out where I'd seen her. She didn't look like the type to buy vintage frocks. Not really her style.

But now I've seen Holly I realise it was Holly who came in, and Barbara was with her. Oh this was six months ago at least." She gave it some thought. "That's right, Holly wanted to get into the '50s mod look and her mother was trying to talk her out of it. Told her she wasn't skinny enough, or something."

"Charming."

"That's what I thought, but then Holly wasn't very nice either if I recall correctly. She swore at her mother. I've never heard a child speak so rudely to a parent before. It was quite shocking; I'd never get away with language like that with my mother. Anyway, Barbara looked like she'd heard it all before, and they took off. But that's not why I remember it. To be honest, I wouldn't have picked Barbara in a line-up, but I'd recognise that whiney teenager anywhere."

They both laughed as they reached the car and let themselves in. As she started up the Torana and began to drive away, Alicia said, "I wonder what their little tiff was all about?"

"Well Barbara thought her daughter wouldn't suit the short hemlines—"

"No, no, I mean Holly and Jake, the coach just now. You know, they were screaming at each other before they spotted us. I just wonder what Holly meant by 'We have to tell him'? Tell *who*? And tell them *what*? Was she talking about her dad?"

Claire tilted her head to one side. "All good questions. And what did he mean by 'You don't even know it was me'? That sounds very suspicious."

They thought about this for a few minutes, driving in silence before Claire sighed softly.

"I wonder if we're reading too much into it. They could be talking about breaking an expensive racquet or something. It mightn't be anything. I can already vouch for Holly's filthy temper—the way she leapt down her mother's throat that day at the shop. It doesn't take much to set her off."

Alicia groaned. "You're right. I've seen her in action, too." She told Claire about the episode in Barbara's kitchen that day she hosted book club, how Holly had screamed at her mother for no apparent reason. "She clearly didn't want us out there on the deck, invading her home. She's obviously got serious anger management issues or something. No, we need to stick to the facts. That's what Hercule Poirot would do."

"So what now? Are you going to take a trip to Balmoral, check out the brother?"

"I'd love to but, sadly, I've got a magazine to put together. Doesn't create itself."

"I know what you mean," said Claire, producing a compact mirror from her handbag and inspecting herself in it. "I'd better get back to work, too; sell a few frocks if I'm going to make the rent this week. It's a pity though, someone really should pay brother Niles a visit."

"Don't worry," said Alicia. "I know just the person for the job."

"Sounds like a silly job to me," said Lynette that night over a chilli concoction that tasted a little like Beef Korma and a lot like Massaman curry. She was calling it Thailandia.

"Get it? It's a cross between a Thai dish and Indian."

"I get it," Alicia replied, mid-mouthful. "And I'll get more of it when I'm done, thank you very much. So, back to 'knucklehead Uncle Niles' then. Surely it won't hurt you to pop down there, order a latté and have a quiet chat to the guy?"

"Yeah, 'cause I've got nothing better to do with my time." She gave her sister an eye roll. "Why me?"

"Well, you're the obvious choice."

"Because I work in a café and can cook?"

"Something like that."

The eyes rolled again. "I'm going to ask about his sister not how to flambé a crepe."

"Still, you're in the same circles, he might warm to a fellow foodie better."

She snorted. "Okay, but let me make a few phone calls first. The Just Beachy sounds kinda familiar."

In fact, the Just Beachy café was notorious in Sydney's café society for being the longest running 'train wreck' on the lower North Shore. After chatting with her boss, Mario, that night, Lynette learned that it was owned by Niles Blakely and was due to go under many times over but was constantly being propped back up.

"Mario reckons it's just never gonna work—badly run, apparently, not great food, either. But somehow it keeps on keeping on."

"I think we have Barbara to thank for that. From what Wanda and Jake say, she's been bailing her brother out for years."

"And now he inherits from her?"

"If she's dead that is."

"True, and we still don't know that for sure." Lynette dropped her fork to the table and sighed heavily. "I know you really thrive on all of this, Lis—"

"*Thrive's* a bit rich, Lynette, I'm not exactly thrilled she's gone missing."

"Sorry, I'm just saying, are you sure you want to get involved? I mean, I'm cool with it, you know me. But you're the one who gets stressy and starts imagining all sorts of gory stuff. I just wonder whether this case might not be the best thing for you."

Alicia placed her own fork down and then picked up her wine glass, took a long sip and said, "I need to do this, Lyn. My imagination's already run wild. You can't imagine the hideous things poor Barbara has already been subjected to in my subconscious. Believe me, finding out the truth will most likely be a relief."

"Fine, fine, just looking out for your mental health."

"That's an oxymoron when it comes to me," she said, only half-joking. "So, about that second helping of Thailandia…"

As Lynette returned to the kitchen, Alicia glanced at her watch. It was just after 7:00 p.m. and she was keen to know if there was more news of Barbara. She jumped up and switched the TV on in the adjoining lounge room, then returned to the dining table.

"Mum and Dad would be most unimpressed," Lynette was saying as she placed two half-filled bowls down in front of them. "Never mix dinner and TV, they always say—"

"Shhh," Alicia hissed.

She'd just spotted Arthur Parlour's face on the ABC news, and he did not look good.

CHAPTER 13

Alicia and Lynette grabbed their bowls and kneeled in front of the TV set, watching, intrigued. Arthur was holding a press conference live from his Woollahra mansion, and was doing a fine job of playing the distraught and devoted husband.

"I urge you, Barbara, please come home," he was saying, staring straight into the camera. "Holly and I are extremely worried. We just want you home, love. We miss you terribly."

The camera then panned to a stern looking fellow who was standing beside Arthur. He was in his late 50s, bulky in a grey suit with an impressive handlebar moustache that was more bikie gang member than a police detective. At the bottom of the screen the name Detective Inspector Kenneth Ward appeared.

"We ask if anyone has any information regarding Mrs Parlour and her whereabouts to please get in touch."

A police hotline number appeared across the bottom of the screen.

"Inspector Ward, are you saying you believe something untoward has happened to Mrs Parlour?" bellowed a male reporter's voice from behind the camera.

"I am saying we are most concerned for Mrs Parlour's safety and ask for any help from the public we can get."

"Mr Parlour, how do you respond to allegations that you were seen having a fight with your wife just before she disappeared?" screamed another voice and the camera swept back to the husband who suddenly looked rattled.

Alicia realised that it was the first time since Barbara had disappeared that he looked genuinely worried.

"I dispute that categorically," he said gruffly. "My wife and I are very much in love and I am most concerned for her."

"What about rumours that you have been having an affair—" began another reporter before the Inspector stepped in.

"That will be all for now, thanks folks."

He pulled a shocked looking Arthur back towards the house while the cameras jostled to follow close behind. Several burly police officers stepped in between them as the image cut off and returned to the anchor desk where a well-dressed blonde woman was leaning forward solemnly. Behind her left shoulder was a snapshot of Barbara and it caught Alicia's breath. It looked nothing like her. Clearly taken back in the '80s, it showed Barbara with a very short, cropped hairdo, fluffed up at the front, which left her looking rather stern and school-ma'amish. Not exactly the most flattering or contemporary photo Arthur could have chosen to give to the media.

"We've just been watching a live press conference from the home of well-known banking identity Arthur Parlour," the anchorwoman said, fiddling through some papers on her desk. "Mr Parlour's wife, Barbara, has been missing since Saturday afternoon and, as we just heard, police hold grave fears for her safety. Um… are you there, Hannah?"

The screen went blank for a split second before an ABC reporter appeared with the Parlour house in the background. She was pressing something to her ear and squinting into the camera.

"Yes I am, go ahead, Fran."

"Did the police say anything more about what they suspect has happened to Mrs Parlour? Whether they have any other clues to her whereabouts?"

"Not at this stage, no. They are not giving too much away but as you say, it is clear there are concerns for her safety." The reporter glanced at some notes in her hand. "Mr Parlour did tell us off camera earlier this evening that he does believe his wife is okay and is hoping she will see the broadcast and come home. However it is clear from the police detectives that they're not quite so optimistic."

"Alright, we'll leave it there. Thanks Hannah."

As the news moved on to an unrelated story the sisters switched it off and returned to the dining table.

"What was that about a quarrel before she left?" asked Lyn and Alicia shrugged.

"That's news to me. But his affairs are obviously out there in the public domain now." Her eyes narrowed. "You know, you always see these distraught family members on TV begging for their 'loved one' to return, then, a few weeks later, that very same person is being hauled away to jail… I just don't know what to believe anymore."

Lynette took a mouthful of curry and considered this for a few minutes, chewing. "Did you get the impression Arthur was talking directly to his wife there, urging her to come home? Like she's in hiding somewhere. I hate to say this, but he's either a really good actor, or he genuinely thinks she's coming back."

"Well, as the reporter said, the cops sure don't. Anyway, I'm glad to see he's finally taking it all seriously."

"He has to, doesn't he? Especially if there's rumours circulating that he's been unfaithful. This won't help his state government pre-selection one bit."

"That's what Wanda said. Maybe that's why Barbara's missing. Maybe she was threatening to tell the press about his carryings-on. Maybe he had to get rid of her."

Lynette was not so sure. "If that's the case it hasn't worked. Now the public not only know about his affairs, they suspect him of being a murderer. That has to be worse, don't you reckon?"

Alicia's stomach tightened. Her sister was right. None of this was adding up and she didn't like it one bit.

~~~~~~

Across town someone else had been watching the news broadcast closely, eyebrows twitching with delight. Arthur could say what he wanted, appeal all he liked but Barbara wasn't coming home.

She turned and glared at Barbara's mute face and then smirked, her top lip curling a little with unabashed glee. *How lucky she had been!* In her wildest dreams, she never would have expected this. Her ship had finally come in.

Finally she was in control. *She was Queen Bee.*

It was her time to shine.

She sniggered then stopped and stared at Barbara again. A shot of fear coursed through her veins, tempering her delight.

"Don't get ahead of yourself," she hissed aloud. *It's not over yet. Not by a long shot.*

She picked up the gleaming pair of scissors she had found in Barbara's sewing case, turned towards the older woman, and began to slice…
~~~~~~

CHAPTER 14

The following morning, a Wednesday, was wet and dreary and Lynette couldn't be happier. She knew the way beach cafes worked and the drearier the day, the less crowded the place would be, and all the more opportunity for her to chat to Niles.

Dressed casually in a creamy pink T-shirt, dangly coloured beads and tiny denim shorts that only someone as leggy and flawless as Lynette could pull off, she borrowed Alicia's Torana and drove across the Sydney Harbour Bridge to Balmoral Beach. A small, meticulously groomed bay on the swanky north side of Sydney, it didn't hold a candle to Bondi Beach, she decided as she parked and made her way on foot along the esplanade. *It was way too clean and boring.*

Several Nike-clad mothers jogged along the footpath, the latest three-wheeled prams in front, designer dogs on leashes behind. There were small groups of well-dressed families picnicking on blankets on the sandy grass, nannies watching over equally well-dressed toddlers at the pristine playground, and some oldies gathered on the beach, dripping from a recent swim. Occasionally, the odd tradesman wandered past, too, burger and coke in hand, wrap-around sunglasses covering his eyes, clearly killing time between plumbing or tiling or whatever job had lured him to this posh end of town.

Lynette noticed that there were several eateries along the esplanade and, as expected, they were all relatively empty today. Just Beachy was the last one on the block before the road ended and a large public park took over. It wasn't hard to find. Lynette had already googled the address on her iPhone GPS. She had also memorised a picture of the owner, Niles Blakely, so she'd have no trouble recognising him when she got there. Judging from the website mug shot, however, he wouldn't be hard to find: he appeared at least a decade younger than his sister and boasted bright red hair and splotchy brown freckles; very easy to pick in a line-up, she thought.

It was just after 10:30 a.m. and the breakfast rush would be over—hence the reason Mario had begrudgingly allowed her a few hours off—but this café was virtually deserted. There was just one customer, an elderly woman braving the elements at an outdoor table with the help of a light green cardigan and steaming pot of tea. Lynette chose a table inside and waited for a red-haired, freckly-faced 40-something to appear, which he did eventually, a dirty dish towel flung across one shoulder.

Niles looked older than his web picture and like he hadn't slept in weeks, grey bags under his eyes and his red hair spiking up in all directions. He had a deep, vertical furrow between his eyebrows that gave the impression he spent a lot of time immersed in dark, unhappy thoughts. One glance at Lynette, however, and the furrow miraculously disappeared.

"Hello there," he said breezily. "Wanna see a menu or just after a coffee today?"

"An espresso'd be great, thank you," she said and waited for him to return with it before launching in.

"I know this is going to sound strange," she began and his eyes lit up. "I'm a friend of Barbara's and I was wondering if we could have a chat?"

The light flickered out and the furrow returned. "Oh, right. You know my sister?"

"Yes, and I'm trying to find her. You don't happen to know where she might be, do you?" He stared at her curiously so she added, "She's gone missing, you do know that, right?"

Niles glanced around, noticed that his customer was preoccupied with the view, and said, "May I?" indicating the chair.

She nodded and he dropped down into it.

"'Course I know. The cops have been in touch and it's got me worried sick. They're asking all sorts of strange questions, like I've been hiding her or something. Ridiculous."

"So they're still in the dark?"

"Yep." He looked her over. "What's your interest in all this? You're not a reporter are you?"

"Oh no. I'm just one of a group of friends who are all very worried about Barbara."

She hoped he wouldn't enquire further, would be embarrassed to reveal she barely knew the woman but she suspected that, like most brothers, he wouldn't really know his sister's friends intimately and would take that on face value. He did and was nodding.

"Yeah, fair enough, it is worrying, eh? She's been gone over four days now and it's just bloody strange."

"So it's not typical?"

"Christ no." He leant in closer. "I can't help wondering what Arthur has to do with it all. You see him on telly last night? *My wife and I are very much in love*'— what a load of bollocks! They couldn't stand the sight of each other. You know what they were like."

Not really, she wanted to tell him but nodded anyway. "When did you last see your sister?"

He didn't hesitate. "About three weeks before she disappeared. Already told the cops all this. It was a Tuesday. She dropped down here to see how I was going, ran some errands and then she left again. Nothing seemed out of the ordinary, she seemed normal. I spoke to her once or twice the next week and then, nothing. She's just vanished. Totally bizarre."

"So you told all this to the police?"

"Yep. They wanted to know where I was when she did her vanishing act."

"When was that, exactly?"

"Good question. According to Arthur, she took off sometime Saturday arvo and never returned. But no one quite knows. I mean, it's not like anyone trusts anything Arthur's got to say."

"You don't like him much, hey?"

"He's a bastard, and that's on a good day. Anyway, I told the coppers I was here, all day Saturday, and Sunday. Which I was."

"Oh, so this place stays open for dinner, too?"

He looked at her blankly. "What? No, well, I mean, I shut up at 5:00 p.m. You probably don't know cafés but—"

"Actually I work at Mario's in Paddington."

"Really?" He looked at her with renewed respect. "Oh, right, yeah, I know that joint, great risotto. Okay, so you know then that we don't just shut the door and skip off into the sunset. I had to stay back and tidy up, do the till, check the stock, that kind of stuff. Apart from the cook, I usually have at least one girl on on weekends, but, well, things've been tight… Anyway, I didn't get out of here 'til really late. Oh, hang on a minute."

He jumped up and raced outside where the customer was waving one hand in the air like she was writing a check. They exchanged words and a brief laugh before he returned inside to see to her bill.

A few minutes later he was back. "Get you another coffee?"

She nodded and, feeling as though she needed to justify her existence, ordered a muffin as well.

"They're a few days old so I'll give it to you for nix," he said, from behind the counter and she tried not to frown.

No wonder his café was struggling. Mario would never just give anything away and he'd certainly never offer up old food. All it did was leave a nasty taste in patron's mouths.

Niles also made himself a coffee and sat down to join her. "They found her wedding ring you know?"

"Really? Where?"

"She'd left it at the house, by her bed."

"Maybe she had a fight with Arthur, threw the ring off and left; is hiding out until things calm down."

He shook his head. "If she did fight with Arthur and decide to leave him, she would have told me, she told me everything. I just can't believe she'd walk out and not say a word. She just wouldn't do that. And she wouldn't leave her ring behind, I can give you the word on that. It cost Arthur a packet, she wouldn't give that up without a fight."

"What if she…" Lynette hesitated, didn't want to upset him any further but he understood where she was going.

"Barbara didn't top herself if that's what you're getting at. If she was that depressed she would have told me, but she never mentioned a thing. Last time I saw her she was as happy as Larry."

He began rubbing the back of his head agitatedly. "I'm a bit stressed, to be honest. The way the coppers were talking, it's not sounding good."

"Well, it has been a few days, anything could have happened."

"What? No, I mean for me." He took a gulp of his macchiato. "I reckon they think I was involved."

"Really? Why?" She tried to keep her tone light but he just shrugged so she said, "Is it because you stand to gain?"

He glared at her for a few seconds before his expression relaxed. "She tell you that, eh? You really were best buds. Yeah, old Barb left me her house. A tiny trust fund for her daughter but, yeah, I get the bulk of her half of the estate, or so the cops tell me."

"I hate to say this but it does kind of sound like motive," Lynette said, wincing slightly because she knew how it would be received.

As expected, he sat forward, anger deepening his furrowed brow even further. "I didn't kill my sister for her bloody house. I love Barbara, she's everything to me, more like a mum than a sister. Hell, I need that woman. She's the reason this place is still standing, damn it. She's helped me so much, never a problem. Why would I do her in?"

"Niles, I'm just saying, I know what money pits restaurants can be. Your sister's wealth could come in handy for a place like this."

"My sister's wealth is no use to me now," he said. "At least not while Arthur's alive."

"What do you mean?"

"This is what I told the coppers. Sure, I get her half of that ugly pile of bricks they call a home, but it's not like Arthur's going anywhere in a hurry. He's hardly about to sell up and pay me out is he?"

"So, even if they do find your poor sister has, well, passed away, you don't get anything?"

He rubbed a hand through his dishevelled hair. "Not unless Arthur drops dead suddenly, no I do not. So, to be perfectly frank, my sister is a lot more help to me alive than she is dead. Or missing, for that matter. Now, if that's all, I've got work to get on with."

He pushed his chair back and stood up with a huff, then disappeared through the back kitchen door. Lynette finished her coffee and muffin then stood up to pay the bill but Niles was still out the back. She called his name then poked her head through the kitchen door to see if she could spot him. He was nowhere to be found and she went to turn back when she noticed a bulging backpack and sleeping bag rolled up against one wall. She wondered if he was heading off somewhere when she felt a light tap her on the shoulder. Lynette swung around to find Niles glaring at her.

"What are you looking at?" he demanded.

She swallowed hard. "Nothing, sorry, I just wanted to pay my bill, that's all."

He stared at her for a few seconds then said, "Don't worry about it. It's on the house."

No wonder he's broke, she thought again, dropping some gold coins in the tip bucket by the coffee machine as she departed.

On her way back to work, Lynette couldn't help thinking that while Niles was certainly a hopeless businessman, and a little creepy at that, he was absolutely right. He had no apparent motive for killing his sister. Not unless Arthur suddenly showed up dead, of course.

And what were the chances of that?

CHAPTER 15

Around the same time that Lynette was interrogating Niles, Missy was busy doing a little snooping of her own. It was just after 11:00 a.m. and she had managed to talk her way into the Parlour mansion with little difficulty, leaving several stunned members of the press languishing on the sidewalk. That was the good thing about being deemed 'ditzy', she thought as she began looking around. People assumed you were harmless and generally believed what you had to say, if only to shut you up.

"You find?" asked Rosa, striding into the lounge room, one hand clutching her iPod Touch, the other pulling the tiny headphones out of her ears. Today she was wearing another tight, revealing dress, her face plastered with make-up, her hair pulled to one side with a plastic pink hibiscus hair clip that clashed horribly with her thick, orange streak.

Missy had given some cock and bull story about a lost book and Rosa had simply looked at her like she had never heard anything so boring and said, "Come, you look." She'd then led her into the lounge room and left her to search alone, saying something about checking her emails.

Missy glanced around from where she'd been checking out a side table and sighed deliberately. "No I have not found my book, and I am going to get in the biggest trouble of my life."

"What is book? What name?"

"It's called *Evil Under the Sun*, but it's a hard cover, an early edition from the library where I work, so it's *really* special and I should never have lent it to Barbara, but she didn't have a copy and she needed it for book club and she promised me she'd get it straight back to me, and oh dear, oh dear, oh dear, I'm dead if I can't locate it. I'll lose my job!"

"Maybe she take book with her?" suggested Rosa, cocking one fake eyebrow, and Missy acted even more alarmed.

"Then I really am in trouble, because, I mean, where is Barbara? Does anyone have any idea?"

Rosa shrugged as if she really didn't care. "Okay," she sighed. "I help you."

"Thank you sooooo much!" gushed Missy, pretending to inspect the bookcase. "I'm really lucky you're still around. I wasn't sure you would be."

Rosa turned back on her, both eyebrows raised sky-high now. "Why not I be here? Who feed Mr Parlour and Miss Holly? Who look after them? Is my job."

Missy was surprised by her vehemence. "Well, yes, until Barbara comes back, of course."

"Pft!" she said, placing the iPod headphones back in place. "Okay I go check bedroom."

Rosa disappeared again giving Missy another chance to inspect the trophies she had been looking at earlier. There were a few token golf trophies of Arthur's and various pre-teen soccer, athletics and swimming medals and trophies that belonged to Holly. But nothing for Barbara. There were no photos of the woman either.

"Who the hell are you and what the hell are you doing in my lounge room?"

Missy swung back around to find Arthur standing at the doorway, hands on his hips, a furious spark in his eyes. He looked like he hadn't shaven in days, and his tie was slung loosely around his neck as though he couldn't quite find the energy to fix it or take it off.

"Oh, hello there," Missy said, ramping up the ditz and bobbing her red locks from side to side. "You must be Barbara's husband? I'm Missy, a friend of your wife's from book club, I'm just—"

"Book club? *Again?*" His jaw dropped and he shook his head disbelievingly. "What is it with you people?"

"Ooh, sorry, I really don't mean to disturb you Mr Parlour, I'm just looking for a book I lent Barbara a few weeks ago…"

Missy explained about the missing Agatha Christie novel but, unlike Rosa, Arthur didn't seem to be buying it. He stared at her sceptically.

"Tried checking the book case have we?" His tone was laced with sarcasm.

"Yes but I just can't see it. Still you know, my mother always says I suffer from domestic blindness—I scream for the salt and pepper when they're sitting right in front of—"

"Look, lady, this is not a good time."

"Oh, of course not, I'm so sorry, I know it's been really difficult what with Barbara missing and all."

Rosa returned then and looked startled to see her boss. She yanked the headphones back out of her ears and thrust the whole device behind her back. Arthur whipped his head around to her and the look on his face even made Missy recoil.

"What the hell are you doing letting some strange woman wander around my house?" he boomed.

"Sorry, er, Mr Parlour, I just thought—"

"Well don't *think*. I don't pay you to *think*. You're not the bloody mistress of this house, you should be checking with me first before anyone comes in here Got it?"

Missy glanced at Rosa. Her face was now bright red and she looked like she was about to cry, so she quickly stepped in.

"Look, sorry, it's not Rosa's fault, really it's not. I insisted she let me in. She was just helping me out."

"It's not her job to help you out. Not her job to do anything but wash my dishes and cook my dinner. Now,   I think it's time you left. If I find the bloody book, I'll let you know."

"Of course, yes, sorry…"

Missy followed him out of the lounge room, down the marble hallway to the front door. As she went she glanced back and the look she saw in Rosa's eyes surprised her. Her embarrassment had dissipated and in its place was something colder and more detached. She wondered if that look was being directed at her or the angry boss.

Arthur swung the door open, stopped, and turned back, his eyes still fiery.

"I have had just about enough of you lot coming here snooping about. If I see one more member of the bloody Jane Austen Book Club—"

"Murder Mystery, actually."

"What?"

"Sorry, it's just that you said Jane Austen, we're the Murder Mystery Book Club. Quite different."

He looked at her like he wanted to wring her neck, and she took note of this. He fired up quickly she thought. As if reading her mind, or perhaps spotting the news crews who were now grappling with their cameras and microphones and rushing towards the gate, looks of disbelief and delight on their faces, he quickly closed the door again and took a deep breath. It was several seconds before he spoke, but when he did he was much more controlled. His tone was softer this time, even a little pleading.

"Look, sorry for lashing out. I hope you understand, it is an extremely trying time for me. I don't know what's happened to my wife but I strongly believe she's okay and she will be home soon."

"I thought you'd be happy to be free of her," Missy said gently, knowing she was entering dangerous waters but feeling buoyed now by his change of demeanour and the cameramen hovering outside. *If he tried anything, they would hear her scream.*

Arthur stared at her surprised. "Free? Why would I want to be free of her? I'm hoping to run a campaign for state government next year; Barbara needs to be beside me, where she belongs. I can't have any kind of scandal hanging over my head. This is the very last thing I want. And you can tell that to your *Murder Mystery* cronies."

~~~~~~~

The aforementioned 'cronies' were not buying it. Or at least Perry wasn't.

"He would say that wouldn't he?" he said, helping himself to some dark chocolate that Claire had just placed in a rose coloured glass bowl on the table. "He's covering his own butt." Perry popped a piece into his mouth and licked his fingers delicately.

The Murder Mystery Book Club were squeezed into the tiny café at the back of the Timeless Vintage Clothing Store on Victoria Street in Potts Point. Determined that the Finlay sisters should not have to do all the hosting work on their own, Claire had kindly offered to hold the next meeting at her shop, hanging the 'Closed' sign on the front door and leading the way through to the café at the back. Although tiny and unobtrusive, the café was a big hit with the customers, and had been since it was installed a few years ago so that bored partners could kill time sipping coffee and reading magazines while their 'other halves' tried on outfit after outfit in peace.

This kept everyone content and the cash register ringing.
~~~~~~~

Alicia glanced around. There was just one round table in the centre of the room, a few delicate wrought iron chairs around it, as well as several chrome and vinyl stools along the walls where racks of magazines and books were stored, and a tiny kitchenette at the back where the coffee was brewed and muffins, friands and other delicacies sold.

The café was separated from the main shop by flowing maroon velvet curtains which, along with a Persian rug, black and white prints, and a glass Tiffany lampshade made you feel like you'd just stepped back into a 1940s Parisian speakeasy. All the furniture had price tags attached.

The boutique itself was bursting with a stunning array of vintage clothes, shoes, handbags and scarves all in excellent condition, and the women, as well as Perry it must be said, found it difficult to ignore the merchandise as they were ushered through. Along the way, Claire explained how she visited her mother in Paris several times a year to scour its fabulous flea-markets for these treasures which she then shipped back home. Sneaking a peek at several price tags on the way, Alicia could see this was not your regular opshop. The prices were hefty for second-hand gear.

Today, Claire looked like she'd just stepped off a Parisian street herself, in a silky black and white polka dot blouse over a black skirt, her hair in a loose chignon. She fetched them all beverages before joining them in a huddle around Alicia's journal, going through the 'evidence so far'.

After hearing about Missy's rendezvous with Arthur in his lounge room, some of the members were not happy.

"You really shouldn't have gone back to Barbara's place without letting one of us know," Anders scolded.

"Sorry, lovely, I just thought I'd help out, that's all. I feel like a third nostril sometimes, just sitting in the library all day, doing nothing. Thought I'd do a little snooping, see what I could see."

"It's great you want to help," said Alicia, soothingly, "it's just that we don't know who we're dealing with here.

I mean what if you'd come to harm and we didn't know where you were?"

"Oh there were plenty of journos hanging around, there's no way Arthur could've done anything. In fact if you watch the Channel Ten news tonight you might spot my fat bottom waddling away."

"Maybe they think you're having an affair with him now?" suggested Perry cheekily and Missy mock gagged.

"No thank you! He's such a pig. All he cares about is his precious political career. That's why I believe him when he says he wants her back. He needs her at home playing The Good Wife."

"It does make sense," agreed Alicia. "So apart from validating his terrible temper, what else did you find?"

"Hm, nothing really, and that's what's so strange."

They looked at Missy perplexed as she scooped her glasses off and began cleaning them with an edge of her light pink, sparkly cotton cardigan.

"I can't put my finger on it, but, well, I couldn't help the feeling that something was missing…"

"Yeah, the wife, Barbara, remember?" said Perry.

"Mmm, maybe that's all it was." She placed the specs back on. "Maybe I should go back in and have another look."

"Nooooo," several of them chorused.

"Alright, alright," Missy said trying not to be offended. "Anyway, I doubt very much Rosa would let me through the front door again. Not after Arthur bit her head off. Oooh he was cranky. You know, now I mention it, she was acting kind of strange, too. Sort of reminded me of my sister's mother-in-law."

"Huh?" they chorused again.

"Well, Mildred, that's the mother-in-law—quite a nice lady if you're not related to her, but sadly, Henny, my sister, is. So, anyway, Henny's away on a girl's weekend, right? And gets back early to find Mildred in her kitchen, cooking up a storm. Now that wouldn't be such a problem, I mean what's not to love about someone filling your freezer with casseroles, right? But it's not just that, she's also re-tuned the radio to her favourite station—some boring classical thingy—and get this, has moved some of the furniture around the way she likes it. She was there two days, max, looking after the kids and she takes over. Rosa was kind've acting like that."

The group stared at her, bemused. Anders coughed discreetly and gave Alicia a pointed look.

"Okay then," said Alicia quickly. "I think you made your point, Missy."

In fact she wasn't sure what Missy's point was at all but she wanted to move things along. She turned to her sister. "Lyn, how about filling us all in on your visit to see Barbara's brother?"

"Sure," said Lynette, "but before I do I have to say, I think Arthur sounds just like Niles. Neither of them is going to win any humanitarian awards but they do seem to be quite sincere in wanting Barbara back and alive. It's in both their interests."

She filled them in on her visit to Niles' café. "He seems genuinely distressed about Barbara's disappearance although, as I say, he's more worried about how it's affecting his life than hers. I mean, who's going to pay his mounting bills now? He's also super stressed about the police and all the questions they're asking. I got a dodgy vibe from the guy, bit of a victim if you know what I mean, but I'm not sure he's a killer."

"We're running out of suspects," said Perry, gloomily.

"There's always that tennis coach," said Claire, and Perry's eyes lit up.

"Yes, I'd forgotten about him. You think he has something to do with it?"

Claire shrugged and then proceeded to tell them about her visit to Woollahra with Alicia, and the strange conversation they had overheard between Holly and Jake. All agreed the words could be construed as suspicious.

"What do you think Holly meant by 'We can't keep this quiet'?" asked Missy.

"Maybe Holly suspects that Jake killed her mum and she wants him to fess up to her Dad?" suggested Perry.

"Or maybe it's completely unrelated," said Claire.

Perry sneered. "You're no fun at all, Miss Hargreaves."

"Of course we might be searching in the wrong direction entirely," Alicia suggested. "Maybe it was someone we have never met who had a gripe with her? Hell, it could easily be the work of a stranger. Maybe she picked up a crazy hitchhiker."

"The majority of murders are committed by people we know," said Missy. "Terribly sad and tragic fact but that's the truth. The difference between love and hate is one very fine line, my darlings. There are endless stories—and I'm not talking Agatha Christie stories—I mean, fair dinkum, real-life tales of wives killing husbands, husbands killing daughters, and I mean it just goes on and on!"

Like you, thought Anders who was clearly wearing thin of the chatty librarian. Aloud he said, "We all need to remember that, at this stage, we don't even know if Barbara is deceased."

A few of them groaned.

"If only they could find the body," said Perry and then, catching Claire's horrified expression, added, "Sorry, Claire, I know it sounds morbid, but let's face facts here. What are the chances she's alive? Really?"

No one had the energy, or naivety, to suggest otherwise. It had been more than four days after all.

"That doesn't mean we can't try and find her… no matter what's happened. She still deserves to be found," said Alicia and they agreed with that.

The problem was, they had no idea where to take the investigation next.

Claire, a stickler for the rules, said, "Personally, I think we need to talk to the police."

"Actually, I'm surprised they haven't called me yet," said Alicia. "I told them about the club, gave them my number."

"Maybe you need to go and see them," suggested Anders.

"And say what, exactly? It's not like we have anything groundbreaking to reveal."

"*Au contraire*," said Perry. "We know a lot more than *they* probably do." He produced a stubby hand and began counting down on his fingers. "For starters, do they even realise that Barbara has the phone number of a battered women's shelter in her house? Maybe there's a history of domestic violence we don't know about?" Another stubby finger went into the air. "Second, do they know that young Holly has obviously been shagging the tennis coach senseless and, from what you tell me, it looks like he's covering something up?"

Now it was Anders' turn to look horrified. "Hang on a minute. That's really personal stuff, Perry. We don't know if it's got anything to do with Barbara's disappearance."

"Exactly," said Perry. "Which is why we need to mention it. It could be a factor."

"He's right," Alicia told Anders. "It's not our job to decide what is and is not relevant to the investigation. But listen, there's one other thing the police should definitely know." She produced a third finger and waved it in the air. "Are they aware that Barbara Parlour was a very miserable woman before she disappeared? I mean, sure, we hardly knew her but contrary to what Arthur is saying, I have written proof that she was not a happy camper."

Alicia flipped to the back of her journal where a small envelope had been wedged, and pulled it out to reveal Barbara's handwritten reply to her newspaper advertisement dated several weeks earlier. She read it aloud:

Dear Alicia. I would dearly love to join your club. I'm just a boring, middle-aged housewife but murder mysteries keep me sane during life's many sad and tragic moments. Perhaps it's because they put my own woes into perspective. I really don't know how I would survive without authors like P.D. James and Ian Rankin and

Agatha Christie. The latter is light when things get dark, a happy ending when I find I have none. She rescues me daily and I do not know how I would get through tomorrow without her.

Warm regards, Barbara Parlour

The group all stared at the letter, speechless.

"I'd forgotten how depressing it was," Alicia said eventually.

"Oh it's tragic," moaned Perry. "Dear God, the woman was crying out for help. If only we'd seen that."

"Hey, Perry," said Lynette. "We can't be blamed for any of this, we'd only met the woman twice. It's her brother who should be beating himself up. Squandered her money on a hopeless café for years and now that she's missing, seems more concerned with saving his own skin, and his sorry excuse for a caf'."

"Not to mention the rest of her family and friends," added Claire. "Why weren't they looking out for her? I don't mean to sound awful but her daughter's an utter nightmare, doesn't seem to care one iota. As for her so-called friend Wanda—she couldn't have distanced herself faster if she'd tried."

"Yeah, they all seem to have such little empathy for Barbara," agreed Alicia.

At that moment they could hear a light tapping coming from inside the shop. Claire jumped up with a radiant smile.

"That'll be Charlie," she announced, sweeping the velvet curtain aside and heading inside the shop to unlock the front door.

"Oh, no," gasped Perry, a bright blush sweeping across his cheeks.

"What's wrong?" asked Alicia.

"Nothing, shhh." He hunched over and covered his face with one hand.

Anders stared at him and then to the others. "Who's Charlie?"

"The fiancé," Missy whispered. "You know, the one who won't marry her."

"Missy! You don't know that," said Alicia.

She held her hands up. "Four years is four years. My cousin Linda was engaged for four years and it all ended disastrously—"

Before she could finish, Claire reappeared with a tall, thin man in a dapper three-piece, pin-stripe suit complete with waistcoat and silk hanky tucked into the jacket pocket. He, too, looked part Asian and was a walking commercial for the vintage clothing biz, and Alicia could see their attraction. At the very least they clearly had a penchant for retro fashion. He smiled politely at the group and ran a hand across the top of his hair which had been styled in a 1950s, Elvis-like quiff.

"Everyone, this is Charlie Szeto, my fiancé," said Claire a little breathlessly. "That's Alicia, the woman who started the club, her sister Lynette, Anders to her right, Perry next to him, oh and Missy at the back."

The group all said hello as Charlie glanced and smiled at each one in turn. When he got to Perry his smile faltered just slightly, or at least that's what Alicia thought, but he recovered so quickly she wondered if she had imagined it. The growing blush on Perry's face, however, gave her pause for thought.

"Sorry to interrupt your little soiree," Charlie said, his eyes firmly back on his fiancé and she shook her head.

"Honestly, it's fine, isn't it guys?" She looked at them imploringly.

"Oh, yeah," said Alicia. "In fact, why don't you join us? We could always do with a fresh perspective."

She felt a swift kick under the table and glanced up to see Perry, fingers splayed across his eyes, giving her a dark stare. His head was shaking very slightly.

"Oh, no, no, I couldn't," Charlie was saying, drawing Claire a little away from the table and lowering his voice. "Darling I have to cancel on tonight anyway, something's come up."

"Really? Again?" She looked bitterly disappointed. "We're almost finished up here."

"Sorry, no choice, I'm afraid. Miller has some last-minute changes to the Grayson manuscript, so I need to get stuck into that." His tone hushed even more so that Alicia had to strain to hear him. "I'm meeting Grayson for dinner to thrash it all out. He can only do tonight, he's heading off to London tomorrow."

She put her head to one side with a puppy dog look in her eyes. "Maybe I could join you for dinner, we won't be long here—"

"No, no," he said again. "It'll be deadly dull. You stay here and do what you need to do." He gave the group another smile. "Nice to meet you all."

There was a fleeting glimpse at Perry again, and this one Alicia knew she had not made up. There was definitely some connection there but when she looked at Perry he was no longer meeting her eyes.

As Claire walked Charlie back through the café, Lynette jumped up to make more coffee and Anders joined her at the espresso machine. Missy, too, stood up, keen to explore the collection of magazines on the side, so Alicia took the opportunity and leaned in towards Perry.

"You want to tell me about it?" she whispered.

He smiled innocently enough. "I don't know what you mean."

She shook her head at him. "Give me a break, Perry. I'm not the founder of the Murder Mystery Book Club for nothing. You know Charlie, don't you?"

Perry's smile turned sly. "I guess that's one way of putting it."

Alicia groaned. *Oh God, this was worse than she thought.* "No way, Perry. I can not believe this."

"Believe what?" asked Claire, returning through the curtains and causing both Alicia and Perry to jump.

"Oh, um, er…" stammered Alicia.

"We were just saying, we can't believe how much the police don't know," said Perry, recovering impressively quickly. "What do you think, Missy?"

Missy looked up from a 1953 edition of the *Australian Women's Weekly* she'd been reading, stared at him blankly then continued to read. She was too engrossed in the coronation of the young Queen Elizabeth to register anything.

"Well I definitely agree they ought to know," said Claire, turning to Anders who was just sitting back down, frothy cup of coffee in hand. "I hear your concerns, Anders, and I agree it's poor form gossiping about Barbara's family, but we just don't know how relevant it all is. It's up to the police to determine that. Not us."

"Fine," he conceded. "Hey, did you want another coffee? Lynette's a demon on the machine."

Claire shook her head, a glossy strand of hair breaking loose from the chignon. She swept it back into place. "No, thank you, I'm charged up enough as it is. So, Alicia, will you do the honours and speak to the police?"

Alicia stopped glaring at Perry and turned back to her. "Yes, I will, Claire, and soon. It's time the cops heard the other side of the story."

As she said those words, though, Alicia couldn't help feeling there was another side to Claire's fiancé, Charlie Szeto, too, and she had a horrible hunch it had something to do with Perry Gordon.

CHAPTER 16

She had expected to be knocked back outright, to be shown the door with a patronising smile, but when Alicia announced herself at the desk of the Woollahra police station the following afternoon, she was ushered straight through to the surprisingly plush office of the detective in charge of the Parlour case. She recognised him immediately from the television news—that handlebar moustache was unmistakable—and he was stroking it firmly as she walked in.

"Detective Inspector Ward," he said, standing to shake her hand and offer her a seat across from his desk. He gave the mo' one last stroke before he sat back down. "I believe you have some important information relating to the Parlours?"

She felt suddenly foolish, wanted to back up and run. What if he laughed in her face, or worse, chastised her for wasting precious police time? Alicia swallowed hard and produced Barbara's letter. As she handed it across to him she explained who she was and where she fit into the missing woman's life. He listened carefully before reading the letter, then pressed a buzzer on his desk. Alicia winced when a young, shaven-haired officer with dimples appeared, expecting to be shown the door, but he simply looked at his boss, eyebrows raised.

"Roger, make a copy of this letter for me, please, then come and sit in on this interview. Bring your notebook."

Alicia was pleasantly surprised. When the policeman returned he introduced himself as Assistant Detective Roger Boyd, and handed her the photocopy of Barbara's letter.

"We'll need to keep the original," Ward explained. "Right, then, let's get your story down."

And so she spent the next 10 minutes telling them everything she knew, from Barbara's first sad appearance at Book Club, to the strange gathering at her house and everything they had noticed there. She told them, too, of the reluctance of Arthur to take his wife's disappearance seriously. All the while the older cop stroked his moustache and the younger cop scribbled notes on a thick pad on his lap.

"I was the one who forced him to call you guys," she said. "He just didn't want to do it. The man was acting way too casual for my liking. I hate to say it but I think he's hiding something."

"Well there was a reason for his reticence," Detective Ward said then asked, "Mrs Parlour never mentioned any trip she was planning?"

"No, quite the contrary. We were all expecting her for Book Club last Sunday. She had specifically asked to present the next book and was supposed to show and provide questions. Why would she do that if she was planning to be away?"

Ward referred to his notes. "The housekeeper, Miss Rosa Lopez, tells us that Mrs Parlour left her Woollahra residence sometime around 14 hundred hours, Saturday afternoon, and her last words were, 'I'm going to London.' So she never mentioned an overseas trip to you?"

"Not a word." Alicia's memory clicked in. "Now you mention it, though, Wanda said something to me about that, too. She'd heard through Arthur that Barbara was flying to Europe. She thought maybe Paris. In any case neither of us believed it."

Both officers glanced at each other and then back at Alicia. Ward said, "And Wanda would be?"

"Oh, um, Wanda Birchin, Barbara's friend, or at least she used to be—they had a falling out apparently, don't ask me what that was about. Anyway, as I say, I doubt very much that Barbara was heading off anywhere. She'd just signed up for our club and seemed intent on being part of it."

"Yes, well in any case the housekeeper assumed she heard incorrectly because her mistress only had a large, black handbag with her, no luggage to speak of."

"There was the mink, sir," said Roger and he earned a scowl from his boss for it.

"Mink?" asked Alicia, intrigued.

He sighed. "It appears Mrs Parlour was also carrying a fur coat when she left the premises."

"How odd," said Alicia. "Summer's about two weeks away. Although of course it's almost winter in London. Maybe she really was heading there."

"With nothing but a handbag and a coat? Besides, we've checked all UK-bound flights for the past five days. No sign of her. Nor do London customs have a record of her arrival."

"So you've got nothing?"

He seemed offended by this. "Well, actually, we do have several sightings of Mrs Parlour on Saturday: parking her car at The Queen Victoria Building in the city around 2:30 p.m., then she was spotted posting a letter about ten minutes later in the mailbox on Pitt Street, and soon after that she goes into a jewellery shop in the Strand Arcade. We have her again on CCTV footage returning to her car and departing the QVB, but she disappears from the radar after that."

"A jewellery shop?" Alicia said.

"Yes. Did Mrs Parlour ever mention needing to get some jewellery repaired to you or any of your group?"

Alicia shook her head. "What sort of jewellery?" she asked and now it was his turn to shake his head.

"I can't comment on that but it gives us further reason to believe she has not left the country or, as the press is now suggesting, harmed herself."

"Then, of course, there's the dumped car," said Alicia.

He nodded. "Yes, located at the Hornsby train station on Monday night. Do you have any idea why she might have gone there? If she knows anyone in the vicinity? Does someone in your club come from there, perhaps?"

Alicia's shoulders drooped. "Sorry, no."

She was starting to feel quite useless and wondered how long before the police chief would realise this and send her packing. For now, she decided to keep him chatting in the hope of gleaning as much information as she could.

"Of course Barbara could have parked at Hornsby station and taken off on a train somewhere," she suggested.

"That is one scenario we are currently looking into," he said. "Unfortunately, at this stage of the investigation, nobody at the station recalls seeing Mrs Parlour arrive or depart, and the cameras do not work."

The look on his face told her exactly what he thought about that.

"So you have no idea *when* she arrived at the station?"

"Or even if she did at all." He shook his head a little. "Look, that's not what I'd like to talk to you about. You said you were in the same book club as Mrs Parlour. I need to know what book you were discussing at your club on the Sunday that she never showed."

"Oh, um, *The Mysterious Affair at Styles*. That's right, the first-ever Poirot."

"Are you sure?"

"Positive, it's the first time she introduces us to the funny little Belgian. Poor Agatha, she never expected him to become quite so popular—"

He coughed discreetly. "No, I mean, are you sure that was the book your club was going to study that Sunday?"

"Oh, sorry, yes, of course I'm sure. Why?"

The policemen exchanged another quick glance. "In Mrs Parlour's vehicle we found the missing mink coat, her driver's license—"

"Well she wouldn't leave those things hanging around, surely? Doesn't that suggest something dodgy has happened?"

Ignoring this question he added, "And we also found this."

Ward reached for a box by his desk and produced a plastic evidence bag in which a book had been sealed.

"Do you know anything about this? Were you intending to discuss it at one of your, er, club meetings?"

He handed the bag to Alicia and she looked it over. Through the thick plastic she could see the book was titled *The Mystery of the Blue Train: A Hercule Poirot Mystery.* The cover illustration showed two train officers peering over the body of a woman, clearly dead and sprawled across a seat in a train compartment. It was classic Agatha Christie.

"Well it's one of Christie's, sure, but it's not on our reading list," Alicia said. "I don't know much about it, certainly never read it, but can only assume Barbara was going to suggest it to us all. Do you think it's important?"

He retrieved the bag from her and placed it back in the box. "Was there anything else, Miss Finlay?"

Alicia hesitated. She wanted to tell Inspector Ward about Wanda's suspicions that Arthur was playing around with the housekeeper but decided against it. She had no proof of this and had already been called a gossipmonger once this week, she didn't need to confirm it. Besides, if the press were onto it, the cops were no doubt close behind. There were two other snippets of so-called gossip, however, that she knew for a fact were true and there was no way she was keeping these to herself. She took another deep breath.

"You should know that the day Barbara held the book club at her house, one of our members spotted her daughter, Holly, kissing the tennis coach."

She felt like a Year Nine schoolgirl and looked at him sheepishly waiting for the eye roll. He showed no expression so she rattled on. "The daughter's 16. The instructor is closer to 30 as far as I can tell." She held her palms up. "I'm just telling you that, I'm not saying it has anything to do with Barbara's disappearance, although I get the impression they're both hiding something…"

She recalled the conversation she and Claire had overheard at the tennis court two days before and repeated it to the policemen now.

Roger, who had been madly writing, his shaved head bobbing up and down as he did so, stopped and said, "Let me get this straight: the daughter, Holly, says, 'We have to tell him. It can't be kept quiet' and the coach says, 'But you can't even prove it was me'?"

Alicia shrugged. "Something like that. That was the gist of it anyway. But, as I say, it could have been perfectly innocent, a discussion over a broken tennis racquet or something."

Ward looked impatient. He'd stopped stroking his mo'. "You let us worry about what is and isn't innocent thanks Miss Finlay. What's the full name of this coach?"

"Jake Smith. That's all I know."

He nodded at Roger who wrote the name down.

"Anything else?"

"Just one other thing. I'm sure you're already onto this but I wanted to mention Barbara's younger brother."

"Niles Blakely? What about him?"

"He's a beneficiary of Barbara's will—"

"And you know this, how?"

She paused. "It seems to be common knowledge actually. Holly mentioned it to me, and then, well, Niles told my sister as much himself. Just yesterday. She called in on him at his café."

Ward's bushy eyebrows bunched together. "Your book club seems to be popping up everywhere."

"We're very worried, that's all. We thought maybe the brother could help us track her down. You do know about his money troubles?"

"Yes, thank you, we do have a few investigative skills of our own." He stood up. "I can't discuss any more details about this case with you, Miss Finlay. At this stage we're not even sure there is a case to answer. For all we know Mrs Parlour may show up safe and well."

"You don't really believe that, right?"

He ignored the question and led her out. At the station door he stopped and turned back. "Miss Finlay, you seem like a smart person but you and your book club need to be very, very careful. This is not some fictitious mystery you can sit down and chat about over cups of tea. Mrs Parlour may have walked out of her own accord or she may be in serious danger. As far as I'm concerned, there are suspicious circumstances and at this stage we hold grave fears for the woman's life."

"I realise that."

"Then stick to what you do best, crime fiction, and leave the real crime to the experts. Got it?"

She promised to do just that but metaphorically her fingers were firmly crossed. There was no way she was giving up on Barbara now. And if she knew the other members of the Murder Mystery Book Club, they would be right behind her.

~~~~~~~~

Just as Alicia was stepping out of the police station, Arthur Parlour was stepping back onto the fairway of his favourite golf course. He'd managed to give the press the slip earlier that afternoon, and was proud of himself for that, but his mood was now dark and petulant as he trudged past the fifth hole, towards the sixth, his golf clubs clattering behind him in his two-wheeled designer leather bag.
~~~~~~~~

That hadn't worked out very well at all, he thought of the quick detour he'd just made. *What a waste of bloody time!* He'd expected her to be happy to see him, it had been days since they'd been together after all, but she'd been a cow.

A first-class bitch, actually, and he was fuming now.

What more did she want from him? He'd needed her; she must have seen that. It had been a horrendous few days. The press was camped at his bloody doorstep, the cops were circling like vultures, and his own daughter could barely look him in the eye.

And now *she* had turned against him, too. It infuriated him. He thought he could trust her. After all this time. But obviously not.

He snarled and pulled the bag up to the teeing ground, then rolled it a little further back so he could get a clear hit. He pulled out the number 1 wood, frowned, then slipped it back in and grabbed the 9-iron, studying it lovingly. It was his favourite golf club, his lucky club if truth be told. He'd pitched a few killer shots with this one recently, surprised the crap out of old Jonsey from Accounts at the last company tournament. Jones had scoffed at the iron, suggested the driver instead, but Arthur had shown him, and shown him good.

He sniggered and stroked the club's shaft, admiring the gleam. It was part of a new set he'd bought just six months ago. They were Callaway—light, aerodynamic and cost a small fortune—but he didn't regret one cent. He knew they were ostentatious, but he also knew he deserved it. Hell, after everything he'd just been through, he deserved it, and more. He grabbed a ball and tee then strode towards the green, pushing the tee into the overgrown grass, and dropping the ball on top.

He stepped back and peered into the distance, down the expansive fairway. There was no one in sight. Good, it was just as he liked it.

He studied the ball, then glanced out at the fairway, and back at the ball again. He adjusted his grip on the club, admiring its shiny, silver lines as he did so, then shifted his feet and jiggled his hips a little. Jiggled them some more.

Then he groaned. He just couldn't get his head into it today.

Bloody hell, now she'd gone and ruined his form. He'd never get a good hit off in this mood.

He dropped the club to the ground, and shook his arms, trying to shake all thought of her away at the same time. A slight noise behind him caught him off guard and he swung around, eyes wide.

"Oh Jesus! It's you, you gave me a bloody fright," he said, visibly relaxing. Then his eyebrows knotted together. "What the hell are you doing out here, anyway? Did you follow me here? You have got to be kidding me."

He turned back, shaking his head and scowling out at the green. Now the day really was a disaster. *Couldn't he have one little golf game in peace?*

"This is bloody unbelievable," he continued ranting, hands on hips. "I haven't got time for this nonsense. I'm not going to tell you again—"

And he was right.

Arthur Parlour never did speak again. Within seconds his head was being smashed to smithereens by his shiny silver golf club.

"**Come,** perch next to me," said Missy as she pushed a few books to the side and made way for Claire who was just joining them at a side table. "Alicia was telling us how a bossy police officer is trying to scare us all off."

"No way?" said Claire.

"Way," said Missy, her bespectacled eyes wide.

It was 6:30 p.m. on Thursday night and they had taken over an entire section at the library, which was now closed to the public. Apart from Anders, who had a medical emergency, the entire book club were present and ready to continue dissecting the case.

"What have I missed?" asked Claire and Alicia quickly filled her in, telling her about Barbara's last sightings and the book she had left behind in her car.

"Unfortunately, none of us have read *The Mystery of the Blue Train,*" said Missy, looking deeply ashamed, as though they had all let Agatha Christie down terribly. "And our only copy is out." Her frown turned to a look of delight. "But you'll never guess who borrowed it?" Before Claire could answer, Missy squealed, "*Barbara.* I looked it up. That copy the police have, the one they found in her car, has to be mine. How spooky is that? Well, not mine, exactly, but you know what I mean, it belongs to this library. I *knew* I recognised her that first day we met, she's definitely been here." She paused. "I wonder why she said she hadn't?" She shrugged, her curly copper locks bobbing about. "Anyway, Barbara borrowed a bunch of books a few weeks ago, before the club even started—"

"Hang on, did you say *The Mystery of the Blue Train*?" interrupted Claire. "That does ring a bell. I think I have read that one."

"Really?" said Alicia. "Can you remember what it's about? Maybe there's a clue in there or she was trying to send us a message. Maybe there was a suicide or a battered wife or something?"

Claire considered this for a moment. "I don't think battered wives were Ms Christie's style, do you? Much too *common*. But let me think…" She swept her black locks back from her face and smudged her glossy lips to one side. "It's about a group of people all chasing some fabulously expensive ruby with an even more fabulous name, and they all end up on that famous Blue Train that used to go to the French Riviera. Oh, I would adore that trip. If I remember rightly, the story featured an exotic dancer, some shifty swindlers, a male impersonator, but, no, definitely no battered wives. A riveting read, though." She paused. "I really can't see what this has got to do with anything. I'm sure if the police searched any of our cars or houses they'd find several old Poirot mysteries lurking about. We are members of the Murder Mystery Book Club after all."

"Too right," said Missy, who had switched to a computer terminal and was madly tapping away. "Okay, so, according to my little digital friend here, *The Mystery of the Blue Train* was first published in 1928, and re-published fairly regularly after that. Um… oh this is interesting, Agatha Christie started writing it two years earlier, in 1926—that's a really long turn-around for her. She usually churned her books out within a year. Just reading the description… ah, yes, Claire, the ruby was called 'the Heart of Fire'. Don't you just love Agatha's imagination? The way she turned things like jewellery and trains into characters of their own?"

"Yeah, yeah, but what's any of this got to do with Barbara's disappearance?" asked Perry, impatiently.

"Well, let me finish. Okay, according to Wikipedia—"

Alicia groaned. "So we're relying on the reputable sources then?"

"Oh they're all right. Now, shhh, this is an interesting quote from some English crime critic. Of the book he says, and I quote, 'Christie's least favourite story, which she struggled with just before and after blah, blah, blah… The international setting blah blah again…' It ends with, 'There are several fruitier candidates for the title of 'worst Christie'.'"

"Oh, I don't think it's her worst book by any means," said Claire. "Not even close. I hated *The Man in the Brown Suit* or whatever it was called."

They launched into a lengthy debate about their least favourite Christie novels before Perry threw a hand up, wearily.

"*Hello?* I have a hot dinner date in half an hour. Can we just get on with it, please?"

"Fine," said Missy. "So, lovely people, why did Barbara leave this particular book—Agatha Christie's least favourite novel no less—in her car before she disappeared? What does it mean?"

"Allow me to do an Anders and say, 'probably nothing'," said Claire. "But I guess it's worth noting."

"Duly noted then," said Alicia, underlining the title in her journal.

At that moment Lynette jumped up, her eyes saucer-like, her mouth agape. "Oh my God," she gasped.

She was staring into her smartphone, startled by something on the screen.

"What is it?" asked Missy looking up from her own screen.

"I was just checking out the online news to see if there were any more developments…"

"*And?*" yelled Perry.

"It's Arthur Parlour."

"Have they arrested him? Has he done a runner?"

Lynette shook her head again, swallowed hard then looked up at them all. "You're not going to believe this…"

"What?" screamed Alicia now.

"He's dead. Arthur Parlour has been found, *dead.*"

CHAPTER 18

For the first time since they met, the Murder Mystery Book Club were speechless. Lynette had just dropped the bombshell and was scrolling through her phone's internet site, desperately trying to find out more while Missy did the same on her computer screen then jumped up and flicked on the library TV. Alicia took over the remote control and began switching through the channels, to no avail. Arthur's death had not yet made the commercial news.

Eventually, Perry broke the silence. "There goes my dinner date," he moaned and Claire shot him a withering look.

Alicia sighed. "I can't believe it. I... I feel terrible, just awful."

"Why?" asked Missy. "What's it got to do with you?"

"Well, I hounded the poor man for days, and then I told the cops he was dodgy... I never suspected he'd be killed."

"Hey, we don't even know if he was killed," said Claire. "Maybe he took his own life or had a terrible accident—"

"Okay here it is," interrupted Lynette, waving her small screen at them. "It's breaking news online... hang on, it just needs to reload. Okay, it says here that it's believed that the body of Arthur Parlour was found late this afternoon, at some golf course... oh, right, the Rose Bay golf club... *'Fatally wounded'*, that's what they say." She scrolled down. "Nope, nope, that's all it says. But that's suspicious—it doesn't sound like suicide to me."

"Where are you getting this from?" asked Missy, fingers flying across her keyboard as she attempted to catch up.

Lynette showed her the web address. "It's a reputable news site but it's obviously just broken, they don't have much. No luck with the TV, Lis?"

"Nothing so far."

"They're such dinosaurs," Lynette scoffed, scrolling through her web browser while Alicia continued to beat herself up.

"Here we were thinking Arthur was a cold-blooded killer and now he's dead. It doesn't make any sense. And still no one knows where Barbara is."

"Oh, God, poor Holly," said Missy. "I mean, sure she was hardly Daughter of the Year but still, for her mum to go AWOL and Dad to show up murdered."

"We still don't know it was murder," said Claire. "It said 'fatally wounded', so it could be manslaughter or a horrific accident. Maybe he got hit by a passing golf ball or something?"

No one was buying it.

"What does all this mean?" asked Perry. "What does this have to do with Barbara's disappearance?"

They stared at him, stunned, not knowing how to answer that.

"Oh, here's another longer story, possums," Missy said and they all huddled around as she read from the screen aloud, scanning the basics.

"Arthur Parlour, respected Eastern suburbs investment manager and prospective state politician, blah blah blah, found dead on the Rose Bay golf course around 5:00 p.m. this evening by club security... um, he was found with a blow to the head in what is believed to be a vicious random attack—"

"Attack?" said Alicia. "That means he was murdered."

"Yes, but random attack?" piped in Perry. "Are they suggesting, *quelle horreur*, that he was just knocked over the noggin by some passing lunatic and left for dead? I mean, they're not connecting the dots to his missing wife? Really?"

"Hush, honey, I'm getting to that bit," Missy said, tapping at the keyboard to move the screen down. "Now, where was I, yes, here we are… um, *'police will not confirm if his death is linked to the recent disappearance of his wife, Barbara Parlour, who has not been seen since Saturday afternoon… However they are not ruling anything out at this stage. They are asking for witnesses to come forward'* etc etc."

"What a joke," he spat.

"Of course they see a connection," said Alicia. "They're just not giving anything away. The question is, how do we all feel about it? Do we think there's a connection between the two cases?"

Every single one of them nodded their heads gravely.

"They have to be connected," said Missy. "It's too coincidental. But how? Why?"

"Maybe the tennis coach really did kill Barbara," said Perry. "Maybe he did as Holly asked and confessed to Arthur and then they came to blows." He stopped, realised how silly that sounded. "No… no, I've got a better idea."

"Here we go," groaned Claire but he ignored her.

"It's a ransom gone wrong. Has to be."

"Sorry?" said Claire.

"Think about it. They're wealthy as all hell. Perfect candidates for that kind of thing. She goes missing, he's very clandestine about it all, doesn't want the coppers involved, assures us she's okay. Maybe she was being held to ransom and he was told not to tell anyone. Maybe the arrogant fool thought he could pay the ransom and get her back on his own. So he agrees to rendezvous at the golf course and instead of getting his wife back, he gets a bang over the head, dead."

Not a bad theory, thought Alicia but Claire wasn't buying it.

"So why wouldn't the kidnapper just hand Barbara back? And are you saying Jake did the kidnapping or someone else? I'm confused."

"Maybe Barbara and Arthur discovered the identity of the kidnapper so they both had to die. I don't know, Claire, I don't have all the answers, I just have the fabulous theories." Perry dropped back into his seat, deflated.

"Well, I for one like the way your mind works, Perry," said Alicia. "It's even freakier than mine."

"Thank you. I think."

"But, listen, I have another theory, and I think you're going to like this one better, Claire." They all gave Alicia their undivided attention. "Lyn, didn't you say that Arthur's body was found at a golf course in Rose Bay?" Her sister nodded. "Guess who lives right next door to a golf course in Rose Bay? Her property fronts the fairway."

Claire gasped. "Oh, yes, of course. *Wanda Birchin.*"

"Exactly. Wanda Birchin. Barbara's so-called ex-BFF. The very same person who told us Arthur was the philandering type. How does she know that? Maybe she was another notch on his bedpost? Maybe they had a lover's quarrel?"

The frown on Claire's face told her she wasn't buying this theory either so Alicia pressed on. "It makes perfect sense to me. Remember, Claire, how Wanda told us that she and Barbara had a falling out, but she wouldn't tell us why. Maybe Barbs caught her sleeping with Arthur?"

"Or maybe Wanda's husband did it!" squealed Missy, suddenly getting in on the action. "She does have a husband, right?"

Claire and Alicia looked at each other blankly. They had no idea. Wanda had never mentioned one, but she certainly behaved like a lady of leisure, which usually meant there was someone in the background, topping up the AMEX.

"Well, assuming that she does, maybe Wanda's husband catches them at it and takes his revenge," said Missy. "Pity we don't know more about the hubby..."

"Pity we don't know whether she was even sleeping around with Arthur or not," added Alicia. "I'm just guessing here."

She slunk back into her seat as they fell into a gloomy silence again.

Eventually Alicia had a thought. "I need to pay Wanda another visit. I need to find out for sure."

Lynette frowned. "I dunno…"

"Sorry, but I need to get some straight answers from her. I reckon Wanda's been playing us from the start. She's the one who invited us over, remember, then fed us all the stuff about Arthur's supposed affair with Rosa. Even tried to implicate Holly in the whole thing—said she was the violent type. Next thing we know, Arthur shows up dead right next door to her house. Nope, that woman's got some questions to answer and I'm not afraid to ask them."

She sat forward, holding her hands prayer-like in front of her. "Listen, guys, I know we're all really busy people and we've spent a lot of time on this already, but Arthur's death takes it to a whole new level. I think we have to step things up considerably if we want to find Barbara alive."

"*If* Barbara's still alive," said Perry, his chin resting on one palm. "I'm sorry, sweetie, but that seems extremely unlikely now. We have to face facts."

"Either way, whether she's alive or dead, we need to find her," persisted Alicia. "And if that means asking some difficult questions, then so be it. Arthur's death clearly proves there's something very dodgy going on over at Chateau Parlour. Come on, gang, are we committed to this or not?"

She glanced at each member and they nodded in turn. While no one knew the woman well, they did know a good mystery when it was staring them in the face, and none of them could resist. And if they could help Barbara at the same time, that was an added bonus.

"So what do you suggest, Poirot?" asked Missy.

"*It is the approach, classic!*" she said, putting on her best Belgian accent. "*The technique of elimination. We eliminate the suspects one by one. We do not scamper around like the puppies.*"

The stared at her, bemused, and she blushed.

"Sorry couldn't help myself. That's a quote from Poirot in *Three Act Tragedy*, I watched it not long ago on TV. What I'm trying to say is, I think we each have to focus on one line of enquiry and work from there. We need to eliminate the suspects, one by one. So, I'll stick with Wanda and see where that takes me."

"And now he's dead, I could go back to Arthur's house and have a look around—" began Missy but Alicia shook her head.

"The cops will be swarming all over the place now, I don't think you'll get past the front gate."

"Well about time, too," she said. "Okay, then possums, I'll stick to what I do best. I'll see if I can unearth more juicy details about the book they found in Barbara's car. I might also look a little more closely at Barbara's account while I'm at it. Maybe there are some clues in there somewhere."

"Is that even legal?" asked Claire and Missy gave her a wicked grin.

"I think it's a great idea," said Alicia, turning to Claire. "As for you, Ms Hargreaves…"

Claire's shapely eyebrows rose slightly. "Yes?"

"You're not going to want to hear this, but I think you need to pay our tennis Lothario a visit. Find out what he really knows about the Parlour family and what his real relationship is with Holly. Maybe find out, if you can, what they were on about that day at the tennis court."

Claire groaned. "Oh, but he's such a sleazebag."

"A sleazebag who took a fancy to you, I'm afraid," she said. "Come on, pull on your tennis whites, it'll be worth it."

"Oh I have just the outfit," she declared, suddenly sounding enthused. "Rightio then but it will have to wait until Saturday, I can't keep closing the shop willy-nilly. I'll go broke."

"What about me?" said Perry, sitting up. "Any sleazebags for me?"

Alicia laughed. "How about you visit that jewellery store in the Strand Arcade? It's one of the last places Barbara was seen alive. Inspector Ward suggested she was getting something repaired but he wouldn't elaborate. Maybe you can find out what that's all about. See if it means anything."

"Excellent idea, what's it called?"

"Oh, damn, Ward didn't say. But how many jewellers can there be in one little arcade?"

"I guess I'll find out, but I'm with Claire on this one—no can do until the weekend. My boss will skin me alive if I take any more time off work."

"Actually, that's ideal," said Alicia. "Barbara was there last Saturday, so you want to make sure you speak to the person who works weekends. Besides, they're less likely to be the owner, so you're more likely to get the goss out of them. Then we could all get back together on, say, Sunday morning and compare notes? Let's meet at my place around 10, so we can give poor Max a little attention, and maybe enjoy Lynette's fabulous cinnamon pancakes…?"

She flashed her sister a questioning glance and Lynette nodded.

"Oh goodie, I'm salivating at the thought," said Missy. "But what about you, Lynette? What are you going to do, possum, apart from cook up a storm, of course?"

"Oh I know exactly what I'm going to do," she said, standing up and stretching out. "I'm going to take another trip across the bridge to Balmoral Beach. As far as I can see, there's one person who should be very happy to hear about Arthur's death, and it's time I paid him another visit."

CHAPTER 19

If Niles Blakely was happy about his brother-in-law's sudden demise, he certainly didn't look it. His hair was even more dishevelled than before, the furrow between his eyes was now a gaping gorge, and the bags under his eyes had turned into luggage. Nor was he very interested in talking to Lynette who was now standing outside his café, her sister in tow.

Lynette had insisted on visiting Niles that very night and, after failing to put her off to the morning, Alicia did a little insisting of her own.

"If you're going this late, I'm coming with you. He could be dangerous."

"I doubt that very much."

"You don't know him, Lynette. Besides, I have a few questions of my own. May as well kill two birds…" She winced, gave her sister an apologetic smile.

And so they had gone straight from the library to their house, first to feed a sorely neglected Max, then to grab a bag of muffins and the old Torana. It would be much faster than public transport.

On the way, Lynette had swiped Alicia's hands away from the muffin bag, receiving a sulky moan in return. "Sorry, sis, but they're a peace offering for Niles. Might also loosen his tongue a bit, if we're lucky."

"So what makes you think he'll even be there?" Alicia glanced at the dashboard clock. It was now almost 10:00 p.m. "I thought you said it wasn't open for dinner."

"Just a hunch."

Lynette's hunch was spot on. Niles was indeed still loitering at his Balmoral café but he was not easily bribed and glared at Lynette's blueberry and white chocolate muffins as though they were laced with arsenic.

"No thank you," he said going to shut the glass sliding door on them.

Lynette wedged her foot in the door and tried for her most sympathetic smile. "Come on, Niles, we're not the enemy here."

"Everyone's the enemy, that's what my lawyer just told me. You hear about Arthur?"

"It's all over the internet."

"Well I didn't do it!"

"I never said you did."

"Yes, but after what I said to you yesterday…" He broke off, blushed crimson red under his freckly white skin.

"That makes me think you *didn't* do it," she said. "You told me you had no motive for killing your sister, unless of course Arthur suddenly showed up dead. Well, you'd hardly say that if you were planning to murder him now would you?"

He stared at her warily then glanced at Alicia who was standing quietly in the shadows.

"This is my sister, Alicia, we're both in Barbara's book club, that's how we know her. Can we come in? Please?" Lynette pushed the muffins towards him. "Freshly baked, *really* tasty. You can flog them off tomorrow if you like. We get five bucks a muffin at Mario's."

He looked at the muffins, clearly doing a little mental arithmetic, then sighed, snatched the bag off her, and opened the door wider so they could enter.

"I can't offer you coffee, the machine's off." He dropped the muffins on the counter. "Want a tea or a cold drink?"

They both shook their heads no, so he sat down with them at a table.

"I couldn't have killed Arthur, you know, I was here all afternoon. Cops have just been, I told them all of this."

"Can anyone corroborate that?" asked Alicia gently and he frowned again.

"No, unfortunately. Barely a soul through all day, same as yesterday. I locked up early today, around 4:00 p.m., been out the back most of the arvo doing the books at exactly the time the poor bastard was supposedly being hit over the head."

"What time was that, do you know?"

"According to 'the filth', his body was found about 5:00 p.m.; they reckon he'd been dead no longer than an hour or two. So, I guess, anytime from four, maybe." He sat up straighter. "I'm not supposed to be talking to you guys about Arthur."

"Then talk to us about your sister instead," said Alicia. "You didn't receive a letter off her this week, did you?"

Both Niles and Lynette looked at her, not quite understanding.

"It's just that I spoke with Inspector Ward today, he's the guy running the case—"

"Yeah I know him. What about him?"

"Well he mentioned that Barbara posted a letter from a city mail box on the day she disappeared. I'm just wondering if that letter was for you?"

He shook his head emphatically. "Ward's already asked me that. I haven't heard a single peep from my sister since she disappeared. I would've said something if I had."

"Fair enough. It's just that you told Lynette that your sister would never do anything without talking to you first.

I just wonder if she, maybe, wrote you about what was happening, how she was feeling…"

"No she did not. Listen, I don't know what happened to her, that's the God's honest truth. Nor do I have anything to do with Arthur's death. I'm not going to pretend I liked the guy, or that I'm even sorry he's gone—he was a pig, most people will tell you that—but I didn't kill him. No way."

He glanced beseechingly from one sister to the other and Lynette placed a hand on his shoulder.

"It's okay, Niles, we're just asking."

"Yeah, well, you're asking a lot of bloody strange questions," he replied, sulkily.

"Can I ask one more?" said Alicia, and, when he didn't respond she added, "About Holly."

He looked up. "Holly? My bratty niece, what about her?"

"Did your sister ever mention anything going on between her daughter and her tennis coach?"

He seemed stumped by the question until a flicker of understanding crossed his face. "Ah, that's right, a slimeball called Jack or Jackson or something."

"Jake Smith."

He nodded his head. "Yep, that's it. I met him once at a family BBQ. Coming on to Barbs, if I recall. Why, you think he's playing up with Holly? She's still a kid."

"She's 16 going on 26, or at least that's how your sister described her."

"Look, I don't know anything about what Holly and some paedophile tennis coach were up to, and I don't remember my sister mentioning it. The only thing she ever said about Holly was that she was a stuck-up little daddy's girl. They weren't real close, not since she hit puberty anyway. What's this got to do with her disappearance? You think Jake did something to her? Or to Arthur?"

Alicia held her hands up. "I'm not saying that, just wondering about him, that's all. And wondering whether Barbara mentioned him."

He shook his head slowly.

"Okay, then," said Lynette breezily, "we'd better get going."

Now it was Alicia's turn to look surprised. Surely Lynette hadn't dragged her all this way so late in the evening for this? These questions could easily have waited until morning. She thought Lynette had some great ace up her sleeve, but clearly she was wrong.

"Can we give you a lift home, Niles?" Lynette was saying, standing up and grabbing hold of Alicia's car keys, which had been flung on the tabletop.

He shook his head quickly. "Nah, still got the books to do."

"You seem to spend a lot of time doing the books," Lynette said. She sat down again and tossed the car keys back on the table. "You're homeless, aren't you?"

Alicia was more stunned by the question than Niles. *So there was an ace after all.*

"Don't know what you're talking about," he replied, his voice deadpan.

"I saw the backpack and sleeping bag, yesterday, Niles, I know you've been bedding down here. I mean, yes, café owners have work to do after hours, but you seem to be spending an insane amount of time here lately. Can't be that much to add up, you're clearly not getting a lot of customers through."

He still wasn't talking so she gave his shoulder another squeeze and asked, "How long?"

After a few moments, he shook his head and groaned. "Got evicted from my Surry Hills apartment Monday arvo. They changed the locks, can't even get in to get my stuff. Bastards. Hardly owed any rent, but you know how landlords can be these days? Stingy buggers."

"Your sister usually bail you out?"

He didn't say anything but the look of shame that crept across his face was all the answer she needed.

"Why don't you just sell this place? Move on? Clear your debts?"

He shrugged. Looked away despondently, so she glanced at her sister.

"Come on, Alicia, we'd better let this poor man get some sleep." She turned back to him. "Good luck with it all, hey?"

He stared after them, bleakly, as they left him sitting alone in the middle of his empty café.

CHAPTER 20

Alicia Finlay stared hard at the 16-page pull-out poster of Lady Gaga that her art director had just designed. It was slightly fuzzy and out of focus, but that's what happened when you blew a digital image up way beyond its original purpose. She wasn't exactly in love with the lime green border either but she knew 12-year-olds would consider it the epitome of style, and that's all that mattered. She gave him the nod and returned to her desk.

It was Friday morning and yet again Alicia was struggling to focus on work. It was becoming a bad habit. She had now finished the kitten mag, these things never took long to whip together, and was onto a one-off poster mag which was failing, miserably, to hold her attention. Alicia had already left two messages at Wanda Birchin's house to no avail and was itching to make some progress on the investigation. She didn't know where to turn. She pushed her chair aside and strolled to the coffee room where, surprise, surprise, Ginny was whipping up a cappuccino. Any excuse to be away from the front desk.

"You look like absolute crap," Ginny said over the gurgling of the milk frother.

"Thanks, Gin, you always make me feel so fabulous."

"Sorry, sweetie, but what's going on? You're spending a lot of time out of the office these days. Gonna get yourself fired if you're not careful."

"Who's to know? Head honcho's in London, remember."

Ginny glanced around. "Yeah but Hamish Keener's not. He's in thick with the Big Boys. I wouldn't put it past him to dob you in."

"He can dob away. The mag's nearly done, I've been catching up at home."

She took a mug out of the cupboard and leant against the bench, waiting for Ginny to finish.

"So what is luring you away so much? Not still stressing about that missing weirdo from your book club are you?"

"Even more so now the husband's shown up dead."

Ginny mock gasped. "I know! I saw that on the Today Show this morning. It's a murky mystery you've landed yourself there, that's for sure. You and book clubs, eh? You've got a bad track record—kicked out of one club, a member missing from another, her husband murdered!"

"I wasn't kicked out of the Monday Night Book Club, thanks, Ginny, I gave them the boot, remember?"

Still, it didn't make her feel any better and she slumped over the kitchen bench with a dramatic sigh.

"Why don't you just leave it to the coppers?" Ginny said, pulling the silver milk jug out of the steamer and fetching a spoon. "Hate to burst your little bubble, baby, but it's *their* job, not yours."

Alicia stood up straight and stared at her. "You're right. My God, you're absolutely right."

She dumped the mug back in the cupboard and ran to her desk to retrieve her handbag.

"Oi, where the bloody hell are you going now?" called Ginny from the corridor, the milk jug still in her hand.

"I'm taking your advice for once!" she called back, jamming one finger on the elevator's down button.

Inspector Ward ushered Alicia into his office with barely a glance, waving her into a chair as he finished something he was typing on the computer in front of him. Eventually he paused and turned to her, giving his moustache a quick pat down as he did so.

"So, it's the book club sleuth back again. Got more insights for me regarding Barbara Parlour?"

She dropped her bag to the floor and shook her head. "Actually, it's about Arthur Parlour."

"You heard about his homicide then."

"It's not possible to hear about anything else. Now the morning shows are camped out at his doorstep, trying to get the first pictures of the distraught daughter, it's disgusting."

"Aren't you a journalist?" he asked, a glint in his eye.

"Yes, but I'd never do that. No amount of money would make me do that."

"Glad to hear it. It certainly doesn't help us do our job either. And nor do constant interruptions from the public." The glint was now gone.

"Okay, okay, I'll get on with it. I just wanted to mention something in case you don't know and it turns out to be important. It's about Wanda Birchin."

"Who?"

"Wanda Birchin, you know Barbara's friend, or ex-friend as the case may be? I mentioned her the other day."

"What about her?"

"I'm not saying she's a suspect or anything—"

"Spit it out, Miss Finlay, I really haven't got time for this."

She nodded. "Sorry. Um, it's just that Wanda lives right next door to the golf club where Arthur's body was found."

His expression changed, he picked up a pen. "Wanda Birchill you say?"

"Birchin, Wanda Birchin." She spelt it for him as he jotted the name down on his note pad. "I'm not saying she has anything to do with it, but she may have seen something. Heard something."

"My men are questioning the neighbours as we speak, but that's good to know. Now, if there's nothing else, I do have work to get on with."

"Well…" He gave her an impatient look. "I probably should have mentioned this last time I was here." The look intensified. "I'm not normally one for gossip and you have probably already heard all of this but I think there might have been something fishy going on between Arthur and his housekeeper."

"Rosa Lopez? How do you mean."

"I think she and Arthur may have been having an affair, I don't know what it means and whether it has anything to do with anything, but I figured I should mention it."

He sighed, had obviously heard this rumour before. "Do you have any actual proof of this alleged affair?"

"Me? Oh, er, not exactly, but Wanda suggested it."

"Wanda Birchin again. And what makes either of you believe Arthur and his housekeeper were intimate?"

"Well, nothing definitive. It's just that they did seem pretty cosy last time I was there. He called her 'baby' and, um, Barbara had told us Rosa usually only worked a few hours in the middle of the day, but she seems to be there round the clock now. Or she was before Arthur died."

"Perhaps, with his wife missing, Arthur employed her full-time to help out," he suggested.

"Perhaps," she agreed. "I'm just telling you so it's off my chest."

"Clearing your conscience so to speak? Okay Miss Finlay, if there's nothing else, I really do have work to get on with."

"Of course you do." She jumped up.

As they walked to the door, he stopped and asked, "When did you last see Arthur Parlour?"

Alicia gave this some thought. "The last time I *spoke* to him would have been Monday evening when I called to get Wanda's details. But I last saw him earlier that day at his house. Just after 1:00 p.m. I think it was— just before your people arrived to chat to him. As I told you, I had nagged him to call you and report Barbara's disappearance. He seemed so reluctant to do it, which is why I suspected him. But now, to find he's been murdered… How's Holly taking it?"

"As you'd expect. She's staying with friends I believe."

"I know one of our club members saw him alive and well around 11:00 a.m. on Wednesday."

"Who?"

"Missy Corner, she's a local librarian. Went over to Barbara's house to look for a book she'd lost."

Alicia knew this was a lie but felt like she needed to keep that bit of information to herself. He had already warned the book club members off once before.

"I see. And this was around 11:00 a.m. you say?"

Alicia looked Missy's number up on her smartphone and read it out to Ward.

"Yes, give her a call. She'll tell you."

Ward wavered. "It probably makes no difference at this point, unless she saw something suspicious."

"Well she did say that Arthur had snapped Rosa's head off." When he raised his eyebrows she quickly added, "Not literally, of course."

Alicia briefly described the altercation at the Woollahra house and Ward stroked his moustache and opened the door.

"A tiff with the servants doesn't usually end in murder, Miss Finlay," he said, the glint back in his eyes. "At least, not outside of an Agatha Christie novel."

CHAPTER 21

The weather was still a little surly when Claire Hargreaves stepped out onto the tennis courts at Rushcutters Bay on Saturday morning, and she pulled her vintage Adidas jacket close around her as she eyed the rain clouds above, threatening to spill their load. She'd also chosen a tiny white wraparound pleated tennis skirt and felt conspicuous in it now. She didn't normally reveal so much leg, Charlie didn't go in for that kind of thing, but she imagined Jake Smith did, and she needed all the help she could get.

As if on cue, Jake appeared on the side of the court and bounded over to her, his eyes sweeping across her legs and up to her jacket. "Cool outfit," he said, his eyes returning to her legs and staying there.

She laughed nervously. "Thanks for meeting me. I've been meaning to get my tennis back up to scratch for years."

"No sweat, it was good to get your call. I thought we had a connection."

He stared into her eyes now, one of those sleazy smiles lingering on his lips, and her nerves quickly dissolved, replaced by indignation and disgust. She had never liked sleazy men, found leering looks, gushing compliments, and even bouquets of flowers quite off-putting. Give her a reserved, up-right gentleman like Charlie any day.

She feigned a warm smile and continued to smile throughout the half hour lesson she had booked with the tennis coach. In fact, Claire didn't need lessons at all, was a very adept tennis player, had learned back in England when she was young, but pretended to miss a few hits and giggled a little girlishly from time to time. She needed him to feel superior if she was going to have him eating out of her hands, but he wasn't falling for her act.

"You're a better player than you made out," he said when the lesson was over and she'd insisted they share a jug of Pimm's and lemonade up at the club bar.

They were seated on a wide, shady balcony looking out over the tennis courts and there were just two other tables occupied, one with a young couple who only had eyes for each other, and the other with a man in a business suit whose own eyes were firmly fixed on a small laptop in front of him. Perhaps he was the manager, Claire thought as she poured the icy drink into two glasses and offered Jake one.

"Oh, thanks Jake, that's nice of you to say," she said, trying hard not to bat her eyelashes. That would be overkill. "So, how long have you been teaching tennis?"

"Few years. Barbara gave me my first break." He paused. "Hey, that was shocking news about Arthur, eh?"

She nodded. "Were you teaching him tennis as well?"

"Nah, he was strictly a golf guy. Suited me just fine."

"You didn't like him?"

He shrugged, picked up his drink and took a gulp.

"So how did Barbara help you?"

"Huh?

"You said she gave you your 'first break'."

Jake nodded, running a hand up the back of his neck. She had seen the manoeuvre before. He was showing off his sizeable biceps, and she couldn't help smiling at his pathetic attempt to win her over. This only encouraged him and he smiled back. She hadn't removed her engagement ring before the lesson, yet this didn't seem to put him off, nor did she suspect that it would. If anything, it probably spurred him on.

"Yeah, you see, I'm a gardener by trade—bloody awful job, digging about in muck and manure, not exactly my idea of fun. Anyway, I'd been doing Barb's backyard for a few months and I noticed that no one ever seemed to be on the court. You know, they've got that fancy court round the side?"

"Yes," said Claire and his smile turned sly.

"'Course you do. You were spying on me just near it."

Spying on *Holly*, actually, she wanted to say but bit her tongue and smiled slyly back.

"So anyway, one day I ask Barbs if she ever played. Hadn't seen her even near the court, let alone on it. Well, she laughed like she'd never heard anything so crazy. Told me the court was all for appearances. She couldn't hit a ball to save her life. I offered to teach her, and well, the rest is history."

"So that's when you set up your business?"

"Tennis Menace, yep, like the name?"

No, she thought, but said instead, "So how many clients do you have now?"

He gave it some thought. "'Bout 20 or so. Barbs helped me recruit all the bored ladies from the local golf club."

"Ah, golf widows."

He laughed. "Desperate housewives more like it."

She raised her eyebrows. "Really? They try it on do they?"

He shrugged lazily. "Doesn't bother me if a beautiful older woman has a flirt."

Claire took a deep breath and asked, "Did Barbara like to have a flirt?"

The question caught him off guard and a dark look flickered across his blue eyes, but he rallied quickly and just shrugged, giving nothing away.

She took another breath. "So is she any good?"

His eyes widened. "What?"

"Barbara, is she any good at tennis?"

"Oh, yeah, um, she's not bad. Took a few months but she got the hang of it eventually. I mean, I'm not going to enter her into Wimbledon any time soon, but she can pull off a decent hit and giggle and that's all those rich socialites are after. The daughter's harder. Holly doesn't listen."

"Sounds like a typical child."

Claire hadn't meant to emphasise the word 'child' but it seemed to have an unsettling effect. His smarmy smile slipped away and the dark look in his eyes was back.

"She's almost 17," he said flatly.

"A little young for you, then."

"I'm teaching her tennis, Claire, not dating her."

"Really? Because that's not how it comes across." He stared hard at her but said nothing, so she quickly added, "You were spotted kissing her, Jake, that Sunday at Book Club."

He looked away, shaking his head impatiently. "Jesus, you guys really are a nosy bunch. So what if we were kissing? We're just mucking around, nothing serious."

"Do you think Barbara would approve?"

"Barbara? What's she got to do with it?"

"She's your boss isn't she? She's also Holly's mum, and I know the type. They usually have a respectable lawyer picked out for their little darlings long before they've even hit private school. You think she wants the tennis boy fraternising with her daughter?"

Jake's eyes squinted, his voice turned cold. "Well Barbara's not around anymore is she? So it's irrelevant."

"You're talking like she's dead," said Claire.

"You don't think she is?"

Claire held her hands up. "I hope not."

"Is that why you called me?"

"Sorry?"

He placed his glass down with a thump and the amorous couple looked around with a start. He leaned in, across the table and said, "Come on, Claire, I didn't come down in the last shower. You don't need tennis lessons, hell you could whop my arse on the court if you tried."

She blushed. "I just wanted to get some practice—"

"You just wanted to find out what I know about Barbara's disappearance. What, you think Barbs caught me with her precious little jodhpur girl and I smacked her over the head or something? Buried her under the tennis court?" He smiled again but it was laced with ice, and his hands were held in two tight fists on top of the table now as though ready for a fight. "Holly was right about you lot. You can go back and tell your book club nerds that the last time I saw Barbara she was alive and well."

"When was that?" she said, knowing she was now pushing her luck.

The smarmy tennis coach had officially lost his charm and now looked more like a small-town thug, his eyes squinted together, his mouth in a mean snarl. Suddenly she could picture him grabbing that racquet and doing something very dangerous with it. Glancing around the balcony, Claire was disappointed to see the couple disappearing inside, but the man in the suit was still there, head up now and also glancing around, so she swallowed her fears and feigned confidence. Perhaps Jake noticed the man, too, because he also lightened up, loosening his fists and giving her a nonchalant shrug.

"Saturday morning if you must know. We had a quick lesson then she said she had to get ready."

"Ready for what?"

He shrugged again. "Beats me. She looked excited, said something about another lesson she was having."

"Lesson? Really? Where?"

"No idea, just mumbled something and left me down at the court. I saw myself out. That was the last I saw of her. I've told the pigs all of this, just ask them. They called me yesterday arvo." He paused. "Apparently someone's been feeding them gossip."

The icy look was back and Claire held her hands up defensively.

"Hey, Jake, I haven't said a thing to the police. Honestly I haven't."

"Yeah, whatever." He stood up, grabbed his racquet and cap. "I've had enough of this crap. I don't have to answer to you or anyone." He glanced at his oversized sportswatch. "Besides, I've got a real client to teach."

"We're just looking out for Barbara, Jake, just worried, that's all."

"So you keep saying. But as far as I can tell, it's Arthur that's dead, not Barbara." He leaned in, inches from Claire's face, his voice barely a whisper. "Maybe Arthur was the one who needed looking out for. Ever thought of that?"

And then he turned and marched away.

Claire took a long gulp of her Pimm's and tried to calm her shaking nerves. She was more wound up than she realised, her heart thumping wildly beneath her jacket. Jake had certainly rattled her, she could see a dangerous side to the man, and was glad the guy in the suit had never left the balcony.

Perhaps things would have been very different if he had.

Claire pulled her mobile phone from her sports bag, took a deep breath and called Alicia, telling her what Jake had just said. Alicia was stunned.

"What? Is he saying that Barbara has something to do with Arthur's murder? That we should be pointing the finger at her?"

"That's what it sounded like."

"Do you think he knows something?"

Claire stared down at the courts where Jake was now showing a middle-aged, skimpily dressed woman how to serve. She could hear her giggling like a schoolgirl.

"I honestly don't know, Alicia. But he's a shifty character and he could just be saying that to get us off his scent."

"So you think he may be involved?"

"Maybe." She told Alicia about his career change from reluctant gardener to entrepreneurial tennis coach. "It seems to me that he has Barbara to thank for all those high-paying clients. If she really had caught him at it with Holly, maybe she threatened to ruin him, call her golf friends and destroy his business. It's one thing for a tennis coach to sleep with a few bored housewives, it's another to meddle with their precious daughters. He was playing with fire, and maybe, just maybe, Barbara's the one who got burnt."

"So where does Arthur fit into all this?"

Claire bit her lip, trying to think. "Maybe they both caught him out. Maybe he's killed both of them, we just haven't found Barbara's body yet."

Alicia shuddered. "It's one possibility I suppose, although it seems a little extreme to me. I mean, surely there are more desperate housewives out there he can coach? Even if Barbara did threaten to call her mates, it's not like he can't source clients elsewhere."

Claire sighed. "I know, it's so unlikely. Still, I found the man quite scary, a little threatening even."

"Did he actually threaten you?"

"No, not quite. It was just his demeanour. He was not happy with my questions, seemed very defensive. There was one other interesting thing he told me, though."

She explained how he had given Barbara a tennis lesson the day she disappeared and how she had mentioned heading off to get ready for some other lesson.

"Hm, that is interesting. What do you think Barbara meant by that?"

"If only we knew... there are so many cryptic clues that make no sense at all."

Alicia agreed and wondered, too, whether it was even true, whether Jake was feeding them red herrings to throw them off his trail. If so, it was very Agatha Christie of him.

"As far as I know," she said, "the police have no record of Barbara going to any other lesson or seeing anyone after the jewellery shop, at least not that they told me."

"Oh dear, I'd better go," said Claire, her voice hushed. "I might be paranoid but Jake's staring up at me now with dagger eyes."

"Yeah, get out of there, Claire, we don't know what that guy's capable of. And thanks, that can't have been easy. Now, I just wonder how Perry is going…"

~~~~~~~~

Perry was having a fabulous time. It was 1:22 p.m. and he had found his way to the only jewellery store in the inner-city luxury shopping strip called The Strand Arcade. He was leaning across the glass counter playing the part of Barbara Parlour's Personal Assistant and, for now, the young shop assistant, a well-dressed lad with bad skin and beady eyes, was buying it.

"I am sorry, sir, but that piece of jewellery has already been repaired and left the shop."

Perry mocked surprise and outrage. "What? *Noooo.* You have to be kidding me. Please tell me you're kidding me?"

"Er, no, sorry. Left on Tuesday."

"Oh. My. God." Perry fanned himself with a brochure from the counter as if he was about to pass out. "This is unbelievable… I had strict instructions from Ms Parlour herself to collect it."

"Must be a crossed wire?"

"More than a crossed wire, young man, I think the whole bloody phone line's down."

The jeweller looked distraught and reached for a book under the bench, scrambling through it as he whimpered, "But I remember really clearly, sir, she was very firm about the address I can assure you…"

"And you spoke to her yourself?"
~~~~~~~~

"Yes I did." He paused, looked jubilant. "Here it is! The Hydro as requested. That's where she wanted it to go, that's where we sent it."

Perry committed this to memory as he shook his head. "Really? The hydro? What else does it say?"

"Just that sir."

"Who was it addressed to?"

The shop assistant went to read it aloud but something made him reconsider. His beady eyes squinted suddenly. "Who did you say you were again?"

"I told you, man. I'm Barbara's PA. Bruno Myers. I run all her errands. In fact I was supposed to drop the jewellery in for her last Saturday, but she was coming into the city anyway so…"

"That was just before she disappeared, you know?" Now the eyes were wide, reaching for gossip.

"Yes, yes, sadly it was. I expect the police have spoken to you?"

"Yes, Mr Myers, they have."

"Good, good, but I can tell you, I expect her to show up very soon and when she does I want to have all her affairs in order. Including retrieving her missing jewels."

"Well, it was just the one, sir."

"What? Oh, yes of course it was. Can I see the, er, receipt?"

The eyes squinted again. He closed the book firmly. "Have you got some ID? A letter of authority?"

His about-face was quite unexpected and Perry pretended to be outraged. "No I do not and nor should I. Our previous jeweller, Henri at Tiffany's would never have asked me such an *impertinent* question. I told Barbs we should have stuck with them. Really can't imagine why she chose to come to this dreary little shop in the first place."

He was making this up of course and began looking around the small store disdainfully. Several customers wandered in at that point and the jeweller held one hand up to placate him.

"I'm sorry if I've put you out," he was saying, his voice lowered. "But we've had a few reporters in here nosing about and my boss tells me I have to, you know, check all ID before offering information." He leaned forward conspiratorially. "One reporter even pretended to be a policeman. Can you believe someone would do such a thing?"

Perry gasped. "No, that is outrageous, impersonating someone else. *Unforgivable.*"

"So you can see, sir, why my boss says I mustn't hand over any personal information. But I can assure you, it's all above board here. I followed Mrs Parlour's specific instructions, I haven't done anything wrong. You could always call the Hydro and enquire with them further?"

Perry sighed loudly and nodded. "Fine, fine, I'll clean up this mess for you."

He strode out, waited until he was clear of the arcade then gave a little whoop. Playing the cranky PA, Bruno, had been a lot of fun, but now he was left with more questions than answers. Like what the hell was 'the Hydro'? And why did Barbara send a piece of jewellery there just before she disappeared?

CHAPTER 22

The Murder Mystery Book Club were settled in for Sunday brunch around the Finlay's tea chest enjoying Lynette's spicy cinnamon pancakes, but no one more so than Missy. She was on to her third helping, long before most people had finished their first.

"You are the luckiest woman alive, Alicia," she said through a bulging mouth, "to have a budding chef under the same roof. Wish my Mum could cook a half-decent pancake."

Perry choked suddenly, spluttering freshly brewed coffee in all directions. "Tell me you're not still living *at home?*" Lynette tossed him a serviette and he began dabbing at the coffee stains down his tight, white sleeveless T-shirt. "You kept that one quiet."

"No I didn't," she said defensively. "Just never came up. Besides, it's all I can afford right now. You know what pittance they pay at the library? Mum says I'd be lucky to meet the annual power bill with that. I'm saving up."

"Good on you," said Claire, who was dressed casually today in a pair of dark blue jeans, a red and blue cowboy shirt tied in a knot in front and her hair in low ponytails.

She looked like she'd just stepped out of an old Western flick. "I couldn't wait to move out of home when I was your age but it was an expensive exercise."

"Yeah and try doing it on your own. At least you've got your fiancé to pay half the bills."

"Oh Charlie and I don't live together," said Claire and this roused Perry's interest.

He stopped dabbing and said, "Really? Why not?"

She shrugged. "Never seemed necessary, I suppose. We're getting married, we'll live together then."

If you get married, Perry was about to say but the frown on Alicia's face shut him up. He simply smacked his lips together and raised his eyebrows knowingly.

Alicia hadn't had the chance to ask Perry any more about his relationship with Claire's fiancé and the very thought of what he might say, sent shudders down her spine. Now, however, was not the time to ask, so she tried changing the subject instead.

"How'd we all go, then? Any good news to report?"

The book club members each took turns to get the others up to speed. Lynette described their visit on Thursday night to the Just Beachy Café and how Niles was now so broke he was homeless.

"At least I'm not holed up on the floor of a café," said Missy, glaring at Perry. "That's totally depressing. I'm not sure how I'd handle that. And eviction, too, soooo demoralising. An ex-colleague of mine from the library got evicted once. Oh she was *shattered*, they threw all her stuff out on the pavement out the front, would you believe? And—"

"How did Niles look?" interrupted Anders, keen to keep on track today.

Alicia noticed that Missy looked aggrieved by this and clamped her lips shut as though trying to keep herself in check.

"Exhausted and stressed, as you would," said Lynette. "How'd you go, Claire, with the tennis sleazebag?"

She winced. "It turned rather nasty in the end, I don't think he'll be sleazing on to me in future."

"Well Charlie will be relieved to hear that," Perry said drolly, and Alicia sighed.

She didn't know what he was playing at, but sensed it was a game where Claire would come out the loser. She liked Claire, enjoyed having her in the club. She had a sharp mind and was not averse to playing the devil's advocate, which both she and Perry desperately needed from time to time to keep them on track and their imaginations in check. She was damned if she was going to let Perry scare her away. He could keep his sordid innuendoes to himself.

"So tell everyone what happened, Claire," she prompted, ignoring Perry this time.

Claire proceeded to describe her meeting with Jake at the tennis club and the way he turned surly very quickly.

"So he didn't buy your student charade then?" asked Lynette.

"Not for one second. Although acting was never my forte."

"Well, I think I earned myself an Oscar yesterday," said Perry. "I fooled the jeweller outright."

He launched into an elaborate account of his time at the inner-city jewellery shop.

"So what's this hydro business?" Anders asked.

"Gee it rings a bell…" said Alicia.

"Well, there's the Snowy Hydro," said Missy. "Isn't that something to do with electricity generation?"

"I'm one step ahead of you, sweetie," Perry said. "I have a theory, wanna hear?"

They all nodded except for Claire who scowled and said, "You and your theories."

"Okay, so, I think our Barbs had a piece of jewellery engraved for her lover who—get this—happens to work for a hydro electricity company! She sent it to him at his office as a gift. Maybe that's where she is now, hiding out with him. If only we knew which company. I Googled it, of course, and there are loads. We don't even know if it's in the same state."

"Hang on, what lover?" asked Anders, also good for proverbial buckets of cold water occasionally. Perry shrugged. "And didn't you say she got something repaired, not engraved?"

"Well, maybe it all comes under the same banner. Zit face jeweller wasn't giving too much away, kind of clamped up on me at the end, if truth be told, but we do know it was one piece. And, I mean, why would she have it sent there?"

"I've heard of the Hydro," Alicia said again, dropping a piece of her pancake into Max's waiting mouth.

"Yes, we've just been told, it's to do with electricity and water—" said Lynette, scowling at her sister and then at Max.

"No, no, I mean, I saw an ad for it somewhere recently. If only I could recall."

"If only you hadn't drunk so much vino in your youth your *leetle grey cells* would be working just fine," her sister said, then ducked as Alicia tossed a cushion at her.

"So, Perry, the jeweller wouldn't tell you who the package was addressed to?" asked Anders.

"Not from want of trying, I can tell you that. No, leave it with me, I'm going to look into it further. Okay, who's next? Oh, Alicia how did you go with Wanda?"

"No luck, I'm afraid. I haven't been able to get through to her, which is why I went to the police but they weren't much use. I have a feeling Wanda's avoiding my calls so I might just have to show up at her house and barge my way in. Might even head over there after this."

"Be sure to take someone with you," Anders said. "Now, if no one else has anything to report I want to show you all something I discovered."

He looked very pleased with himself as he produced a crumpled newspaper clipping from his back pocket, straightened it out and placed it on the coffee table for them to see.

"It's from Tuesday's *Herald*," he explained. "I only spotted it when I was helping my receptionist clear away the old papers from the reception area at work. It's from the classifieds section."

"What is it?" asked Claire.

He began to read: *"Friends and relatives of Rosa Lopez, late of the Philippines—"*

"Rosa? That has to be Barbara's housekeeper, surely?" said Missy.

"That's what I thought," he said, starting again. *"Friends and relatives of Rosa Lopez, late of the Philippines, please communicate. Write P.O. Box 268, Sydney 2001."*

You could have heard a pin drop. Even Max, who had enjoyed all this unexpected company, looked stunned, glancing from Alicia to Lynette and back again.

Eventually, Alicia said, "This case is just too weird for words. I wonder if that's our Rosa and, if so, why she would put an ad in the *Herald*?"

"Exactly my thoughts," said Anders. "Very strange. It's like we keep finding all these little clues that don't seem to mean anything or amount to much and yet…"

"And yet maybe they do," said Missy. "Maybe they will all add up in the end. Like an Agatha Christie novel. You need to show the police this."

Anders scoffed. "What's the point? I mean, I just can't see what it's got to do with anything."

"What I can't understand," said Lynette, picking up the newspaper clipping and studying it closely, "is why Rosa would use the *Herald* classies and some postal box. I mean, she seems like a pretty modern chick to me. Didn't you say she was checking her emails and listening to an iPod when you were last there, Missy?"

"So, doesn't mean she can't put an ad in a broadsheet," retorted Alicia. "I can traverse both worlds. It is physically possible."

"Yeah but you're a weirdo," said Lynette and Alicia went to throw another cushion at her.

Anders grabbed it off her before she could do any damage and gave her a cheeky grin that made her blush.

He turned to Lynette. "What would you do then?"

"Jump online, of course. Facebook is so much faster— you can find all your friends there in about five seconds flat. Or tweet or Google them. You don't need to place a newspaper ad to find people these days. It's so slow and old-fashioned."

"It's so *Agatha Christie*," said Missy again.

Alicia grabbed the letter from her sister. "Why don't we just ask Rosa? Maybe there's a perfectly reasonable explanation. Maybe she's having a family reunion and the oldies don't read tweets." She directed that last comment to Anders, hoping he'd be charmed by her logic. "Can I keep this for my files?" He nodded. "Now, moving things along, I have a little task for you, Anders, if you're up for it."

This time he smiled warmly at her. "Anything. You name it."

"Ooh, there's a proposition," said Perry and Alicia blushed again.

"Shut up, Perry. Now, Anders, it'd be great to find out more about Arthur's murder. The papers haven't got very much and the police clearly aren't saying. I was wondering whether you'd have any access, you know, to the medical files, that sort of thing?"

He shook his head slowly. "Not really, I mean, I might be a doctor, but this sort of stuff is always confidential and it's not like I can just access his files… although," he stopped, paused for a few seconds. "Now I think about it, I may have a way in. Yes, yes, I know exactly who to ask. She's an appalling gossip so if anyone has the scoop, Gorgeous Georgie will."

"Oh, great," said Alicia who was wondering why the sound of 'Gorgeous Georgie' made her want to rip someone's heart out.

He glanced at his watch and jumped up as though his pants were on fire. "But I've got to be quick, she's always down at Bondi on Sunday mornings, having a swim."

Of course she is, thought Alicia, *probably in a tiny little string bikini, just waiting for you to show up.*

"If I run now I can catch her," Anders was saying. "I'll pretend to run into her, that'll be less obvious."

"Pretend, pretend. Run, run," said Perry, jumping up to shoo him out.

"Just let us know how you go," Alicia called out after him. She turned back to the room where at least two people were sniggering at her. She ignored both Lynette and Perry and said, "Okay, that's him sorted. Now, what else do we need to discuss?"

"Actually, I have something to say," said Missy. "I think we need to go back to Agatha Christie herself."

Claire groaned and Perry said, "You want us to have a séance? Wake Agatha from the dead and ask her *whodunit*?"

"No, silly. I mean *learn* from her. Don't you see, that's why I went back to Barbara's house the other day? It's like in *Hallowe'en Party*..."

They were all looking at her wearily again but she was used to those kinds of looks and pressed on. "You know, the Christie novel? It's been a long time since I read it but if my own *'leetle grey cells'* serve me correctly, I recall a line in there where Poirot says that to solve a crime, it's important to reveal who the victim really is, warts and all. *'You have to return to the victim'*—something like that. Don't you see? I think we need to work out who exactly Barbara Parlour *was*."

They were still staring, mutely, so she pushed her zebra print spectacles in place and said, "Think about it, possums, who the hell is she? On the one hand we met a really sweet, gracious but clearly depressed woman who looked like she wouldn't hurt a fly, on the other hand her friends and family seem to depict her as a total drama queen who's about as deep as a puddle." She paused, blushed slightly. "Sorry, I know I ramble on but—"

"No, you're absolutely right," said Alicia. "The truth is probably somewhere in between, people are rarely such extremes, but it would be good to find out more about Barbara. It just might help."

It made sense to Claire, too. "But how do we do that? Apart from foraging through her house again."

"I don't know, exactly," said Missy. "But that's the reason I went to her house, and why I was looking up the book that was found in her car. What does it tell us about the real Barbara Parlour?"

The group stared at Missy, still not sure how to respond. Eventually, Perry suggested, "Maybe we should talk to her friends again."

"Except who are they?" said Claire. "We thought Wanda was her BFF but she wasn't having a bar of it."

"What about the brother?" said Lynette. "He seems to be the closest person to her, or at least that's what he says. Maybe I should pay him another visit, get the real story on his sister this time."

"A least you won't have any trouble tracking him down," said Alicia.

"True, but it'll have to wait 'til tomorrow. I have some recipes I want to work on today."

"Fair enough," said Claire, stretching out. "In fact, it mightn't hurt all of us to stop thinking about this so much and get back to our own lives; do what Poirot used to do and let the brain cells stew on it for a while."

"Wish I could," said Alicia. "Unfortunately, I'm yet to talk to Wanda and I really want to tick that off. I'm gonna head over there after this. I think she's hiding something and I intend to find out what."

CHAPTER 23

Wanda Birchin took one look at Alicia through the plate-glass window by her front door and promptly turned away. Funny the way the Murder Mystery Book Club members were starting to have this effect on people, Alicia thought, banging loudly on the door again.

"Come on, Wanda!" she called out. "I know you're in there." She was met by stony silence. "I just saw you, Wanda. Please, it's really important!"

A minute later the door swung open and Wanda stood before her in yet another flowing kaftan, but this time she didn't look quite so relaxed.

"Are you trying to get me into trouble?" she demanded.

"Sorry?"

"The police! They called me in yesterday, said they'd had a lovely little chat to you and were suddenly asking me all sorts of unexpected questions. Like I have anything to do with any of it! I will tell you again what I told them, I am not Barbara's buddy."

"No, but you were Arthur's, right?"

The older woman glared at her. "I don't know what you're talking about."

The construction work on Wanda's face ensured she gave little away but Alicia wasn't letting her off that easily.

"You laughed at Claire and me when we came to visit last time, said we were clueless. Well, I'm not quite so clueless now, Wanda." She waved one hand inside. "Please, can I come in? It's important."

Wanda stared at Alicia for a few moments then, sighing dramatically, let her in, leading her back through the house, this time to the kitchen where she began to open the fridge before turning back.

"White wine?"

"White coffee would be better, thanks."

She mock snored and then pulled out a coffee plunger and proceeded to make a pot. She also produced two large white cups, some skim milk and a bowl of sugar.

"So what did the police want?" asked Alicia.

Wanda's eyes snapped from the plunger to Alicia and back again. "A million and one questions. *When had I last seen Barbara? When had I last seen Arthur? Where was I at such and such a time?* Then, to make matters worse, they started grilling me about the blasted housekeeper. I mean, honestly, Alicia, I don't know for a *fact* that he was sleeping with the woman, I just assumed that's all. It's one thing to gossip about it over a few drinks in the cabana, it's quite another to be making accusations like that at the police station. Can't you see, you could get someone in serious trouble."

"What, more serious than murder?" said Alicia. Wanda looked away. "I'm not going to apologise for passing on your suspicions, Wanda. If Arthur was being unfaithful, it opens a whole new can of worms."

"I don't see how. Milk? Sugar?"

"Just milk, thanks. Look, Arthur could have been killed by a jealous lover or husband. You just don't know."

She laughed, that same, expressionless laugh. "Oh for goodness' sake you are being so melodramatic. What's an affair between consenting adults?"

"You tell me."

She turned around to face Alicia. "There you go again. What are you suggesting?s"

Alicia took a punt. "You were seeing him, weren't you? Arthur, I mean. That's why you fell out with Barbara. You were bonking her husband behind her back."

Wanda hesitated before saying, "You make it sound so romantic. And don't give me that look. It was hardly behind Barbara's back. She knew all about it, or if she didn't she was a bigger moron that I thought."

"So were you the one who kept phoning the house and then hanging up when Barbara picked up?"

Wanda looked outraged. "Why on earth would I do that? I'm not some pathetic little thing. Arthur and I are both adults; it's just a bit of fun." She paused. "Well, it *was* a bit of fun... We used to joke about it. Pretend we were going to dump our partners' sorry butts and hook up, but we weren't serious. I didn't want to leave my husband and certainly not for *Arthur*. He'd be sleeping around on me in minutes. And for some Godforsaken reason Arthur wanted to stick with Barbara. I was fine with it and so was he. End of story."

"Did you tell this little story of yours to the police?"

She paused, turned back towards the cabinet. "Of course I didn't. I'm not stupid."

"Oh, Wanda. You have to tell them the truth."

Wanda snapped back around. Her eyes were fiery. "What and land myself firmly in it? I don't bloody think so!"

"But if you've got nothing to hide—"

"I've got everything to hide, you silly girl. I happen to have the terrible misfortune of being at the wrong place at the wrong time."

"How do you mean?"

She paused, handed Alicia the coffee cup then sighed. "Oh God I might as well tell you. I was with Arthur not ten minutes before he died."

Alicia was stunned. "Oh, I see."

"You see nothing! It was totally innocent but if the police know I'd seen him that day, they'll try and pin it on me.

They'll tell my husband, it'll destroy my marriage… what's left of it." She stared into her coffee cup glumly. "Grant will have a fit if he finds out."

"Your husband? He doesn't know?"

"Of course he doesn't bloody know! I'm not as careless as Arthur, not so cavalier. Although I'm sure it'll all come out now, thanks to you."

"Hey, I'm not the one sleeping around. But can we back up a bit? So you were with Arthur just before he was killed?"

She groaned. "Apparently so. But not for long! He was doing his usual golf round, this house is close to the fifth hole in case you haven't noticed, and he likes to drop in, sometimes."

"Is that what they're calling it these days?"

Wanda smirked at her. "He was here less than ten minutes."

"Ooh that is a quickie."

"Oh give me *some* credit. I have much better form than that. We didn't *do* anything. Actually, I was rather annoyed with him if you must know. I'd distinctly told him not to come." She took a small sip of her coffee. "I'd called him at his house after lunch to see how he was coping and he said he'd drop in; I said, don't you dare, Grant's home early today. So, naturally, he ignores me and shows up, starts fawning all over me, declaring his undying love as usual. I sent him packing."

"What time did he show up? Exactly?"

"At 4:20 p.m. I know because I had ten minutes to get him out of here before Grant was due home. His pulse was well and truly pumping when he left me, I can tell you that. And it wasn't the only thing."

Now it was Alicia's turn to groan. "So your husband was around, too, when Arthur was killed?"

"He was here at the house, so?"

Alicia placed her cup down and stared at her. *She hadn't connected the dots?* "Sorry but aren't you worried that Grant saw Arthur 'fawning' all over you and followed him back to the green and killed him in a fit of jealousy?"

"My God, you could write a murder mystery yourself! No, that's ludicrous. He came home at precisely 4:30 p.m. as planned—he's always punctual, it's rather annoying but you learn to cope—and he showed absolutely no signs of jealousy or anger or whatever you're supposed to show if you've just seen your wife snogging another man. He was happy, had had some drinks at work, apparently. We simply shared a cocktail and then had dinner."

"So you can account for his whereabouts the whole evening?"

She paused. "Well, most of it. I mean, he did go for a swim while I heated up dinner. Florrie had prepared quite a lovely salmon dish—"

"Swim?"

"Yes, Grant does laps in the evening. Stress relief, or so he says."

"And he definitely did his laps that afternoon? You know this for a fact?"

"I didn't stand around holding his towel if that's what you mean. But he came in huffing and red-faced, oh about 30 minutes later."

"Just like he'd look if he'd killed someone."

She gasped. "I resent that. Grant did not kill Arthur, he's not some sort of psychopath who can smash someone's head in with a 9-iron and then sit down calmly to eat dinner. Honestly."

Alicia stared at her. "How do you know it was a 9-iron?"

"I don't! I'm just guessing."

She let it drop, pushing her cup away. "I'm not trying to stress you out, Wanda, I'm just trying to get all the facts straight. You really need to go back to the police. Tell them all of this, about your meeting with Arthur, about the affair."

She shook her head wildly. "No! No I will not. Who made you jury, judge and executioner? Lives are a lot messier than you realise and when you finally become a grown-up you might understand that."

"I'm 30, Wanda, not 13."

"Then start acting like it. My affairs are my own damn business and they have nothing—I repeat, nothing—to do with you, your blasted book club, or any of this. You'll soon see. They'll discover who killed Arthur, and my husband will be none the wiser."

"And what about Barbara? Where will she be?"

She sighed impatiently. "Look, I'm sorry about Barbara, I have no idea where she is, honestly I don't. And I'm sorry about Arthur, too." Her eyes welled with tears, catching Alicia by surprise. She brushed them away angrily. "Okay, so I had a soft spot for the silly bugger, lock me up if you want to, but I didn't hurt him, or his wife for that matter. I can tell you this, none of it has anything to do with me."

"Or your husband, Grant?"

"*Especially* Grant."

"I hope you're right, Wanda," Alicia said, getting up to leave. "Otherwise, you could be harbouring a killer, right under your perfect little nose."

This time a flicker of fear managed to break through Wanda's rigid brow.

CHAPTER 24

As she manoeuvred her Torana along Rose Bay's winding streets towards home, Alicia's mobile phone began to ring. She glanced in her rear vision mirror to check for police then, noticing none, scooped it up and answered. It was Anders and he sounded breathless.

"How'd you go?" she asked.

"Great," he replied, the line just slightly crackly. "Gorgeous Georgie was just as gossipy as I remembered, she already has her finger on the pulse. She's amazing that woman."

"Yay for her," Alicia said through clenched teeth. "So what'd she have to say?"

"Well, it's a long story. Want to meet up?"

Her heart skipped a beat. "Sure, what did you have in mind?"

"How about a drink, my shout?"

She glanced at the car clock. It was now almost 4:00 p.m. Time to put the killjoy to bed.

"Love to, where?"

"How about the Woolly Hotel near your place, make it easy for you?"

"Sounds great. Shall I call the others?"

He hesitated. "Um, no, I don't think it's that important… No need to bother them all this late on a Sunday."

She couldn't help beaming. "Oh, right, okay. Well, I'll see you there in about, oh, ten."

They clicked off and she did a little jiggle behind the wheel as she drove. A one-on-one with Dr Anders! She couldn't wait.

Now don't start reading anything into it. She chastised herself. Anders probably just wanted to offload what he'd just learned; it was no doubt perfectly innocent. Still, as she drove back towards home, she couldn't help hoping it was anything but.

It took Alicia several minutes to find Anders when she first stepped into the Woolly Hotel. The place was packed to the rafters. A popular rock band was playing, wedged up on a small stage in one corner, and the sweaty hordes that swarmed the dance floor and bar were the largest she had seen in a long while.

Great, she thought, *this will be real romantic.*

After several minutes she spotted Anders standing on the other side of the pub, staring at the band with a slight, confused frown, two glasses of red wine in his hands. He was wearing black jeans and a checked shirt rolled up at the sleeves but still managed to look like a duck out of water. Alicia watched him for a moment from a distance, wondering how such a tall, athletic man could come across so soft and vulnerable. Where did that come from, she wondered?

He sensed her staring at him and looked around, his frown instantly replaced by the most breathtaking smile. Alicia's heart did that annoying double beat thing again. She pushed through the throng towards him.

"You really are always early aren't you?" she hollered above the noise when she reached him.

"I tell you, it's a curse!" He laughed. "Hope you like cab cav! I grabbed you one, figured it'd be a decade before I managed to get back to the bar."

"Love it, thanks!"

"Shall we head out back? Probably a bit quieter there!"

"Sure!"

Alicia took one glass and followed Anders as he led the way through the crowd and out to the beer garden at the back. He was right, the garden was almost deserted, the music luring most revellers inside, and they were grateful for it. There was just one other couple, well into their 60s, perched at another table and looking utterly bored. The woman glanced at them hopefully, the man coughed loudly, rolled his eyes a little and looked away. They clearly weren't enjoying the ambience. Anders chose a back table, placed his glass down on a coaster and pulled a chair out for Alicia to sit down.

"So, you want to go first?"

She wasn't sure what he meant having momentarily lost herself in the fact that she was now alone at a table with Doctor Dreamy. Or at least she would be alone if only the older couple would rack off.

"Sorry?" she said, batting her eyelashes shamelessly.

"I rang your house," he explained. "Spoke to Lynette. She told me you were over at Wanda's, accusing her of hiding something, and you were doing it without any backup."

Alicia blushed. "Oh, yes, Wanda Birchin, of course!" She took a quick gulp of her wine, trying to refocus. "Right, well, I had a feeling there was more to Ms Birchin than she was letting on. And I was right. Wanda has been having an affair with Arthur Parlour, had been for some time."

"Seriously?"

"Well, it wasn't very serious now you mention it, more like quickies between holes if you know what I mean. She lives right next door to his golf club, so it was way too convenient for both of them. But here's the thing: Wanda saw Arthur just minutes before he died."

His deep brown eyes widened. "What? They were together?"

"Wanda tells me nothing happened, that her husband was due home and she sent Arthur packing. And she insists he was perfectly fine when he left."

"And you believe her?"

She nodded. "Yeah, I think I do."

"Still, it sounds very suspect to me. Do the police know?"

"Not yet, I'm hoping she'll tell them the truth. I gave her until the end of the day to 'fess up or I told her I'd call Inspector Ward myself. She looked ready to kill me."

He placed his glass down and frowned. "Be careful, Alicia, this isn't a game."

"That's what the good detective said. Don't worry, Wanda Birchin is little more than a middle-aged Stepford Wife. She's harmless."

"Not if she's a Stepford Wife she's not—have you *seen* that movie?"

She laughed. "Nah, Wanda's alright. I can't say the same for her husband, though."

"Jealous kind?"

"I haven't met the guy but she seemed terrified of getting caught. I guess you would if you'd been sleeping around behind someone's back. Pathetic behaviour."

Anders choked on his wine then, spilling a little of the red liquid down the front of his shirt.

"Damn it!" he said and Alicia jumped up to grab some serviettes that were with the cutlery on a side table. She handed them over and he dabbed away.

"Sorry, stupid of me."

"You okay? You look like you've just seen a ghost."

Alicia recalled the flicker of emotion that had crossed his face just moments before he choked. What was that look, she wondered? Guilt? Shame? It was the same look that

Perry had flashed that first book club meeting. Like he was hiding something, something he wasn't exactly proud of.

Oh Alicia, she thought. *You are so melodramatic!* She tried to douse her overactive imagination as she watched him dab away at his shirt.

She touched his hand to calm him down. "Don't worry about it, Anders, it's just a dingy old pub. It's not like the Queen's about to walk in, inspect the troops."

They both laughed a little, disarming the tension. The elderly couple at the other table stared at them for a moment, then watched as Anders rolled the soaked serviettes into a ball and tossed them into a bin nearby.

"Hate this shirt anyway," he was saying. "My wife gave it to—"

He stopped. Blushed crimson red. Looked flustered again.

"You're *married?*" She almost leapt up when she said it, surprised by his admission and feeling suddenly very confused. She was sure he'd said he was single at that first club meeting.

Had she misheard him?

Had he lied?

Anders stammered, "Oh, no… I mean yes, I mean…"

Alicia stared at him. "You're either married or you're not, Anders. It's pretty simple." She half laughed, pretending it really didn't matter that much.

"Actually, it's not that simple at all."

He looked away but before he did she spotted that same sense of guilt or shame or whatever it was she had seen earlier.

It wasn't all in her mind; something really was going on. *Like Wanda, had he also slept around on his partner? Was he still trying to?*

Anders took a very large swig of his wine this time, almost demolishing it in one gulp. Then set the glass back down with both hands, as if afraid it would fall over again.

"Look, do you mind if we don't talk about this? It's not why I wanted to get together today."

She stared at him confused, her heart feeling wrenched in every direction. "I just thought…"

"What?"

"Nothing, sorry, stupid of me. I just misunderstood… Anyway, it's really none of my business. I mean, it's not like you and I…"

She let the sentence dangle as he watched her, his brown eyes piercing.

"Never mind," she said, desperate to change the subject, "so how'd you go with your friend?" She felt flat. A little numb. Stupid, mostly.

"Huh?"

"The gorgeous one." Now her tone was surly and it caught him off guard.

"You okay?"

"I'm fine. I just can't stay long so let's get on with it. What did your friend Georgie have to say?"

"Oh, um, okay. So, yes, as I said, I did manage to catch her—she was still at Bondi, doing a little sun-baking—"

"Yeah, yeah, spit it out." Alicia was not in the mood for more news of other women in Anders' life.

"Right, well, she did have the goss. You want it in layman's terms?"

"Hm-mm."

"According to her sources, and I know for a fact they're reliable, Arthur died from blunt force trauma to the back of the head. Believed to be from a golf club."

"A 9-iron?" she asked hopefully.

"Sorry, didn't get quite that much detail. Why'd you ask?"

"Never mind, go on."

"Not much more to say. No defensive wounds. Coroner suspects he was taken by surprise. Certainly no indication he fought back."

"No DNA under the nails then?"

He almost laughed. "Nope."

"Well, I guess that's only fair. Agatha Christie had to work it all out pre-DNA, so now it's our turn."

He went to say something and then stopped.

"What?" she asked.

"It's just that… well, I wanted to talk to you about something a bit, um delicate. It's the reason I asked you here."

"Oh?"

"I'm worried."

"Worried? About what?"

"I just wonder whether we really should be interfering in all of this. The Murder Mystery Book Club, I mean."

A feeling of dread crept up on her. "What do you mean?"

"Well, it's not what we all signed up for is it? It was just supposed to be a bit of fun, discussing crime fiction once every fortnight. I didn't think we'd end up interviewing real-life killers, you know?"

Alicia felt her temper rise. This rendezvous wasn't turning out at all as she'd hoped. First Anders had confessed to a mysterious wife, now he was trying to weasel his way out of the club.

"Nobody said you had to investigate, Anders. You can opt out any time you like."

She tried to sound casual, didn't quite pull it off. Anders stared at her, frowning as she took a large gulp of her wine and tried to calm down. She felt like a fool. Alicia had thought the book club members were enjoying the process as much as she was. She thought they were all committed to this investigation. Clearly she was wrong.

He softened his tone. "That's not what I'm saying, Alicia."

"Then what are you saying?"

"I'm just saying I'm worried—"

"Well stop worrying, Anders! This is not your problem to worry about. Just walk away, find another book club, one you can have *loads* of fun with. Hey, you might even find yourself a bit on the side and you won't have to put your life in danger for it."

She knew it was a ridiculous comment, completely unjustified—what did she know about this man and his life? The hurt and confusion that swept across his face now made her insides shrivel. She felt terrible, and suddenly very drained, so she pushed her wine glass aside and stood up.

"Sorry, Anders, I shouldn't have said that. I'm just tired. I need to go."

"What… where are you going?" He struggled to his feet.

"Look, it's nothing personal, I just need to get to the DVD shop before it closes." She stopped, turned back. "I know you don't want to investigate but I do and I know something that might help."

"Alicia, you don't understand—"

She held one hand up. "Don't worry about it, honestly. It doesn't matter. You're right. It wasn't supposed to be about missing people and murder. Hell, even Missy got run over; that wasn't supposed to happen. It was just supposed to be fun. And if you're not having any you need to quit." She feigned a smile. "Thanks for the wine."

Alicia strode quickly out through a side gate and onto the street while Anders stood there, watching her go, his heart now firmly in his stomach. He felt confused and anguished and sat back down with a thud, staring forlornly into his empty wine glass.

He'd botched that up big time.

Behind him the elderly couple was openly gaping, thrilled by the afternoon's unexpected entertainment.

~~~~~~~~

Later that evening, as she sat sipping hot chocolate in her lounge room, Lynette beside her, Max snoring by their feet, the rain bucketing down outside, Alicia began watching a new copy of a very old Agatha Christie movie remake of
~~~~~~~~

Hallowe'en Party. She was still smarting from Anders' comments and feeling confused and angry, mostly at herself. It had been foolish of her to think she could have a relationship with this man. *What did she know of him? Really?*

And it had been even more foolish of her to assume that all the book club members wanted to spend their precious downtime investigating the disappearance of a woman they knew even less. Anders was right. All they had really signed up for was a bit of light reading. To expect more from them was pure fantasy, and she would tell them so next time they met up. Maybe other members were feeling the same way.

Maybe they all needed an escape clause?

She shook Anders' sad, crumpled face out of her mind and concentrated on the flick. Intrigued by what Missy had said earlier about going back to the victim, she had decided to rent the movie to hear Poirot's quote for herself. Of course it would have been better to refer directly to the book, but it was Sunday night, the library was closed and time was of the essence. Perhaps the film version would be just as enlightening.

It was certainly entertaining and the Finlay sisters were so caught up in the plot that they almost missed the pivotal quote when it finally came. One of the main characters, mystery writer Ariadne Oliver, was criticising a child murder victim when she stops herself and asks Poirot if it's unkind. He looks at her po-faced and declares, *"In a murder it is not unkind to say what the victim is like."*

"A-ha!" squealed Alicia, grabbing the remote and rewinding it. They listened again, then later for the line Missy had recalled:

"The personality of the victim is the cause of many a murder."

When the film ended, Lynette sat forward and looked at her sister. "But how does this help us? I mean, what's the point?"

"Well, like Missy said, we don't really know the victim at all. One person tells us she was a nightmare, another says she's a saint. I think what Poirot's trying to say is it's important to be honest about a victim if you're going to solve their murder or disappearance or whatever. Think about Arthur for instance. I mean, he wasn't murdered because he was a lovely bloke. Quite the opposite, I'm sure, and it won't help investigators to pretend otherwise. If you want to get at the truth you need to face it, head on. It's most likely someone had had enough of Arthur's patronising behaviour or his affairs or whatever."

"But if it's a random attack, a mugging…" began Lynette.

"Then that's different, obviously. But if someone is murdered in cold blood, there's usually a good reason, and it's usually because someone had a beef with them. Obviously. It's called motive. So what did Arthur do to piss someone off so badly that they took a golf club to his head? And, more importantly, what did Barbara do?"

Lynette sat back and thought about this. "But, but she might not have done anything. She might just have been in the way."

"In whose way?" Alicia asked. "That's why we need to find out more about her. We've all been delusional! Missy can be irritating sometimes, the way she blabs on, but in this case she is spot on. We don't know Barbara Parlour at all. How could we? We met her twice for a few hours each time. We only saw what she wanted us to see, or not see as the case may be. But who is Barbara really? And what did she do that caused her disappearance? The same could be said for everyone in the book club. What do we know about any of them? They're all a bit, I dunno, *strange*. It's like they're all hiding something…"

Lynette looked completely confused now. "What do you mean?"

"Well, take Perry. He's got some bee in his bonnet about Claire, God knows what that's about. I'm too terrified to ask. And Claire… well, what's her story? Seems like a bit of a control freak to me, and why hasn't she married her fiancé? As for Missy—say what you like but it's not every day that someone tries to run you over. What the hell was *that* about?

And don't get me started on bloody Anders. He tells us he's single, turns out he's not."

"He's not?"

"No he bloody well is not. He's married. There. It's out."

Lynette stared hard at her sister. "Are you okay?"

"Of course I'm *okay*. Why wouldn't I be *okay*? What's any of this got to do with me?"

"Alright, take a chill pill." Lynette held up her hands to placate her. "It's just that I thought that you and him, you know?"

"No! No, not at all."

"Well, if you insist—"

Lynette did not get a chance to finish her sentence as the phone began screeching from the other side of the room. Alicia jumped, staring at it and back at her sister. It was just after 11:00 p.m. Too late for a social call. Her first thought was that Anders was ringing to quit the book club. *Good riddance!* She thought even as her heart did a lurch. Then it occurred to her that something dreadful might have happened to her parents or her brother. *A violent home invasion in Cairns, where they lived? A car crash, perhaps?* Her heart lurched again.

"I'll get it," Lynette said breezily, never as perturbed by late callers as her older sister. "Hello?"

She spoke for just a few seconds when her eyes widened and she began clicking her fingers, pointing at something on the coffee table.

Alicia shook her head. "What?" she mouthed, confused.

"The remote!" Lynette said, holding one hand over the mouthpiece. "Put the TV on the ABC!"

Alicia did as requested while Lynette held onto the phone. It was the late news bulletin and a bedraggled looking reporter was standing under an umbrella outside the Parlour mansion in Woollahra. She sounded flustered.

"Yes, James," she was saying, "that's correct. Unfortunately, we don't know any more at this stage but we'll keep you posted."

The visual than clicked back to a well-groomed man at the station. "Thanks for that Verity. That was Verity Velour there reporting from Woollahra. We'll have more on this breaking story as it unfolds. Now, to business matters and the ASX 100—"

Alicia pressed mute and turned back to her sister who was speaking into the phone, shaking her head.

"What? *Really?* Oh my God. Alicia was with her just hours ago… Yep, yep… Okay, well, you let the others know and… oh, absolutely, we need to meet again. Let's try tomorrow… Got it… You will? Fantastic, I appreciate it. Have you got all their numbers? Excellent, okay… Yep, okay see you then. Thanks Missy. Bye."

She hung up and turned back to her wide-eyed sister.

"Please don't tell me they've found Barbara's body."

"No, no, it's not that at all." Lynette sat back down, looking mystified.

"Then what?"

"It's about Arthur."

"Now what?"

"They're holding someone in connection with his murder."

Alicia relaxed a little. "Great. Who?"

"Wanda Birchin." Lynette squeezed her eyes shut, waiting for the scream, which came very quickly.

"*No way,*" Alicia cried. "Why? When?"

"Don't know much more than that. Missy just heard it on the news. It said something about holding her for questioning."

"Which we all know is police speak for being under arrest. *Arrrrgh.* I just can't believe it. She must have spoken to the cops like I asked her to. Oh God, I feel terrible."

"Don't you dare," said Lynette. "They wouldn't be holding her if she didn't have something to do with it. They must have searched her place and found something. Or maybe they got her to confess."

"I can't believe that."

"Maybe it was manslaughter or she's an accessory after the fact, covering up for the hubby?"

"Hmm, maybe. Still, I can't help feeling responsible. Bloody hell, I really thought she was innocent. I thought she'd confess her affair, maybe ruin her marriage, and that'd be it…"

She thought then of what Anders had said and realised that she had spent the afternoon in the house of a killer. He wasn't over-reacting after all.

"You don't really know Wanda," Lynette was saying, reading her thoughts. "It's exactly what you were just saying, and you're right. We're all relative strangers in this. Apart from you and me, none of us really know each other, let alone Wanda or Barbara or Arthur. Think about it, you met Wanda, what, twice?"

"Still, you think your instincts will start clanging away or something. I just didn't pick her for a murderer, that's all. I wonder what they found."

Lynette grabbed the remote from her and began flicking through the TV channels, trying to find more news. "You know, it makes sense if you connect the dots, Lis'. Think about it. She was having an affair with Arthur, we know that for a fact. We also know he didn't want a whiff of a scandal in the lead up to his political campaign, he told Missy that himself. So why would he go to Wanda's house and try and play around again? He knows the press are on to him; that would be stupid. Maybe Wanda lied to you about that afternoon. Maybe Arthur went to her house to break it off with her and Wanda wasn't having it. Maybe she was so furious she killed him in a moment of blind passion. Or… or… maybe she killed Barbara first so she could be with him and when he found out he confronted her and she killed him, too. Maybe that's why he dropped in to see her that day?" She stopped. "God, now I sound like you and Perry."

Alicia let out a long, sad sigh but she was no longer listening to her sister. Instead she was recalling another line from the film they'd just watched, another pearl of wisdom from the incomparable Hercule Poirot:

"Old sins have long shadows."

She wondered now, which of Wanda Birchin's many sins had finally caught up with her.

CHAPTER 25

The start of the new week was as glorious as a day could be—the sun was warm, the breeze was gentle, and the two Finlay sisters were not in the mood for work. It never helped when the weather was this good, but it was especially hard in the light of last night's events. How on earth were they going to concentrate on something as mundane as *work*?

Lynette was already holding up the white flag and had decided to take the morning off. Dressed in an extremely mini, yellow sundress and insanely high, wedge sandals, she was just hanging up the phone from her unimpressed boss when her sister appeared for breakfast.

"You're late for work," Alicia mumbled, reaching for a cereal bowl.

She'd had a terrible night's sleep, tossing and turning with feelings of both guilt and anger. Guilt because she'd forced Wanda to go to the police in the first place, and anger because the woman had so blatantly lied to her face, over and over.

Then, of course, there was that tiff with Anders. She kept replaying it in her mind. *Did this mean he was no longer part of the*

195

Murder Mystery Book Club? And why did he tell them all he was single when he was not?

Perhaps Anders and his wife were separated, she thought hopefully. She had certainly seen no signs of another woman in his house that day he hosted book club. *But if that was the case, why didn't he just say that yesterday? Why keep her in the dark?* Her heart did its usual twist. Maybe Anders wanted to reconcile with his wife, maybe they were still in love? She shuddered, trying to erase him from her mind.

"I've just told Mario not to expect me this morning," Lynette said, cutting through. "He's spitting chips, of course, but tough luck. I'm determined to see Niles again, if it kills me!"

"Having a little dip down at Balmoral while you're there?" Alicia indicated the bikini strap that was poking out from beneath her sister's sundress.

"Why not? If this horrible affair has taught us one thing, Lis', it's to enjoy life while we can. Fancy joining me? We can get fish and chips afterwards. There's a great fish place down there."

Alicia poured some muesli and milk into the bowl and dropped onto a kitchen stool to eat. "Sorry, you're on your own. I want to go back to the house—"

"Barbara's house? I thought we'd all agreed to stay clear of the place."

"That was before Wanda murdered Arthur. Now I *have* to go back, see if we've missed anything. Besides, I want to see if Rosa's there, ask her about that strange advertisement she put in the classifieds."

She took a mouthful of muesli and stared into her bowl glumly.

"You okay?" asked Lynette, eyes squinting. "You look like crap."

"Gee, thanks Lynny."

"Sorry, but you look exhausted and, well, you were pretty bloody cranky last night. Want to tell me what's going on?"

"I'm fine, just had trouble sleeping that's all."

"Going over the case, eh?"

She shrugged. "Something like that."

"Well that's hardly going to help you sleep."

"I know, I know."

Lynette grabbed her handbag and over-sized sunglasses. She slipped them on and then bent down to give Max a cuddle.

"Gotta go, got work to do."

"Yes, all that swimming will be most taxing," Alicia said. "Just be careful. Promise!"

"I promise," Lynette called back, then slammed the front door and made her way to the bus stop.

The trip between Woolloomooloo and Balmoral is a long one, requiring at least two bus changes, but Lynette was prepared. She had grabbed a copy of Agatha Christie's *Murder on the Orient Express* on her way out and started reading as she went. It had been scheduled for the upcoming Sunday's book club and while she wasn't sure they would even be holding it anymore, she was determined to read it just in case. It had been many years since Lynette had taken that fateful train journey with Poirot and 12 angry suspects, and the details were now hazy.

She had considered swatting up by watching the film— the fabulous Albert Finney version with a cast of vintage Hollywood stars including Lauren Bacall, Ingrid Bergman and Sean Connery—but she knew that film adaptations never quite stuck to the original story, so thought better of it. This was a *book* club after all!

By the time Lynette's bus chugged the final leg down to the esplanade at Balmoral, a good hour later, she was so engrossed in the novel she barely noticed. Along the way she had come across another classic Poirot quote that got her thinking about the Barbara Parlour case. After inspecting the compartment of the murdered man and discovering a monogrammed handkerchief, a pipe cleaner, a gold watch (conveniently stopped at the time of the murder) and other interesting items, he quips, *"One cannot complain of having no clues in this case. There are clues here in abundance."*

That's just like Barbara's case, she thought, making a note in the margin. She sat back and thought about this for a bit. There were so many clues cluttering the case—on the whiteboard in Barbara's kitchen, all that stuff left in her car—yet none of it seemed to make any sense. She wondered, as Poirot does, if that was deliberate.

"Last stop, Ma'am!" came the bus driver's voice from the front and Lynette looked up with a start. The bus was empty and they were parked at the curb.

"Oops, sorry!" she called out, thrusting the book in her bag and grappling to get out.

She jumped onto the pavement, glanced around, got her bearings then began to make her way along the esplanade to the Just Beachy Café.

It was bustling when she arrived, as it should be on such a glorious day, and Niles looked run off his feet. She looked around for another waitress but it was clear he was flying solo.

"I haven't got time for you," he hissed as he brushed past her on his way to the espresso machine. "It's chaos today."

She followed him into the café, dumped her handbag in the back room and grabbed an apron she saw hanging on a hook.

"Okay, where do you want me to start?"

He looked up from the coffee machine with surprise. "You're going to help me?"

"That's what I keep telling you. But let's start by clearing this place a little. Orders all taken outside?"

"Tables 3 and 6 are still waiting. And they're not looking happy."

"I'll soon change that."

He threw her an order pad and pencil, and she dashed outside.

After about 30 minutes, Lynette noticed that the café was fast running out of supplies, things like serviettes and sugar sachets, and she couldn't see any sign of them in the storeroom.

"Oh bugger it. I did pick up some yesterday," said Niles when she enquired. "Haven't had a chance to unload them yet." He reached for some car keys that had been placed under the counter. "Do you mind? It's the old Beamer out the back."

She grabbed the keys and dashed through the kitchen, past the harried looking cook who was wrestling with a hot frypan and some eggs, to the back door where she spotted his black BMW. As she went to unload the boxes from the boot, a small bell began ringing in her head, but there was no time to think. She had to get back to the hungry hordes. She lifted up the boxes and hauled them inside.

It took another 20 minutes but the place finally settled down. The breakfast rush was over and most customers were finishing the dregs of their coffee before heading off to the gym or Bridge club or wherever it was the idle rich go when they don't have to worry about the rent. Lynette returned inside with a tray of dirty dishes and cups.

"Just dump them in the kitchen, I'll deal with them later," Niles said. "And thank you."

"Don't thank me too soon, it'll probably fire up again for lunch you know?"

"I know, I know, I've already called Annie in. She'll be here any minute."

"Good, then you and I can sit down and chat."

He shot her a worried glance but said nothing. Once the young waitress arrived, looking like she'd just crawled out of bed, Niles made Lynette and himself a latté then they sat down at a back table. He let out a long, weary sigh.

"That's the problem with this business. Drought one day, flood the next and it always seems to rain when I haven't got any staff on."

"Such glorious weather, Niles, surely you expected it to be busy today?"

He shrugged. He clearly had no business acumen, and had probably avoided putting staff on to skimp on costs. She decided not to go into any of that, it wasn't her *raison d'etre*. Instead, she asked about Barbara.

"What do you want to know?"

"I want to know what she was like."

"I thought you guys knew her."

"So did I, but I'm wondering whether there was another side to Barbara that we didn't know."

She took a sip of the latté, nearly burning her tongue in the process and pushed it aside to let it cool down. Lattés were not supposed to be boiling hot, she wanted to tell him, but again she resisted. There was no saving this guy from himself.

Instead she said, "It's just that we seem to be getting such diverse descriptions of your sister. I wonder whether the side she showed us at the book club might be very different to the side she showed others."

He looked confused and rubbed his tired eyes.

"I just want to know what she's really like, Niles. Not the saccharine, air-brushed studio photo version. I want to know about the real Barbara Parlour. Tell me about her."

He stopped rubbing his eyes and thought about this for a moment. "My sister was… is…" He paused again, looking suddenly distraught. "Jesus, I don't even know how to refer to her anymore. You think she's okay?"

She shrugged. She couldn't offer him that solace, she didn't know.

"Alright, let me start again. Barbara is a good person, she's just made a few bad decisions in life."

"Like Arthur Parlour?"

"Exactly. You're not supposed to talk ill of the dead and all that, but the man was a total bastard. All he cared about was being the Big Cheese in society. I told you he was turning politician, right?" She nodded. "He would've been right at home with those scumbags. Slept around on her, too. Made her furious."

"Did he ever hit her?"

Niles looked surprised. "Christ no. I woulda smashed his face in if he even tried." He caught himself and stopped. "But I didn't! I mean, I never touched the man—"

"Yeah, I know, we've been through that." She wasn't in the mood for his innocent victim routine today. The ocean outside was beckoning. "So why did your sister stay with Arthur if he was so unfaithful?"

"Didn't really have a lot of choices. I mean, we're not old money you know. Come from the wrong side of the tracks. Neither of us is very educated, never made uni, and I know for a fact that Barbara doesn't want to have to work again. She tried her hand at various things, PR, acting, writing… but prefers to be a lady of leisure." There was slight disdain in his voice then. "Guess it was just easier to stay with him. Giant house, steady income, all that."

"Couldn't she sue him for divorce? Take him for half his money and set herself up somewhere else?"

"And then do what? Plus she had Holly to consider."

"But Holly's practically an adult, she's 16. She'd be fine."

"I dunno." He hesitated. "There was something, um, *bitter* about my sister I s'pose you could say. She was always angry at Arthur but, I dunno…"

"What, Niles? What are you trying to say?"

"Don't quote me on this."

Lynette held up her hands. "Do you see a tape recorder? A camera? I'm not a reporter, Niles, I've told you that before. I'm a friend."

"I know. Look, I love my sister, I owe her big time, don't get me wrong, but sometimes I wondered whether the real reason she kept helping me out with loans was to get back at Arthur. She certainly made sure he knew about it. Rubbed his face in it all the time. I guess what I'm trying to say is, I think my sister's loathing of her husband fuelled her, gave her purpose, you know? Well, that and this café of course."

"And Arthur had no problem with her using *his* money to pay *your* bills?"

He began massaging the line between his eyebrows. "He had no choice. I guess you could call it guilt money."

"So let me see if I've got this straight. Are you saying your sister enjoyed splashing Arthur's money about? Did it to taunt him?"

He stopped massaging and shrugged. "Yeah, I reckon she did. I remember she bought a giant ruby ring once, ugly reddish black thing in a clunky gold casing. When I commented on it she just laughed and told me she doesn't even like rubies, just wanted to stick it to Arthur. As I say, I love my sis, but she ain't no saint, that's for sure." Niles' tired eyes looked imploring. "Do you think she's okay? Still alive, I mean?"

It was the second time he had asked and Lynette suddenly felt pity on him and placed a hand over his.

"I honestly don't know, Niles. I'd like to say yes but I have no idea. That's why I'm here. Is there anything else you can tell me about your sister? Anything that might help?"

He thought about this for a few minutes, glancing back out to the café, which was starting to fill up again. "Not that I can think of."

"Fine, well, you've got my number if you think of anything at all. No matter how small, just call me, okay?"

"Okay, look, I better get back."

"I'll leave you to it then."

"Hang on, how much do I owe you for today? For helping out?"

He reached into his pocket as if going for his wallet and she waved him away.

"Don't be stupid. Just shout me the coffee, okay?"

He nodded a silent thank you, his hands together prayer-like, then dashed off towards an incoming customer while Lynette gathered her stuff and headed for the beach outside.

The sun was now much stronger and Lynette dumped her towel on the warm, white sand and slipped out of her sundress to reveal a pink and white-checked bikini underneath. Several men around her turned to stare, mesmerised by her milky brown skin and long, lithe legs, but Lynette did not notice. She rarely noticed the attention she got from men, unless of course they were older, richer and ready to promote her to 'Princess' status and pop her on a pedestal. Then she would turn to them with a wide smile, flick her silky blond hair, and step on up.

Lynette expected complete adoration from the men she dated. The problem with this arrangement, at least as far as her older sister was concerned, was that it never lasted long. Eventually the richer, older bloke would start treating Lynette less like royalty and more like the human being that she actually was, and Lynette would grow indignant and dump him for another pedestal-wielding, richer, older man. And so the vicious cycle continued.

For now though, men of all persuasions were far from Lynette's mind as she lathered herself in sunscreen then strode into the water for a dip. It was glorious. As she lay on her back, the ripples bobbing her about, she considered what Niles had just told her, and she began to see a pattern. There was another side to Barbara Parlour, a darker, more devious side that she had clearly not shown to the Book Club. To them, she had appeared soft, nervous and vulnerable.

Just like a victim.

Yet Niles described a woman who knew exactly what she wanted and was very much in control. Almost into playing games, she thought. In fact, hadn't he mentioned that she used to act, once? That correlated with something both Arthur and Wanda had said of Barbara. They had both called her a drama queen.

Lynette stood up with a start nearly toppling over an ogling body-boarder nearby.

Had Barbara been playing a role with the Murder Mystery Book Club? Hiding her true self? Acting like someone she was not? *And if so, why?*

As Lynette strode back to her towel and laid down on it to dry, she couldn't help wondering who—or what—it was that Barbara Parlour was trying so desperately to hide.

An hour later, as Lynette gathered her things to go, she heard the jangling of keys in her handbag. It surprised her. She hadn't taken Alicia's car and her house key did not make that much noise. She reached in and realised then that she must have inadvertently popped Niles' keys in her handbag after fetching the supplies from his car. She groaned, not in the mood for more of his self-pity and puppy dog eyes, then reluctantly headed back towards his café. As she did so, the bell that had been ringing in the back of her head began clanging louder and louder.

That's when it hit her, and she stopped and gasped, shaking her head.

It couldn't be.

Lynette detoured around the café to the back car park where she took a closer look at Niles' BMW and gasped again. It had dark, tinted windows and there were several dents along one side, some paint missing where it had clearly collided with something.

Or someone.

A shot of electricity raced through Lynette's body as she recalled Missy's words after her hit and run a few weeks ago: *"All I could see was an old dark-coloured BMW… it had dark, Drug Dealer Windows."*

"Hey, you're still here!" came Niles' voice from the kitchen door and Lynette swung around to see him watching her closely, his hands in his pockets, an inscrutable expression on his face

"Oh, um, I forgot to get your keys back to you," she stammered, her heart pounding as she tossed them across the car park to him.

He caught them in one hand. "Thanks. You off now?"

She nodded, hesitated then took a deep breath. Alicia would never forgive her if she didn't ask.

"So what happened to your car?" She indicated the dented side and tried to sound casual.

He shrugged. "No idea. Just found it like that."

"Really?" Casual had turned to accusing.

"Yeah, really. Why?" A dark look crossed his eyes.

"You didn't accidentally hit something… or someone?"

He stared hard at her. "'Course not. I'd remember something like that wouldn't I? What's this about?"

"I'm just wondering how you could dent your car so badly and not notice," Lynette said trying to sound light.

"Obviously some idiot must have side swiped me while I was parked and didn't bother to leave their details," he spat. "Not my fault."

No, she thought, *nothing ever is*. Lynette studied his face, unable to read him. Did he look culpable or just confused?

She decided to leave it for now; she was not even sure how any of this fitted in with Arthur's death or Barbara's disappearance. Why on earth would Niles try to hurt poor Missy? How could that help with either of those outcomes? It had Lynette's head spinning, and her head had been doing way too much spinning today, so she decided to let it rest for now.

Besides, Niles might look exhausted but he could still beat her in a punch up. Of that she was certain.

Lynette waved him goodbye and turned to go, but as she left him standing there, staring curiously at his car, she couldn't help wondering if Niles Blakely was as innocent as he made out.

CHAPTER 26

As Alicia entered work late that same Monday morning, she made a decision that surprised her. She was not going to go to Woollahra today, she was not going to chat to Rosa Lopez or have anything to do with Barbara Parlour and her murdered philandering husband. Not today. Today she was going to do as Claire and Lynette had done yesterday, and take a well-earned break.

Perhaps in his own infuriating way, Anders was right. She was taking it all too seriously. Perhaps she needed some distance if she was going to get some perspective. Besides, her editing work was really starting to pile up.

At the front desk she waved a quick hello to Ginny who was flirting with a spandex-clad courier from *Deliver it, Express!* He was holding a bike helmet in one hand and popping her details into his phone with the other, and she had to shake her head as she made her way to her desk. Ginny certainly didn't muck around.

She wouldn't be sitting around pining for a married doctor, she thought.

After her computer whirred to life, Alicia watched a seemingly endless stream of new emails begin cluttering her inbox. She chose to ignore them as she set to work, putting the final details on the Lady Gaga magazine and trying hard to concoct some witty coverlines. It was tricky coming up with great lines when you were dealing with a vacuous pop star, and she battled to keep the sarcasm from her tone.

Gaga for Gaga had been done to death and she didn't think anyone would appreciate *The Lady is a tramp*. She sighed and kept thinking…

Two hours and countless exclamation marks later, she put the cover aside and turned back to her email. Better clear the inbox before it spills over, she thought, picking through the messages as you would a carcass, looking for the tasty morsels and dumping the spam.

It was the 21st email that caught her eye. Her English publisher had an idea for her next project and wanted to run it by her. She clicked the email open but only got as far as the first sentence.

"You're hitting summer over there," he wrote, *"just wondering whether a Spa Special might be in order?"*

That's when all her good intentions went awry.

Alicia sat back, eyes wide, then clicked the email shut, grabbed her handbag, and retraced her steps. Ginny was still giggling beside the courier, who clearly wasn't living up to the 'Express' part on his contract. *Or was this another courier?* Alicia wondered, giving Ginny a quick wave and marvelling yet again at her strike rate.

"Where you off to now?" Ginny called out but there was no time to explain.

Thanks to her publisher's email, Alicia had finally remembered where she'd seen the word 'Hydro' and why it had rung a bell. She had to get back to the Parlour house, and she had to get back there pronto.

On the way Alicia put a quick call in to her sister who was also in transit, this time making her way back from Balmoral Beach.

"Just letting you know where I'll be," Alicia said. "I brought the car to work today, haven't got the energy for pubic transport, so I'm driving there now."

She glanced down at her thighs and scowled. They had been sorely neglected of late. Perhaps it was time to renew her gym membership?

"Great," said Lynette, her voice just slightly crackly, "but why don't you take someone with you? Give Anders a call."

"Anders? Why should I?" She felt her hackles rising. "I don't need a man to protect me."

"Easy, tiger. I'm just saying, might be more fun that's all. I thought you and Anders were, well, you know…"

"Well you're wrong," she said. "How many times do I have to tell you, there's nothing going on between us. He's married."

"Yeah, about that, I think you have that all wrong—"

"No, no I do not." She calmed her tone a little. "He told me so himself, just yesterday. Besides he's not very interested in all of this."

"All of what?"

"This investigation. Barbara Parlour. I think he's about to quit the club."

"Really? That's not the impression I got."

"Yeah well that makes one of you then. How'd you go with Niles?" She wanted to change the subject, was not interested in Anders' behaviour right now.

"It was very interesting, actually." Lynette relayed the words Niles had said about his sister and her bitterness towards her husband. "But there's one really big thing I have to tell you."

"You better be quick, I'm almost there."

"Okay, okay," said Lynette who then lowered her voice as though avoiding eavesdropping fellow passengers. "So remember what Missy said about her hit and run the other week?"

"Missy? What does Niles have to do with Missy?"

"Just humour me. Do you remember what she said or not?"

"Yes, she said some hoon in a dark BMW tried to take her out. Why?"

"I know a hoon with a black BMW. And it's got dents all over it."

"Oh my God! Niles?"

"The very one."

Alicia gave this some thought. "But… but why would he want to hurt Missy? That's illogical. As far as I know they've never even met."

"Good question, I have no idea," said Lynette. She sighed long and low. "Look, the more I think about it, the more I think it has to be a coincidence. A strange one, that's for sure. Still, it's worth noting…"

"God my journal's turning into a novel with all these ridiculous little 'notes' that seem to add up to diddly-squat. Oh, I'd better go, I'm getting close and no doubt there'll be coppers swarming the place. Don't want to get done for phone-driving!"

"Okay, fine. Just be careful, Alicia, okay?"

She promised she would then hung up and began searching for a park.

Despite Alicia's expectations, there wasn't so much as a flimsy blue and white ribbon anywhere near the Parlour mansion when she arrived and the media had all cleared off. She felt a flicker of relief as she walked up to the front door and pressed the now-familiar buzzer. Then a sudden stab of panic.

She imagined Arthur swinging the door open, a bloody gash across his head, a frown upon his forehead, ready to berate her yet again for interrupting his perfect, polished life. Alicia felt deep regret. *What had she done to the poor man? Why hadn't she left him alone? Maybe he'd still be alive if she had?*

A second later, much to her surprise, Holly answered the door. While she was very much alive, Holly was dressed today like someone from the living dead—black top, black leggings, black tutu over the leggings, giant black, stomper boots on her feet, and thick, black eyeliner smudging her eyes. (Lots of black, in case it wasn't obvious.) She had also put a purplish-black tint through her already dark hair, which was hanging in greasy strands around her face, and there was a poorly drawn tattoo of a tiny black cross on her arm that Alicia hadn't noticed before. She was either in deep mourning or had turned 'Emo' overnight, but in any case the look did not suit her.

Alicia felt her heart pang for the poor, confused child.

"Hi Holly," she said, trying not to stare at her gothic transformation. "I'm so sorry about your dad."

"Really?" said Holly, her upper lip curling slightly. "I thought you were gunning for him."

"Not at all! I was just trying to find your mum, that's all. How are you holding up? I thought you were staying with friends."

"No way, man! Heidi's mum treats her like a child, much better here. Besides, I'm, like, 16 you know, old enough to live on my own."

"Rosa's not here?"

"As if! Took off days ago."

"Really? Isn't that odd?"

"Nope. Why would you stay around this place? It's cursed."

"So who's going to look after you? I mean, I know you can look after yourself and all…"

She pulled a face. "My Dad's sister Harriet is on her way from Adelaide. Yawn."

"Well, it's probably for the best."

"I'm not scared being on my own. They did catch the killer, you know."

"Yes. So I heard. Wanda Birchin, apparently. That is, if she did it."

"'Course she did it! The cops told me Dad's fingerprints are all over her house, and, get this, her fingerprints are, like, all over the golf club that killed him! So CSI."

"Which golf club?" she asked.

"Huh?"

"Was it a 9-iron?"

Holly had that you're-a-nutter look on her face again. "Who gives a toss? Whatever it was, it killed him…" She choked back a sob now, tried to fight it, determined not to cry in front of her mother's boring friend. "I always thought Wanda Bitchface was dodgy. Always real sleazy with Dad when she called up."

"I heard she phoned your house the day your Dad died. After lunch some time. Did you answer it?"

"Why would I? That's Rosa's job. Well… it was."

"So Rosa was still around then?"

"Dunno." Her claggy black eyelashes scrunched together. "What's it all got to do with you anyway?"

"Listen, Holly, I'm not trying to be sneaky or get the goss. I genuinely want to help; all of us at your mum's book club do. We're good people and we want to find her. You do want to find your mum, don't you?"

"'Course I do!" She sniffed loudly. "I thought she was just being a cow. But now, well, after they found Dad…"

Unable to dam the flow any longer, Holly began to cry, great gulping, snotty snobs, and Alicia pulled her into a hug. The young girl did not fight back. She might think she's all grown up, but really Holly was still very much a child. Still reeling from her mother's mysterious disappearance, her father's death must have come as an enormous shock.

No amount of teenage bravado, or gothic gear, was going to change that.

After a while, Holly struggled free looking excruciatingly embarrassed and glanced around as if worried someone had seen her.

"Can I come in?" Alicia asked gently. "There's something inside I really need to look at. I promise, it will help your mum."

Holly wiped a hand across her nose and let her in. Alicia headed straight for the kitchen fridge and the magnetised advertisements she had seen there the day that Barbara hosted that first official Book Club.

It was just as she'd expected. One of the magnets was advertising a luxury spa called the Hydro Majestic in the Blue Mountains, just northwest of Sydney. She plucked it off and studied it.

"What's this got to do with anything?" asked Holly, snatching it from her.

"Did your Mum know anyone at this spa, the Hydro Majestic, do you know?"

She shrugged. "Her usual place was the Golden Door up in Queensland. Why she needed to go to a spa when she did f-all I'll never know."

Holly stopped, bit her lip and choked back a sob. Bitching about her mother wasn't so much fun now that the poor woman was missing.

"Oh, *where* is she?" she wailed again. "Where could she be?"

Alicia gave her hand a quick squeeze. "I'm not sure, Holly, but I have a hunch this place holds the key. Can I keep this?"

Holly shrugged, handing it back. Alicia was about to turn away when something else on the fridge caught her attention. Or, rather, something that wasn't there.

"Where are the pictures of your mum, Holly?" she asked.

Holly followed her eyes to the fridge and her own eyes widened a little. The usual cluster of family photos were still there, but this time only those of Arthur and the young Holly. There were none of Barbara.

"Hm, that's strange. Wonder where Mum's pix got to…"

"Did she maybe take them with her, that Saturday that she left?"

Holly shook her head furiously. "Nuh, I definitely saw them after that because I was so narky with her I wanted to take them off and rip them up…" She must have seen Alicia's startled expression. "But, hey, don't look at me, I didn't touch them! I swear!"

"Then who did? Your Dad?"

She shrugged again. "Maybe, he was angry, too. Maybe he wanted to get rid of her."

"Yes, except he told my friend Missy that he wanted your mum home, 'back where she belongs', so why would he remove her photos?" She had a sudden thought. "Did someone give them to the police or the press, for identification, maybe?"

Holly thought about this. "Maybe. I know I didn't, and it's not like I've seen them on the news."

Alicia hadn't seen them either. The pictures of Barbara she'd seen on the TV news had obviously been taken out of an old photo album circa 1982. "Do you mind if I look in the lounge room?"

Without waiting for an answer Alicia strode through, and gasped aloud. Several photos of Barbara had also been removed from the top of the mantelpiece and the side table, and her tennis trophy was also gone. Then she spotted the stilted family portrait that was hanging above the grand piano, and froze. This time, instead of a cheesy picture of three faux happy people, she saw just Arthur with his daughter standing in front. Alicia stepped towards it to take a closer look, and gasped again.

Barbara had been crudely chopped out of the frame; you could still see a little of one shoulder and part of her bleached blond hair.

Someone had sliced the rest of her away.

"Oh my God!" said Holly, behind her, a nail-bitten hand to her mouth. "That's creepy! It's like someone's trying to get rid of her."

"That's exactly what it's like," said Alicia, turning back to Holly. "When was Rosa last here?"

"Rosa? Um, I dunno, the cops came around on Thursday night to tell me about… um, about… Dad."

"And was Rosa here then, Holly?"

"No, she'd taken off."

Alicia blinked several times. "So when did Rosa actually leave?" Holly shrugged non-committal. "This is really important, Holly, try to think. Let's start at the beginning. What time did you get home the Thursday that your father died?"

"Okay, okay, chillax! Um, I'd been at school, and got back about 2-ish—we had, like, a free period after lunch. Um, that's right, Rosa was here then, had just made popcorn so she gave me a bowl. I don't know after that as I went up to my room to, you know, hit the computer and stuff. Dad was still around when I got home, too, but he told me he was heading off to play golf and would see me later for dinner… I didn't think anything of it…"

Alicia needed to keep the girl on track. "So when did you next see Rosa?"

She considered this. "Um, that's right, I came down to watch *Neighbours* on the big screen."

"So what, that's on about 5:00 p.m?"

"Yep. Dad was gone but Rosa was still here. As soon as I came down she said she had to leave, that she had a family crisis or some bollocks story. She had, like, a suitcase with her. I knew she was pissing off for good. Knew it was gonna happen sooner or later. I mean, like, we were the cursed family with the missing mother…"

Alicia gripped her by the shoulders hoping to ward off another tearful outburst.

"Holly, this is extremely important. Tell me, do you know if Rosa was home before *Neighbours* started, around 4—4:30 p.m? Did you see or hear her anytime between 2-ish when you went to your bedroom, and 5:00 p.m. when you came down to watch TV?"

Holly looked a little alarmed now, choked back a sob. "I don't know! Honest I don't! As I said, I was in my room then, had my earphones on listening to some iTunes and stuff. I came out just after *Neighbours* had started. What's all this about? Why're you asking all these questions about Rosa?"

Alicia gave Holly's shoulders a squeeze. "Not sure Holly, but if Rosa comes back, call the cops. Got it?"

Holly's eyes filled with fear and she looked 12 all over again. Alicia glanced at her watch. It was lunchtime. She had to get Holly out of here. Just in case.

"Aren't you supposed to be at school now?" she asked.

"Yeah, like, so?"

"So it mightn't hurt to go, be a good distraction from all of this. Must be pretty lonely here by yourself. Be good to see your friends."

Holly thought about this, did a half shrug. "Jake was gonna come over… hours ago." She sniffed. "He's ignoring my calls, my texts, I thought he… Like, I just thought…"

She let the sentence dangle and Alicia pulled her to the couch and forced her to sit down. "What's going on with you guys?" she asked softly and Holly just looked away.

It was time to get some straight answers, Alicia decided, so she said, "It's pretty obvious you two were having an affair."

"It's not an *affair*," she scoffed. "We're not, like, 105 or married or something. Besides, he loves me."

Alicia felt her heart break for the foolish young thing. The first in a long line of heart breaks, she wanted to tell her but said, instead, "Jake Smith loves no one but himself, Holly, I'm sorry to tell you that. I wouldn't be waiting for him to come rescue you."

"I'm not!" She looked indignant, but there was vulnerability there, too, in those smudged, black-lined eyes.

"So what were you screaming about with Jake that day Claire and I saw you on the tennis court?"

Holly automatically reached for her stomach, a blush creeping across her chubby cheeks, and the penny finally dropped.

"Oh, I see," said Alicia softly. "You're pregnant."

Holly dropped her hand and scowled. "No I'm *not*. Or… at least, not anymore. I thought I was… I was just late."

"So *that's* what you were screaming about? You wanted Jake to tell your Dad that you were pregnant with his baby?"

"But he wouldn't. Said he couldn't even be sure the baby was his! *Like I'm some ho'*. Anyway, it doesn't matter now. He doesn't even want to know me anymore. I thought… I thought he loved me…"

She sobbed heartily again and Alicia sat there for several minutes, this time letting her get it all out.

"You know, the world is made up of good guys and bastards," she told the crying teen. "Jake falls into the second category. Always did, always will. You're better off without him."

She sniffed loudly. "That's what Mum said."

"Your mum knew about—"

"No way!" She looked mortified, swiping away the tears. "Well, I dunno… she might have suspected, I'm not sure. But I didn't want her to know. That's why I went to see a different doctor. One my friend Sara goes to in the city. He's really cool."

For Alicia, another penny dropped, but for now she let it stay there as Holly rattled on.

"I couldn't go see Mum's doctor, stupid interfering biddy. She'd dob me in for sure, tells Mum, like, *everything*. But I reckon Mum'd worked it out anyway. Told me Jake wasn't, like, good enough, *responsible* enough. I told her where she could shove that." Tears began streaming down her face again. "The last time I saw Mum I screamed at her! Dad didn't fight with Mum the day she disappeared, like all the TV shows are saying. I did! It was me!" She gulped hard. "Dad didn't tell them that because he was trying to protect me. He was a good man, he didn't deserve…" She broke off and sobbed some more.

Alicia waited a few minutes then grabbed the girl's hands and pulled her up. "Come on, you're going to school.

Go and pop your uniform on and I'll drop you in. Honestly, even algebra has to be better than sitting around here moping all day."

Much to Alicia's surprise, Holly did as she was told, returning after ten minutes in a crumpled uniform, hitched too high above the knees, and her backpack slung across one shoulder. She had tied her black hair into a tight ponytail on top of her head, removed the nose ring and covered up the tattoo, clearly not *de rigueur* at her swanky private girls' school.

Within 20 minutes Alicia had dropped Holly off and was making her way to the Woollahra police station. She had just solved the case of the dead husband, and the police had it completely wrong.

CHAPTER 27

Alicia's third visit to the Woollahra police station was not received as warmly as she'd come to expect. Instead of being shown straight through to Inspector Ward's office, this time his sidekick, Roger, appeared and ushered her into the busy station and over to his messy, paper-strewn desk right in the middle of the room. He indicated for her to take a seat across from him and stared at her, trying to look tough. He didn't succeed. Roger had a kind of cute, baby-face look about him, not helped by the tiny little dimples in his cheeks. Bad cop was not his forte.

"I really need to speak to Inspector Ward urgently," she said. "It's about Arthur Parlour."

Roger looked suddenly smug, grinning from ear to ear. "We're one step ahead of you, Alicia. We've got Wanda Birchill in custody now."

"It's Wanda Birchin! Birchin! My God what is wrong with you people? You could at least get the poor woman's name right if you're going to lock her up and throw away the key. Anyway, that's beside the point, she didn't do it."

He looked at her sideways.

"I mean it, Roger. You've got the wrong woman. Listen, can I ask you a question?"

He nodded tentatively.

"Was Arthur killed with a 9-iron?"

"Sorry?"

"He was hit on the head, right? Was it a 9-iron golf club?"

"A-ha!" He grinned smugly again. "No it was not. It was a putter."

"Just as I thought," Alicia said, wiping the smile from his face. "Come on, Roger, you *have* to get me in to see your boss. I know who killed Arthur Parlour, and it was not Wanda Birchill, I mean Birchin! Bloody hell, you've got me doing it now!"

~~~~~~~

The Murder Mystery Book Club were now gathered at The Orient Express restaurant in Potts Point, a venue chosen as much for its name as its delectable, traditional Chinese cuisine. The food was outstanding, and it needed to be, this was a celebratory dinner of sorts. Thanks to Alicia's keen eye, they had helped solve the mystery of Arthur's recent murder. Sadly, however, Barbara remained missing so no one was popping the champagne corks just yet.

Rosa Lopez was now in police custody, under arrest for the murder of Arthur Parlour, and Wanda Birchin had been released and was no doubt home, licking her wounds and facing the wrath of a jealous husband. She probably had Alicia's face on a dart board somewhere, and the younger woman felt a tinge of guilt which was being quickly washed away by cheap chardonnay and back slaps from her fellow book clubbers.

"You are truly amazing, Miss Finlay," Claire said a little breathlessly as she took her seat, grabbed some chopsticks and began surveying the food. There was crispy skin duck, ginger beef, twice-cooked pork and a large platter of mixed
~~~~~~~

entrees. She had arrived late, saying something about a "squabble" with her fiancé, and the group had let it go for now, even Perry who usually couldn't resist a dig.

It had been a busy week for the amateur sleuths, and all of them were beginning to face growing impatience from partners, flatmates, work colleagues and the like. Alicia wasn't even sure Max was still talking to her or Lynette at this stage. Not even homemade treats could cheer him up.

Anders had also shown up late, choosing the chair furthest from Alicia, and she was surprised to see him, offering him a clipped hello, then returning to the rest of the group. She was in too good a mood to let him get her down tonight.

"So how did you know Rosa 'done it' so to speak?" Claire asked, her chopsticks settling on a vegetarian spring roll.

Alicia swallowed her mouthful of ginger beef and explained. "It was the missing photos and trophy, Claire. You know, Missy, you almost picked it yourself. Remember when you made that impromptu visit to Barbara's house and we all got cranky with you? You said you felt like something was missing?"

"Oh my god, yes!" said Missy. "I couldn't work out what it was, but something wasn't right. So you think Barbara's stuff had been taken by then? *Really?*"

"I can't say for sure, but Rosa had probably started to remove them one by one so no one noticed. It was Rosa's way of cleansing the place of the 'demon wife'. By the end of the week there was no trace of her."

"But why didn't Arthur say something?"

"He probably didn't even notice," said Alicia. "I know that Holly hadn't."

"Oh, how simply depressing," said Perry, waving a scallop in the air. "Poor Barbara, no wonder she was crying out for our help. Her family are monstrous!"

"One of them is dead, Perry, and the other's an orphan," said Claire.

"Doesn't change the fact," he replied, thrusting the mollusc into his mouth.

"Perry's right," said Lynette. "As Poirot says, it's not unkind to say what the victim is like. In fact, it's the kindest thing you can do if you want to catch their killer. Missy was on the ball there, too. Being honest about the victim helps to explain why they got bopped over the head in the first place."

"Precisely," he said, sneering at Claire. "If Arthur hadn't been such an utter bastard to Rosa, let alone his *wife*, sleeping with anything with a pulse, he'd probably still be alive and kicking as we speak."

"Having an affair is certainly vile," Claire said stiffly, "but it does not justify murder. No way."

"Anyway guys, can we get back to the subject please?" said Alicia, throwing Anders a quick glance. He hadn't yet said a word, was just staring at the table as he chewed his food, his mood sullen. She glanced away again. "Here's how I think it went down, and the police tend to agree with me. Arthur was obviously having an affair with Rosa, I mean we can all accept that's a given, judging by his track record. So, when Barbara disappeared, Rosa was overjoyed. She probably assumed that she now had Arthur all to herself. She could stop being the domestic slave and step into the role of mistress of the house. And in fact, that's what we noticed. Suddenly she was always there, she'd dropped the apron, was dressing all sexy, acting like she owned the place. And, we now know, ridding the mansion of reminders of Barbara. She's the one who sliced Barbara's face out of the family photos. Took great delight in it, too, I can imagine."

She turned to Missy again. "Once again you picked it and none of us caught on."

Missy gave her an enquiring look.

"Remember you were raving on about your sister's mother-in-law was it? The one who came in and took over?"

"Oh, yes, Mildred!" said Missy. "She was minding my sister's kids for a weekend but acted like she'd moved in permanently, changing the radio station, the furniture. That was the exact same vibe I got from Rosa. She was acting like Lady of the Manor, except Arthur wasn't buying it. I heard him tell her to get back in her box, or words to that effect."

"Exactly! And you said she looked pissed off."

"Majorly."

"Right, and that's probably when Rosa began to realise that Arthur was never going to marry her—no matter what happened to Barbara. It must have finally dawned on Rosa that she would always be seen as the hired help, just a bit of rump on the side."

Perry sneered at Claire again. "See, utter bastard. So, what, Rosa followed him to the golf course?"

"Yep. We know that Wanda phoned Arthur earlier that fatal afternoon—the police have confirmed her call came in around 2:30 p.m. Holly was in her bedroom, heard the phone ring but didn't answer it. My guess is, Rosa answered and then eavesdropped in on Arthur's conversation with Wanda. That's when she overheard Arthur say he wanted to rendezvous with Wanda during his afternoon golf game. Rosa must have been furious, perhaps she had thought she was now the only one. In any case, she followed Arthur to the golf course and then over to Wanda's house."

"But didn't Wanda tell you nothing actually happened that afternoon between her and Arthur?" asked Lynette.

"Still, he was there long enough to kiss Wanda, and Rosa probably saw that. Worse still, he declared his undying love and demanded that Wanda break up with her hubby. He didn't mean it, of course. Wanda said they always spoke like that to each other, it was just a silly game they played."

"But Rosa didn't know that."

"Exactamondo!"

Lynette waved a waitress over to order more rice. "Anyone want anything else while we're at it?"

"I'll have some more wine," said Anders, speaking for the first time.

"Oh and some more of those deep fried wontons!" called out Perry, as the waitress scurried away. "*Wanton* indeed!"

"Anyway," continued Alicia, "Rosa must have spotted Wanda and Arthur kissing and become enraged. She then followed Arthur back onto the fairway, probably confronted him or, more likely snuck up on him unawares, and belted him over the head with the putting stick."

"Not the 9-iron then?" said Anders and she looked at him surprised.

"No, that's partly why I suspected Wanda was innocent. Without thinking she rattled off the word '9-iron', it seemed really spontaneous. She told me she was just guessing and I believed her. If she had really done it, she would've known it was a putter and accidentally said that. It got me wondering. Then I spotted all those missing fridge photos and trophies of Barbara at her house, and that eerie family photo with Barbara cut out. That's when it occurred to me: the only person who could have had access to them was Rosa."

"Well, there was also Holly," said Perry.

"You've always had it in for her, haven't you?" said Anders.

"And you've always stood up for her," said Alicia, eyebrows raised. "Want to explain why?"

He shifted in his seat, couldn't quite meet her eyes. "No, I do not."

"Something to do with doctor/patient confidentiality perhaps?" His eyes snapped towards her, surprised. "Holly told me today, Anders. She was pregnant with Jake's baby, or at least she was for a few weeks before she miscarried."

"Really?" said Claire. "So that's what they were fighting about at the tennis court?"

"Yep. Holly wanted to tell her father and Jake didn't believe it was even his baby."

"Pig!" said Missy.

"You were treating her, weren't you?" Alicia said to Anders, who now looked almost relieved, like a man who had been carrying a load for too long and had finally let it drop. "Holly told me she was seeing some city doctor. It has to be you. You obviously recognised Barbara that first day at book club, I could tell there was something there that you were hiding. Then, when we had book club at her house, you seemed a bit edgy."

"I was worried about running into poor Holly. She didn't need her doctor showing up on her doorstep. Luckily, we didn't cross paths."

"Actually, that's not true," said Alicia. "Holly did spot you out on the terrace and came back into the kitchen and screamed at her mother. I didn't know what she was on about at the time but she thought her mother had deliberately brought you here, to taunt her I suppose."

Anders shook his head. "Oh, God, I didn't realise that. The poor thing. I really should not have attended that club meet, should have stayed away. Given her some privacy."

"But how did you know Barbara was Holly's mother if you hadn't met?" asked Missy, scraping the dregs of the rice into her bowl.

"When I was treating Holly she explained how devastating this would be to her parents and I recognised their names from the social pages."

"Why didn't you tell us all of this?" demanded Perry.

Anders looked around at their startled expressions. "I'm sorry, guys, I couldn't tell you. It's against my oath…"

Perry looked disgusted. "We were dealing with murder, Anders. I think the Hippocratic oath takes a back seat."

"Look, if I really believed Holly had something to do with all of this I would have spoken up, I would have. But I felt for the poor child. She's just a mixed up, screwed up kid who turned to a lowlife for love and was treated shabbily. When she found the courage to come to me she was extremely distressed. And she came to me in confidence, I couldn't go around telling her secret to an entire book club."

Perry snorted at this but Alicia felt some sympathy for the doctor. Something to do with a rock and a hard place.

"I understand that, Anders," she said gently. "I also couldn't believe Holly would kill her father. Niles had already told us she was a daddy's girl, through and through. It just didn't seem right."

Lynette was over this line of conversation. "Look, I'm sorry about Holly, really I am, but didn't you say it was a false alarm anyway, Alicia?"

Anders spoke up. "She was pregnant but only briefly. Obviously the stress of all of this has taken its toll."

"Again, I'm super sorry," said Lynette. "But can we get back to Rosa, please? I still have so many questions. Like, how did you know she followed Arthur to the golf course, Alicia?"

Alicia took a quick sip of her wine. "Well, like I said, Rosa answered the phone that afternoon when Wanda called. So Rosa is the one that could have overheard where Arthur was going. But most telling is the fact that she's got no alibi. There's no one to account for her whereabouts during that pivotal time, around 4:30 p.m. when Arthur was killed."

The waitress appeared with a fresh bowl of steaming rice in one hand and the bottle of wine in the other. They made room for them and then she left to fetch the wontons.

"More wine anyone?" asked Anders, and several of them raised their glasses for him to refill. He did so then took a large gulp of the Sémillon and cocked one thick brown eyebrow at Alicia. "So, based on everything you said, the police simply released Wanda and arrested Rosa? I don't mean to sound rude, Alicia, but a few missing happy snaps isn't exactly a smoking gun. I mean, it's all just circumstantial evidence."

She glared at him. *So that's how he wanted to play it, eh?*

"Yes, Anders," she spat back. "I realise it's not enough to convict a person. I'm not an idiot. I mean, a chopped up family photo doesn't exactly incriminate anyone, and the police certainly weren't taking my word for it. Inspector Ward thinks I'm a meddling pain in the backside as it is."

She gave Anders a particularly pointed look. "But the cops were already on Rosa's trail."

Several of the group glanced between Anders and Alicia, wondering what was going on, so she turned her attention back to them and softened her tone a little. "You see, apart from Wanda's fingerprints on the golf club—she says she must have inadvertently touched it when he popped in during his golf game—they also found Rosa's paw prints everywhere. The problem was, they didn't think much of it at first because, well, she was the housekeeper after all. Her fingerprints *would* be on the golf clubs, especially if she cleaned them and put them away."

"So why do they suddenly suspect Rosa now?" Missy asked, helping herself to the wontons that had just arrived. Perry snapped at her chopsticks with his own and then grabbed the bowl from her, smiling cheekily.

"Well, here's the clincher," said Alicia. "About the time I was talking to Roger—he's my buddy down at the police station—his boss, Inspector Ward, was reviewing CCTV footage of the car park at the golf club. They have someone who looks a lot like Rosa on camera, leaving at precisely 4:37 p.m."

She flashed Anders another look.

"Sprung!" said Missy excitedly.

"Exactly, and then with the evidence of the affair—apparently they found a bunch of saucy texts from Arthur on Rosa's phone when they picked her up—it's motive, means and opportunity."

"The holly trinity!" gasped Claire, clapping her hands with delight.

Lynette sat forward. "What I still don't get, though, is where Niles fits into all of this?"

Alicia shrugged. "He doesn't, he's perfectly innocent. At least, when it comes to Arthur's death."

"So why did he ram into Missy then?"

"*What?*" cried Missy, and Lynette held a hand up to placate her.

"I'm being melodramatic. It was probably just a strange coincidence." She proceeded to tell them all about Niles' battered black BMW. "The more I think about it, the more I think that it *has* to be a coincidence. I mean, there has to be more than one old battered Beamer in this city, right? Otherwise it doesn't make any sense."

When Missy looked at her, not quite buying it, she added, "Why, pray tell, would Niles want to hurt you, Missy? He doesn't even know you, does he?"

"No, I've never even seen the guy," she said.

This seemed to relax her a little and she chomped on her wine glass giving it some thought.

Eventually, Anders sat back and said, "Well you Finlay girls have certainly done some good sleuthing. Especially you Alicia. You should be proud of yourself."

"Don't be silly," she said. "We didn't do this alone. We can all give ourselves a pat on the back. It was a *team* effort."

"True, but having said that I hate to put a dampener on it all—"

"But you will," interrupted Perry, glaring at him.

"Yes, I'm sorry but I will. Where, exactly, does all of this leave poor Barbara?"

The group turned to Alicia, hopeful she had the answers to this riddle, too, but she held her palms out, empty handed, then sat back in her own chair, deflated.

"Sorry, guys, but that I do not know."

CHAPTER 28

"Rosa murdered Barbara," Perry declared dramatically. "She *must* have. Surely this proves that she would do anything to have Arthur to herself. Must have kidnapped Barbara to get her out of the way, and stashed her body somewhere, probably up near Hornsby station."

"That's certainly what the police think, and they're interrogating her as we speak." Alicia hesitated. "I'm just not convinced."

"Why?" he demanded. "This is categorical proof that Rosa has a violent streak. I'm just glad I didn't spill any crumbs on the carpet last time we were there." He mock shuddered.

Alicia was shaking her head. "I know, it would be very convenient if we could point the finger at Rosa. But Roger tells me that she is taking no responsibility for that one, adamantly refuses to take the blame for Barbara. Insists she has no idea where the woman is. And, for some reason, I believe her."

"If that's true, and I'm not saying I think it is," said Anders, "then that leaves us back at square one."

They all looked deflated and sat sipping their wine for several minutes, the celebratory air now dissipated.

"Maybe we have to accept," Anders said eventually, "that we'll never know what happened to Barbara. Maybe Rosa did kill her and will never confess. Or maybe Arthur had something to do with it and with his death goes the secret we've been looking for."

"Oh you're so optimistic this evening," groaned Perry.

"Sorry, but we need to face facts. Maybe we've taken this search as far as we can, people."

He looked around the table and they began to nod one by one, all except for Alicia. She was not willing to give up just yet and she was furious with Anders for trying to turn the rest of them.

"Anders I told you before, if you want to walk away—"

"I'm just saying—"

She held her hands up to him and then turned to the group, who were now frowning, wondering what was going on between these two.

"Listen, if anyone else wants to opt out now, please do. This amateur investigation of ours is not compulsory. Never was. It's certainly not what you signed up for." Her eyes flickered to Anders and back again. "The way I see it, we can still find Barbara. There are still some valuable clues we haven't even looked into."

"Like what?" This was Lynette.

"Like the missing letter."

Alicia knew she was grasping at straws, but she couldn't just let it drop, not when it felt like they were so close.

"What missing letter?" asked Perry, stifling a yawn.

"Remember the police said that Barbara posted a letter from a post box on Pitt Street the day she disappeared? What was in that letter? Whatever happened to it? We never did find out."

"Could've been a bill, something dull and unrelated," suggested Claire.

"Or it could have been a suicide note," countered Perry.

"No way," said Lynette. "Niles told me she wouldn't just do that, she'd tell him first. She told him everything."

"Maybe she did," said Perry. "Maybe that's what was in the missing letter."

"Then why didn't Niles tell us? Or the cops? You asked him about the letter, Alicia, and he said she hadn't sent him one."

Alicia sat forward. "No, no, he said he hadn't *received* one. That's quite a different thing."

"What do you mean?" Lynette asked and then stopped. "Oh, of course, he couldn't have received the letter. I can't believe we didn't think of that earlier."

The other club members looked from sister to sister confused, so Alicia explained: "Barbara was seen posting the letter on the Saturday that she disappeared, right? But we all know that mail doesn't get sent on weekends. So that post box would not have been emptied until the following Monday. So, by the time it got sent—"

"It wouldn't have got into Niles' mailbox until the Tuesday at the earliest," interrupted Lynette. "But Niles was evicted from his place the day before, on the *Monday*. He probably hasn't even been back since then—he said the landlord had changed the locks, so chances are he can't even get into the building to check his mail. Oh. My. God. The letter could be sitting at his old apartment block, just waiting for someone to discover it. It could hold all the answers."

They began to chatter excitedly, their enthusiasm miraculously renewed. All except for Anders who was leaning back in his chair, drinking his wine and looking depressed.

"We need to get hold of that letter," said Alicia cutting through the noise.

"I'll call Niles now," said Lynette, reaching for her handbag. "Get him to rush over and get it."

While Lynette found her phone, looked up the number for the Just Beachy Café and then stepped outside to place the call, the other members of the book club continued to talk excitedly between mouthfuls of wine and the final scraps from the platters. Within minutes Lynette was back but the look on her face was not encouraging.

"You want the good news or the bad news?"

"Both!" screamed Missy.

"The good news is, we were right. Niles hasn't been back to get his mail since he got kicked out. The bad news is, the ex-landlord is way too efficient, and called Niles just today to tell him he was redirecting his mail to the café."

Alicia's heart flagged. "So are you saying it's out there in snail mail land somewhere?"

Lynette nodded gloomily. "I think so. I asked Niles to call his landlord pronto to see if it's already left, but I don't like our chances."

She sat back down and began munching on a stray alfalfa sprout despondently. Within minutes her phone was beeping loudly. She stared at it.

"It's a text from Niles," she told them, tapping to retrieve the message. "Damn it. The mail was redirected this morning, won't get to Balmoral until tomorrow arvo if we're lucky. Niles also says the landlord can't recall if there was any letter from Barbara. He didn't notice."

They all groaned.

"This is far too frustrating," said Claire. "Now I can really empathise with Hercule Poirot and Jane Marple. Investigating is so *gruelling*."

"While we're chasing up loose ends," said Anders suddenly. "We never did work out why Rosa would place an ad in the newspaper classifieds. Anyone got any thoughts on that?"

Alicia stared at him, confounded. She could not work the guy out at all. One minute he was cold, the next he was hot.

"You're right, Anders, what was *that* about?" said Lynette. "You know, it's funny the way there's all these odd little clues that seem to lead us absolutely nowhere.

I was telling Alicia how it reminds me of a line I just read in *Murder on the Orient Express*."

"Oh?" said Missy, intrigued.

"You know the drill: they're on the train and Poirot has just found the body of a man stabbed 12 times in his compartment. He looks around and there's a bunch of clues just sitting there by the dead body—a monogrammed hanky, a pipe cleaner, a burnt letter, that kind of thing. He says something like, *There are too many clues in this room*.'" She paused. "I was thinking about this earlier today. That's exactly what this case is like: too many clues. They're confusing us."

"Maybe they're supposed to," said Missy.

"Speaking of clues," said Perry. "We never did track down that missing jewel, either. You know, the one that was sent to somebody who works in Hydro, or something like that."

"Hydro!" said Alicia, dropping her glass to the table and almost spilling the contents across it. "Oh my god, with all the excitement over Rosa, I forgot all about it!"

She leaned down and grabbed her handbag that had been wedged underneath her chair, and within seconds was showing off the magnetic ad for the Hydro Majestic.

"According to this, it's a luxury spa," she told them. "Holly tells me it's not her mum's normal hang. I meant to Google it at work but forgot all about it."

"Oh, I remember this place," said Claire, taking it from her. "It's a stunning spa resort up in the Blue Mountains. I would have mentioned it the other day when we were discussing the Hydro but I thought it had closed down."

"Then why are they advertising?" asked Alicia. "This doesn't look old and see at the bottom, there, Claire, it says, 'Now taking bookings'."

"Let's find out," said Lynette grabbing it from Claire and then keying the name into her smartphone. She logged online and began tapping away.

"Yep, here is it. Oh it looks very fancy schmancy."

She held the phone out so they could see the image of a stunning, whitewashed hotel on its tiny screen. Alicia jumped up and peered over her sister's shoulder as she scrolled down the page to find out more.

"Says it's been refurbished. Only just reopened about a month ago."

Alicia threw one hand to her mouth. "Oh my. That's it! I've been so blind. What's the contact number for it, Lynette?"

"Hang on, I'll find out." She pressed a link and a phone number and address popped up.

Alicia grabbed her own phone again and dialled the number while the rest of the group stared at her, open-mouthed, not quite sure what she was up to, but electrified nonetheless. Even Anders looked reinvigorated and had stopped clutching onto his wine glass like a buoy.

"Good evening, this is the Hydro Majestic, how can I help you?" came a chirpy man's voice from the other end.

"Oh, hello there," Alicia said breezily, winking at the others. "I'm looking for Barbara Parlour."

Perry gasped, Anders' eyes narrowed and the others just looked confused.

"I'm sorry?" came the voice at the other end of the line.

"Um, could you put me through to Barbara Parlour's room, please?"

Alicia crossed her fingers and waited.

CHAPTER 29

Most members of the book club had now deserted the restaurant, anxious to get home and appease loved ones. All that remained were Missy, who was gathering her things to go, Lynette, who was counting the cash they had all dumped in front of her, and Alicia who was leaning across the table, head in her hands, looking dejected.

"Well what did you expect?" said Lynette, giving her a prod. "Did you really think that Barbara was hanging out at some luxury spa oblivious to the fact that there's an international search underway for her? Not to mention a dead husband and an orphaned child?"

Alicia groaned. "Alright, alright it's a bit out there, I know, but it does happen."

"When, Alicia, when does it happen?"

Missy, who was just standing up to go said, rather flippantly, "Well, it happened to Agatha Christie of course." She stopped and giggled. "But there I go again, rabbiting on about Agatha Christie! Okay you two, try to cheer up and I'll see you—"

Alicia sat up. "What did you just say, Missy?"

Missy stopped and looked at her, a little flustered now. "Oh, sorry, I'm just saying, you know, that Agatha Christie did exactly that. A million years ago of course."

When both sisters stared at her, baffled, she added, "You guys must have heard that story before? You know, when she disappeared in real life? Went walkabout for a week or so. There's a good book about it in the library, actually. Called *Missing for Ten Days* or something like that. It has all the juicy details—"

"Just tell us what happened," interrupted Alicia. "To Agatha. This vaguely rings a bell."

Missy dropped her bag on the table and sat back down. "Well, that's the thing; it was such a mystery at the time. And involving the queen of mystery herself! You couldn't have made up a better story. You see, one day, back in 1925 or thereabouts, Agatha Christie just took off in her car and no one had a clue where she'd disappeared to. She just had a coat and handbag, nothing else apparently, and the police became suspicious that she'd been murdered. There was a giant manhunt for her body. They all assumed the cheating first husband, Archie Christie, had killed her and dumped her body in some lake. Police even drained it, looking for her, would you believe?"

"So what had happened to her?" asked Lynette, enthralled.

"Well, possum, it turns out she was hiding out at some luxury spa pretending to be someone else. Claims she had amnesia or something, but no one really knows, and Agatha has never spoken about it. So the mystery lives on."

"God, this sounds so familiar, I do know this story," stammered Alicia. "I just can't remember all the details."

"But hang on," said Lynette. "What was she doing there if she didn't have amnesia?"

"Personally, I reckon she was teaching the unfaithful husband a lesson."

"Let me get this straight," said Lynette. "You're saying that in real life, Agatha Christie disappeared and was hanging out for over a week at some hotel and no one knew who she was? Sorry, Missy, but that sounds a bit far-fetched. I mean she was a pretty famous author even while she was alive."

"Her *name* was famous," Missy reminded her. "But you have to understand this was before the internet and TV gossip shows and the like. Celebrities, especially authors, weren't so recognisable back then. You didn't have a million pictures of them popping up everywhere. It's not like today where everyone knows exactly what J.K. Rowling looks like. Besides she was using a pseudonym remember."

"That's it!" squealed Alicia. "Why didn't I see it earlier?" She turned back to Missy. "Do you know what name Agatha went under?"

"At the spa? Not off the top of my head, no." She paused. "Pity Barbara's missing. She would know. I looked up her file again at the library the other day and she took that very book out, the one I just mentioned, *Missing for 10 Days*, oh about a month before the book club started. The story would be fresh in her mind."

The look of shock that crossed Alicia's face was priceless. "Oh my God, oh my God, oh my God!" she squealed, catching the eyes of the few remaining patrons and staff. "Has she returned it?"

"Yeah, why?"

Alicia glanced at her watch then grabbed her handbag and jumped to her feet. "Come on, we've got to go!"

"Go? Where?" said Missy and Lynette in unison.

"To the library, of course! We need to get that book out and we need to get it now!"

CHAPTER 30

Ten minutes later the three women were standing out the front of the library where Missy worked. She had her keys in her hand and a deep frown across her brow.

"I can not believe I let you talk me into this," she told Alicia who was tapping her toes impatiently beside her. "Geraldine will have my hide if she finds out I'm opening up now. It's 10:45 p.m! I mean, it's one thing to let you guys hang out a bit late one evening—I could just pretend I was catching up on filing, it's not like I ever have my work done on time—but to illegally open this late? Not sure how I'm going to explain this one, and she's looking for any excuse to get rid of me."

"It will all be worth it in the long run, I promise you," said Alicia. "I really appreciate this, Missy."

"It can't wait until tomorrow?"

"Nope, no way. I need that Agatha Christie book and I need it *now*. Can't you see? She's following it like a script. But I don't have all the details…"

Missy didn't quite know what Alicia was talking about but took the keys and opened the door anyway, rushing inside to turn off the alarm, before ushering the sisters in. "I know I said to go back to Agatha Christie but I didn't mean it this literally." Alicia smiled. "I'm not going to turn the main lights on, they'll get spotted from the street, but here…"

She strode over to a back room and flicked the switch there. "This will give us enough light to go by. Okay, let's be quick, me lovelies. Now, it's called *Missing for 10 Days* or *Ten Missing Days* or something like that, and I'm pretty sure it's in reference…" She strode across to the relevant section. "Not going to switch the computers on either, that's a dead giveaway. We can find it if we hunt around."

"You don't know the author's name?" asked Lynette.

"Normally I do. It's right on the tip of my tongue, but all this excitement is turning my brain to mush… Doesn't matter, if we search we should be able to find it. It's a smallish book, white cover, picture of Agatha on the front." She stopped and giggled. "Duh! It'll be under C for Christie. I am such a dunce tonight."

She raced along the aisle and began scanning the shelf marked 'C'. It did not take long for Missy to give a little yelp. She promptly shooshed herself.

"Here it is," she whispered, pulling a book out and holding it up for them to see.

Titled *Eleven Missing Days: The Agatha Christie Mystery*, it was written by C.G. Johnson and was quite a slim book, clearly devoted to that specific time in Christie's life.

"This shouldn't take too long," said Lynette grabbing it from her and flicking through the pages. "What are you hoping to find in here, Alicia?"

"More clues." She turned to Missy. "Do you need to check it out?"

"No way, José. It'll record the time and then I really will be in trouble. No, as far as I'm concerned you stole it earlier today and it has nothing to do with me! Just get it back quietly and no one will ever know."

She snatched the book from Lynette and thrust it into Alicia's hands as though it was a hot potato.

"Fine by me," said Alicia. "Come on, let's get out of here. I've got some serious reading to do."

Later that night, as Missy made her way home and Lynette headed off to bed, Alicia returned to her own room, changed into pyjamas, slipped under her bed covers and began to read. The story that unravelled before her was enthralling.

It also sent prickles of anger racing through her body.

CHAPTER 31

The Blue Mountains is a pleasant train ride from Central Station in the heart of Sydney, and it took Alicia just under two hours to reach Medlow Bath, home to the wondrous Hydro Majestic Hotel. She had brought *Eleven Missing Days* with her to pass the time, but couldn't help thinking instead of Anders, and his morning visit.

The doctor had shown up just before 8:00 a.m. Both sisters were awake and getting ready when they heard a firm knock on the front door. Lynette was preparing for work, she couldn't take any more time off if she wanted to survive the week at Mario's, but Alicia had already called Ginny to tell her she would not be in. It was time to put the mystery to bed at last.

"Hey, Lis! It's Anders, for you," called Lynette from downstairs.

Alicia looked up with a start from the sink where she was brushing her teeth. She quickly finished up, checked her reflection in the mirror, pulling a hand through her tousled hair, and padded down the stairs. Anders was standing at the bottom, his lank frame leaning against the wall, his old gym bag by his feet. He gave her a shy smile and she tried to smile back but she was still smarting from the night before.

"Have you got a minute?" he asked.

She glanced at her watch.

"Twenty of them, then I have to run. I've got a train to catch."

"That's all I need," he said and followed her inside.

Alicia led the way through the lounge room and out to the tiny backyard. Tiny was an understatement. It was *minuscule*. But Alicia loved it, nonetheless. It was fenced in by tall brick walls on three sides, all of which were covered in a lush mixture of hot pink bougainvillea and fluorescent green vines. There were two wooden deck chairs around a small rotting wicker table, which was overflowing with various citronella candles, books and magazines. A slightly mouldy, striped hammock was dangling from a hook on one wall, waiting to be connected. When it was hung it swallowed up the entire space, but was well worth it if you were on your own and felt like floating on air. Today Alicia chose one of the chairs and indicated for Anders to take the other, which he did.

He was obviously dressed for work in a smart dark blue fitted suit and crisp white shirt. His steel-grey tie was loose around his neck, waiting to be tightened. He rubbed a hand through his own tousled hair and looked at her sheepishly.

"I've come to apologise."

"No need—" she said but he cut her off.

"No, let me say this, please, Alicia. Let me get it all out before you say anything, promise?"

She nodded and sat back.

"What I was trying to say at the pub on Sunday… I stuffed it up big time. It all came out wrong…"

"Anders—"

"Hey! You promised I could finish."

She pretended to zip her lips shut and he half smiled.

"I was not saying I *don't* want to be part of the book club. Jesus, I love this club. I haven't had so much fun in ages.

I know that sounds awful, I feel bad for the Parlours, I just mean, it's invigorating being part of all of this."

She nodded. She felt the same way.

He smiled again. "Well, if truth be told, Missy and Perry both drive me nuts half the time, but I don't want out. Not at all." He took a deep breath. "What I was trying to say so appallingly was that I am worried about you."

"Me? Oops, sorry!" She flung a hand to her mouth. She'd forgotten she wasn't to speak.

"Yes, you. You seem to be doing most of the heavy lifting in this investigation and I'm worried you'll get hurt." He looked into her eyes then and there was an intensity she hadn't seen before. "When I phoned your house the other day and Lynette told me you were going to see Wanda… going to accuse her of God knows what, well I got really worried. I just wish you'd asked me, or anyone to go along with you. To back you up. You shouldn't have to do all this by yourself. And it's potentially dangerous. I mean, sure, Wanda ended up getting let off, but even the police thought she was a killer at one point. You need to be careful, to stop and not rush in. This was supposed to be a bit of fun, it wasn't supposed to be life threatening. That's all I was trying to say. And Jesus I botched it up badly…"

He shook his head at himself and gave her another of his breathtaking, heart-stopping, cold shower-inducing smiles. Alicia held a hand up to speak and he laughed then gave her the go-ahead.

"Anders, first up, I also need to apologise—"

"No, you—"

She wagged a finger at him. "Hey! Now it's my turn to speak, zip it!"

He smiled and shut his mouth.

"I never gave you a chance to finish what you were saying at the pub. I just leapt up and jumped down your throat. I read you all wrong and I'm sorry."

He nodded, showing he accepted her apology.

"However," she said. "You must not worry about me. I am touched by your concern, really I am, but I am perfectly safe."

"How do you know that?"

"I know that because, while you may be the first person to turn up to every event, I am the first person to see danger, even when it's not there." She sighed. "Almost always when it's not there." He looked at her confused. "It's hard to explain, but I have a very dark mind. Ask Lynette. I'm a glass-is-half-empty, guilty-until-proven-innocent kind of girl. That's my burden to bear. I always see the worst in people and events. I am not going to get myself into any kind of danger because I will conjure it up long before it actually occurs."

He stared at her, eyes squinting slightly through an unruly fringe. "I don't know what you're on about," he said at last. "Just promise me you'll take care."

"I promise. I'll be fine. Why are you so worried about me, anyway? Do I really come across as little Miss Vulnerable?"

He laughed. "Quite the opposite."

"Good, so stop worrying! You're worse than my mother and she's over 2,000 kilometres away. I can take care of myself, Anders."

"I know, I know. I… I just care about you, that's all."

Her heart squeezed. She felt breathless and she felt angry, too, because he had a wife and he shouldn't be caring about her. She glanced at her watch. "I should probably get my skates on."

"It's just, well there was one other thing…"

"Yes?"

"It's about my wife."

She held a hand up. "Look, it's really none of my business—"

"Please, I need to tell you this."

She nodded and sat back, waiting for him to gather his thoughts, just as Lynette appeared at the sliding door.

"Hey, guys, hate to break up your D&M," she said, "but can I have a quick word, Alicia?"

Anders stared at her curiously as she got up and stepped back inside with her sister.

Alicia asked, "Did you hear back from Niles?"

Lynette nodded, smiling widely. "It's just like you thought. Niles did lend his car to his sister. That last Tuesday he saw Barbara, when she drove to his café, she pretended her car was playing up and asked to borrow his old Beamer to 'run some errands'. Or so she said. He reckons she had it a good hour or so. Easily could have done it."

Now Alicia was smiling. "I knew it! The pieces are all falling into place."

"But why would she—"

"I'll explain it all later, I promise. I'd better get back out there." She nodded her head to where Anders was sitting quietly watching them through the glass door.

"Alright then. I've got to go anyway, I'm running late and you will be too if you don't hurry things up." They exchanged a quick hug. "Promise me you'll be super careful? And call me the second you get back?"

"I promise," she said.

"And good luck," Lynette said, also indicating the man outside.

Alicia smirked at her, then stepped outside and returned to her seat across from Anders. He waited until he heard Lynette slam the front door shut before he continued.

"We're separated," he said eventually. "My wife, Vanessa, and I. She's moved out."

"Oh," Alicia said. She didn't know how she felt about that. Separations could be messy. They could also be reconciled.

"We're not getting back together," he said, as if reading her mind. "It's over, well and truly over. Believe me…" He hesitated. "God this sounds like the plot of a really bad Gwyneth Paltrow movie. It's the reason I didn't want to talk about it at the pub, it's pathetic really."

"What?"

"I found Vanessa in bed…" He paused again. "She and my brother…"

He couldn't meet her eyes suddenly, but she could read the shame in his tense jaw and the way his shoulders hunched over. He looked battered, defensive, humiliated, and she wanted to reach over and embrace him.

Instead she placed one hand over his and said, "Your wife was sleeping with your brother?" He nodded. "I'm so sorry. When was this?

"Three months ago."

Oh, that makes it raw, she thought, bleeding for him and herself at the same time. He wouldn't be too keen on any woman at this point in the game. How could he be? It was the ultimate betrayal.

"Are they…?"

"Still together? Yep. The plot gets even better than that. She's pregnant now."

"Oh God."

Anders looked away, his eyes sheepish, then back at her.

"It's not really something I like to talk about, it's the reason I didn't tell you at the pub. But I should have and I'm sorry. It's just so bloody humiliating, and it's split my family in two as you can imagine. I'd… I'd appreciate it if you didn't mention this to anyone at Book Club."

"Of course not." She smiled at him warmly. "Thanks for letting me know."

He nodded then stood up. "Anyway, I'd better let you go. Sounds like you've got a train to catch. Where you off to?"

Alicia hesitated. She wanted to tell him where she was going, wanted to elaborate on what she had discovered last night but she had a hunch he would try to talk her out of it. Or, worse, come with her. She didn't want that. Not now. She needed to get her head together. She needed to ignore his advice.

"I'll explain it all later," she said instead and guided him back through the house to the front door.

He looked at her suspiciously but let it drop.

"Let's talk later, okay?"

"Absolutely," she said, and was rewarded with his electric smile in return.

Alicia couldn't help smiling to herself now as she sat, staring out of the train window as it made its way up the mountain towards Medlow Bath. She tried to shake Anders from her mind but couldn't stop feeling happy and relieved in equal measure. She was not only relieved he was staying in the club, she was happy he'd confided in her about his wife. She didn't know what that meant for her, what he really felt for her, but it opened a door she had thought was firmly shut. *Perhaps she and the good doctor had a chance, after all?*

"Stop it!" she hissed to herself out loud, catching the eye of a fellow passenger. Ignoring him she returned to staring, smiling, out at the view.

When the train arrived at Medlow Bath station, Alicia finally put all thoughts of Anders aside, grabbed her bag and jumped off. She glanced around then began walking south on the Great Western Highway, towards Bellevue Crescent. Within minutes she was standing outside a sprawling, whitewashed hotel that clung to the escarpment like an aging Hollywood beauty. She took a deep breath, strode into the lobby and grinned.

It was as though she had just stepped back in time, back to the halcyon days of Agatha Christie herself. Or even earlier, to Jane Austen's time.

The Hydro Majestic is aptly named with extensive marbled floors, rich carpets and extravagant art deco arches and dome. It began life as a humble Edwardian house hotel and Australia's first hydropathic resort back in 1904, and reached its peak after World War 2 when it was considered one of the grandest hotels in the country. It soon became a favourite haunt for Prime Ministers, opera singers and even Sherlock Holmes' creator Sir Arthur Conan Doyle.

Eventually, however, time and neglect saw its beauty fade and it began to crumble into insignificance over recent times.

Looking around her now, it was clear to Alicia that this most recent makeover had restored it to its former glory. Today there was a magnificent ballroom, convention rooms, plush lounges, a spa and gleaming restaurant with a gilded ceiling and café, but she bypassed them all and headed straight for the front desk where a receptionist was smiling politely.

"Yes Ma'am, how can I help you?"

"Hi there, I'm looking for Teresa Neele, please."

The receptionist glanced into her screen and began tapping at the keyboard. Still smiling she said, "I'm sorry, but there's no one here by that name. Can you spell it?"

Alicia did and the computer still said no. She deflated, feeling like her heart had stopped. *So much for that theory,* she thought.

Teresa Neele had been the name that Agatha Christie had used at the Harrogate Hydro where she hid in December 1926—during 11 long days while all of England held their breaths and searched for her. According to the book, the name Agatha chose was really a variation of Nancy Neele, the real name of her husband's mistress at the time.

Teresa Neele was also the name Agatha used when she placed a mysterious advertisement in a newspaper while she was in hiding. That ad had read: *Friends and relatives of Teresa Neele, late of South Africa, please communicate. Write Box R702, The Times, EC4.'* It was almost a replica of the ad that Anders had found referring to Rosa Lopez of the Philippines.

That's when the penny dropped. Alicia's heart started pumping again. *How could she be so stupid?* She turned back to the receptionist.

"How about Rosa Lopez?"

The woman smiled, a little less warmly this time, and glanced back at her screen. Within seconds she was nodding her head.

"Yes, we do have a Rosa Lopez here. Shall I give her room a call?"

"Don't bother," said Alicia. "I think I know where she is. Room five, right?"

The receptionist glanced at the screen and looked surprised so Alicia took this as confirmation and strode across the lobby towards a sign marked 'Accommodation'.

At Room 5 she knocked loudly. There was no answer. Alicia knocked again to no avail. But she would not be beaten, not after all the hard work she'd done. After a few minutes, Alicia returned to the foyer and glanced across at the spacious café on one side. It was now just after 10:00 a.m. and she could hear the clink of china cups.

High Tea time.

How appropriate, she thought.

As Alicia entered the café, she spotted her, sitting alone at a corner table, beside a large glass window. Alicia took another deep breath, waved the waitress away and strode over.

"Hello Barbara," she said. "I thought I'd find you here."

CHAPTER 32

Barbara Parlour looked up from her book with a start and for one brief moment looked like she had her own case of amnesia, staring at Alicia blankly before recognition flooded across her face.

"Oh, *Alicia Finlay*. Fancy meeting you here." She smiled as though greeting an old friend and indicated the chair beside her. "Will you join me? I've just ordered a Darjeeling. Much lighter than English Breakfast. Doesn't even need milk."

Alicia stared at her for a few seconds, bewildered by her reaction. *So that was how she was going to play it, eh?*

She sat down as the older woman placed her book to one side and called the waitress over. She placed another tea order then they stared at each other for a few minutes without speaking.

Today Barbara looked dramatically different from the first time Alicia had met her. Her ash blond hair had been recently streaked with bright, golden highlights and blow-waved into a voluminous curled bob around her face. She had a bright red silk blouse on with red and green beads dangling around her neck, and deep red lipstick which made her look bold and confident; the antithesis of bashful Book Club Barbara.

Beside her was a lavish three-tiered plate of delicate, iced cupcakes, powdery Turkish Delight, cream-laden scones, and sandwiches crammed with smoked salmon and capers. She offered one to Alicia, who shook her head no.

"So," Barbara said eventually, "how did you find me?"

Her tone was more confident, too, the nervousness gone.

"It took a while, obviously, but we worked it out."

"God knows I left enough clues. I thought you'd be quicker, to be frank. You people are no match for Hercule Poirot!"

Alicia frowned, anger bubbling inside. She swallowed it back down and waited until the tea had been brought before speaking again.

"You led us on a very merry chase, Barbara. We all feel a little stupid to be honest, and pretty pissed off." Barbara looked surprised by this. "What did you think? We were worried about you, Barbara! We honestly thought someone had kidnapped you or worse. We even suspected poor Arthur—"

"*Poor Arthur* my foot," she hissed back.

"He's dead, you know."

Barbara glanced out of the window at the glorious mountain view. It was such a clear day you could see right across to the Three Sisters rock formation and beyond. She glanced back.

"Yes, well, I did hear that. But it wasn't my intention."

"It wasn't your *intention*?" Alicia couldn't believe the woman's utter lack of emotion. "He was found clubbed over the head. Your daughter is distraught."

"Oh Holly'll survive," she said dismissively then picked up her teacup and took a long, slow sip.

Alicia shook her head in astonishment. This woman was a monster, but screaming at her was not going to get any answers. Instead, she calmed herself down and said, "Did you do all this just to get back at Arthur?"

Barbara took another sip of tea and shrugged. "He could come across as charming when he wanted to, but Arthur Parlour was a bastard. He started sleeping around on me almost from the start. We'd been back from our honeymoon two weeks when I found lipstick on his collar." She gave a wry smile. "How cliché."

"So why didn't you divorce him?"

"He wouldn't let me, said it would ruin his chances of promotion at work, and later, at the ballot box."

Alicia scoffed. "That is ridiculous. It's not 1926 anymore, Barbara. Nobody cares about divorce these days; besides, you could easily have left *him*. But you didn't want to leave him, did you? Just like your husband told us…" She paused, almost laughed. "Hell, *everyone* told us! Wanda, Holly, even your own brother. They all told us you were a drama queen, Barbara, you *relished* the drama. And we didn't believe them. Our silly little book club stood up for you. Fought tooth and nail for you. Tell me, Barbara, did you delight in knowing that we were all out there worried about you? Frantically trying to find you? Did you think about your daughter during any of this?"

Barbara's eyes flared up, a scowl crossed her face. "Stop acting like she's some sort of saint! Holly never gave me a thought, so why should I consider her?"

"Because you're her *mother*, Barbara. You're supposed to be the grown-up. Or at least, I thought you were."

"You don't know me at all," she snapped, clunking her teacup down so loudly several people looked around. She took a deep, calming breath of her own. "All I wanted to do was give my husband a wake-up call." Her eyes suddenly lit up, her mood excited now. "I had been reading a book about Agatha Christie, how she took off and scared her husband half to death. I thought, what a grand idea! I'll disappear for a bit, see if he even notices." She smiled. "You can blame Agatha Christie! She's the one who popped the idea into my head. If I hadn't read that book…"

"Is that why you ran down poor Missy?"

Barbara stopped smiling. "Sorry?"

"I know you were the one who tried to run Missy over with the BMW."

Her eyes darted back and forth. "I don't know what you're talking about. I don't even own a BMW. As for Missy, why would I want to—"

"Oh give me a break, Barbara. You recognised Missy that first day at Book Club. Or rather, she recognised you from the library and it freaked you out. I noticed it straight away. Why was that?"

Barbara was obviously wrestling with her conscience, or what little she had of one, and had turned very quiet so Alicia ploughed on, desperate to keep her talking.

"We know how it went down, Barbara. Your brother owns the BMW. Lynette spotted it a few days ago at his café with dents all over it. We know that you borrowed it the Tuesday before you hosted Book Club, the Tuesday that Missy got run over. Niles has already confirmed all of this so don't bother denying it. You pretended your car was playing up and took his Beamer which, conveniently, had tinted windows, and drove back across the Harbour Bridge, waited for Missy's scheduled lunch break—which you'd already ascertained was at noon because she told us about it at that first book club gathering at my place. Then you tried to kill her."

"No! No, I just wanted to hurt her, that's all."

"*Why?*"

Barbara sighed and placed her hands on the table, admiring her long, polished nails as she did so. They looked like they had only recently been manicured.

"You're right, I was quite startled to see Missy at that first get-together at your place. What were the chances? She recognised me instantly, of course, from the library, and I panicked that she'd look up my library file and discover I took that bloody book out. The one on Agatha Christie's disappearance. Then she'd put two and two together and give the game away far too quickly. I needed to buy some extra time."

Alicia dug into her handbag and produced *Eleven Missing Days*, dropping it onto the table in front of Barbara. The older woman smiled and picked it up.

"Yes, this is the one." She flicked through it, a slight smile on her lips. "How ironic. I use a library well out of my local area and I still get busted." The smile deflated. "But that's all it was, honestly. I didn't want to kill her, really I didn't. I was hoping maybe she'd break a leg or twist an ankle and couldn't come to the next book club. I just wanted to scare her off until I had set my plan in motion."

"So that's why you joined our club? Hoping to drag us all into your little scheme. Why? Because you figured we'd be inquisitive, mystery-loving types?"

"Exactly. I needed somebody to notice when I disappeared. I couldn't rely on Arthur for that. He wouldn't have reported me missing for weeks. This spa bill would be through the roof." She smiled, looking shameless again. "I'd been plotting this for ages, was thinking of enlisting my brother in the whole scheme but he can't be relied on at the best of times. Then I spotted your silly little advertisement in the classifieds. You can't imagine how excited I was! I had such fun writing to you, all soppy and depressed. I knew I'd hook you in, and I knew my sudden disappearance would catch your eye. You couldn't help but investigate."

Alicia frowned, not sure if she was being complimented or criticised. "We were genuinely worried Barbara. We've all spent hours and hours on this trying to find you. We've neglected our own friends, families, jobs." She paused and took a sip of her tea, trying again to calm down. "So that number for the battered women's shelter on the white board—you left that for us to see? To make Arthur look dangerous?"

"Yes I did, and I make no apology for it. I knew Holly wouldn't notice. She wouldn't notice if the bloody house was on fire. Don't you see, I *had* to get you guys involved.

That's why I insisted on holding the first club at my house. I needed to plant the clues. I knew you'd spot that kind of stuff and hoped you'd mention it to the police or, better yet, to the press. I wanted Arthur to get a rude shock. I wanted him to come under suspicion, to get questioned and accused of doing away with me. I wanted to teach him a lesson."

"Ahh," said Alicia. "That's what you meant the day you disappeared, when you told Jake, the tennis coach, that you had another lesson on. You meant you were about to teach Arthur a lesson." Barbara nodded smugly. "But it's just so extreme—"

"He *deserved* it. He treated me appallingly. He needed to learn a lesson."

"But he never did beat you up, did he?" She shook her head no. "And the scarves around the neck, the nervousness?"

"All an act. I did a little theatre work in my time, you know?"

There was a sickening blush of pride in her cheeks and Alicia wanted to stand up and swipe it away. "I know," she said instead. "We all missed that clue initially. Glaring as it was. Everyone told us you were a drama queen. Yet still we didn't take it literally. I have to admit, you were good, you had us all convinced. We really believed you were a victim, a vulnerable, hapless victim."

"Ha! Never!" She waved a salmon sandwich in the air.

"So tell me, the mysterious phone call you got the day you hosted Book Club? The hang-up that Lynette and I witnessed…?"

"That was me." The blush of pride deepened. "I called from my mobile phone in the bedroom while you were fetching the lemonade in the kitchen. Clever aren't I?"

"And your suggestion for that Sunday's book club, *The Mysterious Affair at Styles*? Deliberate?"

She nodded, laughing. "Let's face it, shall we, I made it pretty damn easy for you! I mean, short of writing it in giant letters in the sky, I was making it all pretty clear that Arthur was a pig. That's why I can't believe it took you so long to work it all out." Then, reading the contempt on Alicia's face she quickly added, "I had to do all that, don't you see? I *had* to make you believe that Arthur was being unfaithful to me. I didn't know how to show you so I thought, what better way than a series of mysterious hang-ups? And he was you know, he was frightfully unfaithful."

"I know, Barbara. That's what got him killed, remember?"

Again she glanced away and out to that mountainous view, soaking it in as if she was simply on holidays.

"So, the newspaper appeal from Rosa Lopez to friends? You?"

Her eyes snapped back to Alicia. "Of course. Well, Agatha Christie did the same thing. She used the name Teresa Neele of course."

"And the jewellery you sent from the Strand Arcade?"

"Another clue. Agatha got a ring repaired and sent that to Teresa Neele at the Harrogate Hydro. Room number five. Oh, I had such luck getting the exact same room number as Agatha Christie! I hadn't expected *that*. An added bonus. I wanted to follow Agatha's path exactly, you see, have a little fun while I was at it. It took me weeks and weeks to think through, to plan and devise. That's why I couldn't have Missy going and giving the game away too quickly. If she mentioned that book at the next book club it'd be too obvious. I needed it to work, I'd had the most thrilling few weeks planning this whole thing. It *had* to work."

Then, noticing Alicia's now unrestrained look of disdain, she quickly added, "I was going to come back. *Of course* I was. I was going to return like nothing had happened, just as Agatha did, and then Arthur would be off the hook, but maybe he'd appreciate my presence a little more when I got back. I know it's juvenile, but hell, it worked for Agatha Christie."

"Er, no it didn't Barbara."

"Sorry?"

Alicia took the book from her and turned to the final chapter. "Sure, when Agatha went missing for 11 days, her husband, Archie, was accused of killing her and his adultery was splashed all over the headlines, but afterwards, when he found her at the spa and they returned home, tails between their legs, nothing had improved. That must have been the final straw. Archie divorced Agatha soon after and married Nancy. There was no happy ending for them." She snapped the book shut. "And there'll be no happy ending for you, either, Barbara."

Barbara sighed, scooping up a Turkish Delight. "Oh, well, I never did finish the book. It started to get boring…" She popped it in her mouth and proceeded to chew. "But, still, I achieved my goal. Arthur's name has been sullied. That's all the happy ending I need."

Alicia felt sick to her stomach. "He's more than 'sullied', Barbara. Your husband is dead. He was murdered."

"Not by me he wasn't. I heard that they're holding Rosa for that. Who knew she was a murderer as well as a traitorous slut? I knew she was sleeping with him. Well, not sleeping so much as having quickies in the pantry, in the bathroom, behind the pergola. Disgusting, juvenile behaviour. They were worse than Holly and Jake."

Alicia's eyebrows rose.

"Oh yes, I knew about them, too, but they were a class act compared to my husband and his whore. At least they had the decency to try to hide their affair. But not Arthur and Rosa. Oh, no, they flaunted it! He used to call her his princess. His 'precious Filipino princess'. Said I was little more than a useless maid. Couldn't even cook. What was the use of me? They laughed at me. Both of them, all the time. I heard them, giggling behind my back. Well, I showed them! I was the one holding Arthur's respectability in my hands. I was the one with all the power. Once I was gone, it was all downhill for him."

"He wanted you back, you know."

"Good. So he should." She sat forward then, a flicker of doubt appearing in her eyes for the first time. "Really? Did he say that?" Alicia nodded. "Well, I was coming back, you have to believe me, Alicia. I didn't even mean to stay away this long, it was just going to be a few days… I wrote a letter to my brother, I told him where I was. I just don't understand why he hasn't spoken up. It's very strange—"

"Niles never got your letter, Barbara. He got evicted from his apartment before it arrived. He has no idea where you are. He's come under suspicion, too, his café's about to fold. He's frantic."

Her jaw dropped. "So *that's* why he never said anything?" She sat back, giving it some thought, then picked up a scone and shoved it into her mouth, cream smudging her lips as she chewed. "In any case," she said, mid-mouthful, "it's not my fault. I wrote, I tried to explain, I can't help it if the letter never arrived."

As if this somehow assuaged her guilt.

"That's not good enough!" Alicia spat now, unable to control her anger any longer. "You could have *phoned*. Contacted the police. Why didn't you come forward when they found Arthur's body on the golf course? Why didn't you come back and see your daughter through all of that horror? She's all alone, Barbara. She's a mess, an absolute mess, and so is your brother."

Several patrons were now staring at the table but Alicia didn't care, and Barbara didn't seem to notice.

"I *was* coming back!" she cried. "I am… I'm checking out tomorrow, just ask the receptionist." She dabbed at her lips with a napkin.

"Not before time."

"I… I panicked, that's all. I… I thought the police might suspect me. I'm not even sure I've got an alibi for the time Arthur was killed, I spent most of that day sightseeing, alone. But now, well, now that they've pinned it on Rosa…"

"Now you think you can slink back and pretend everything is okay?"

Alicia felt furious again. It occurred to her now as she watched the 'miserable housewife' stuff herself full of sweets, oblivious to the depth of pain and trouble she had wreaked, that Barbara Parlour had actually been extraordinarily successful. She had achieved the ultimate revenge—her philandering husband was dead, his reputation destroyed, and his mistress was locked up for his murder. She could not have planned it any better. Alicia wondered whether Barbara knew about Wanda's affair with Arthur. She was certainly not going to mention it, but in any case Wanda, too, had been maimed along the way, her reputation ruined and her marriage in tatters.

She pushed her teacup aside and stood up. As she did so, she realised that Arthur, Rosa and Wanda were not the real victims in all of this, just as Archie Christie was not the true victim when Agatha did her own disappearing act all those years ago. In both stories, there was a young girl caught in the middle. Had any of these supposed 'grown-ups' stopped to consider how their behaviour would impact their children?

"You're heading off? So soon?" said Barbara, looking genuinely surprised.

Had she really believed that Alicia would sit back, sip Darjeeling and enjoy the scenery? Alicia shook her head at her again, nothing left to say. Then picked up the book, placed it back in her bag and walked away, feelings of anger and disgust bursting to the surface now.

As she strode out of the majestic hotel and back towards the train station, Hercule Poirot's words kept echoing in Alicia's head.

"Old sins have long shadows."

What lingering effect would this have on the already troubled Holly Parlour? That was the true legacy of Barbara Parlour's deadly charade.

PART 3

It was Sunday, 2:10 p.m. The third official meeting of the Murder Mystery Book Club was just getting under way, and the various members of the club were settling into deck chairs in the shady backyard of Perry's stylish terrace house. He had only recently renovated the place and, unlike many of the old terraces around Surry Hills, it was bright and breezy thanks to strategically placed skylights and an entire glassed wall at the back that afforded a great view of the small, lush backyard. There, Perry had placed an assortment of *hors d'oeuvres* and drinks, including gin and tonic and a fruit punch.

His flatmate, the 'randy author' he'd warned them about at that first book club, was nowhere to be seen and when Alicia asked about him, Perry exhaled loudly.

"Jonathan's in the UK at the mo', working with the cover designer on his new book."

"That's lucky," she said.

"You have no idea," he replied, disappearing into the kitchen before she could enquire further.

She glanced at Lynette who'd already got the full story and said, "I'll tell you all about it later."

Several members had brought copies of today's book, *Murder on the Orient Express*, but before they started dissecting it, they had the small matter of Barbara Parlour's reappearance to discuss. No one was interested in fiction when there was a real-life mystery to catch up on.

By now they all knew that Alicia had located Barbara alive and well, but several members still had plenty of questions and were leaning over Missy as she flicked through *Eleven Missing Days*, the same book that helped click the final pieces of the puzzle into place.

"So let me get this straight," said Perry who was still smarting from the whole affair. "Barbara staged her own disappearance and left a bunch of clues around so we'd be interested enough to investigate? And she got the idea from reading this book about Agatha Christie?"

"Yep," said Missy. "That's why she did all those strange things like get a ring repaired and sent to the hotel where she was staying. It's exactly what Agatha did all those decades ago. Except, in Barbara's case she addressed the ring to Rosa Lopez, her husband's lover, just as Agatha had addressed hers to Archie's lover. I guess it was to throw suspicion on Rosa. But yes, as Alicia says, she followed the script almost exactly. Get this…" Missy turned to a page that had been marked in the book. "According to this, before she disappeared, Agatha Christie left her wedding ring in her bedroom, then swept out of the house telling her maid that she was going to London."

"Ah! So that's why Barbara mentioned London to Rosa?" said Claire.

"Exactly. A fantastic red herring if ever I heard one. Agatha was also wearing a fur coat and carrying a large black bag, no luggage. She then drove off and her car was later found dumped near a quarry."

"And we know that Barbara took a fur coat, no luggage and dumped her car near a train station," said Lynette.

"She really did follow the story, almost exactly to the word," said Anders, sounding impressed. "That must have taken an amazing amount of planning."

"What I find even more amazing," said Alicia, "was how the same stuff-up that happened to Agatha Christie, also happened to Barbara Parlour."

"What do you mean?"

"I mean the letter to her brother. Back in 1926, just before she disappeared, Agatha Christie wrote her brother-in-law a letter telling him she was feeling distressed and going to a spa in Yorkshire. Except he didn't really take the letter seriously and apparently burned it, so it was never used to help find her."

"Oh I see." said Claire. "That's similar to what happened to Barbara. She wrote to her brother but that letter also got lost along the way."

"He's got it now though," Lynette said. "I spoke to Niles a few days ago, and we were right. In her letter Barbara tells him she's unhappy and going away for a while, to a hotel in the Blue Mountains. But he never got it, so it was no use to anyone."

"Least of all Arthur and Holly," said Alicia.

"In any case, Niles sounds enormously relieved that she's shown up in one piece, even if it does mean he doesn't get her inheritance. Maybe he's not as bad as I thought. Oh and he swears black and blue that he had no idea his car was used to run you down, Missy. His sister borrowed it under false pretences and he never suspected a thing. Reckons he didn't even notice the dents for a day or two, so just assumed it had happened at the café car park."

She scoffed. "Sure, I believe him. *Not.*"

"Speaking of cars, was there any significance to the book that Barbara left in her Mercedes when she disappeared?" asked Claire. "You know, there was that Poirot novel *The Mystery of the Blue Train.* Was that deliberate?"

"Oh I know!" said Missy, referring back to the book she had been scanning while they talked. "I'd actually picked up on this days ago but didn't think anything of it. That was the book Agatha had started writing around the time she disappeared. She usually dashed books off in a matter of months, but she really struggled with that one, and now we know why—she was going through marital problems at the time. Barbara obviously left it as a clue for us, but we didn't connect the dots."

"I feel like a bit of a dunce to be honest," said Alicia. "It seems so obvious now."

Anders scoffed. "Not at all. I mean, it was a huge stretch for her to think that we would know all the intimate details of Agatha Christie's own disappearance some 90 years ago. That we'd somehow put the two together. I'm stunned that you eventually did. I never would have twigged. Never."

"We are the Murder Mystery Book Club, Anders," said Missy and still he shook his head. "I'm just kicking myself I didn't look up her library file earlier."

"In any case, it didn't really matter," said Alicia, "because she honestly expected her brother to get her letter after a few days and the whole ordeal would be over. All she really wanted was for us to alert the police that she was missing and put Arthur under suspicion. That's why she acted so nervously around him and gave us the idea that he was beating her up—wearing the scarf around her neck, acting all jittery. She knew we were the types to notice these things and would go to the police. And you have to give her credit for that. She was right. If it wasn't for us, Arthur probably never would have said anything, he wouldn't have gone to the cops, the story might never have broken and his reputation never would have got trashed."

"He'd also probably still be alive," said Claire, her head to one side.

"We don't know that, Claire," said Lynette. "Maybe Barbara's disappearance only accelerated what would have happened anyway. Rosa Lopez is a nasty piece of work and there's no way Arthur was going to hide his affair with Wanda forever. She might have found out eventually and still attacked him."

Alicia shuddered. "Guess we'll never know but I can tell you one thing, Barbara swears black and blue that she did not want Arthur dead. That was not her intention. Says she just wanted to teach him a lesson."

"Tell that to the judge," said Perry as he handed around a platter of cheeses and olives.

Anders nodded. "Yes, sounds like justification to me. She led every one of us, including her family and the police force, on a wild-goose chase. She should be punished for it."

"Oh I think she will be," said Alicia. "Roger tells me Ward's considering laying charges of wasting valuable police time."

"And what about *our* valuable time?" demanded Perry, holding the platter towards her now.

"We didn't have to look into it," Alicia reminded him, helping herself to a marinated olive. "It's our own fault for being so bloody nosey."

Claire stood up and poured herself a punch. "I make no apologies for trying to look out for Barbara. I mean, for all we knew, she was a poor, neglected woman who could have been kidnapped."

"I almost wish she had been," hissed Perry who was clearly going to take some time to get over this one. "So tell me, how is little Miss Holly?"

Alicia scrunched her lips to the side. "Not sure. I called her house yesterday to see how she was doing but she was out with friends. I spoke to her aunt Harriet—Arthur's sister has been staying there. Anyway she tells me Holly is relieved her mum's alive, but furious at the same time. Currently not talking to her, and I can't say I blame her."

"Poor kid," said Perry. He clapped his hands suddenly. "Okay gang, Barbara Parlour has taken up more than enough of our time already. Let's get on with the next book club. It's time to get lost in storyland again!"

"Hear, hear!" said Anders.

"Well, before we do," said Alicia, "I have one very important question to ask." They all looked at her. "How are we all feeling about this book club?"

Uncertainty crossed their faces.

"I mean, you're all here and I really appreciate that, but if anyone feels that it's all been a bit much and wants to opt out of the club, well, I wouldn't hold it against you."

Several members laughed and Perry slapped her gently across the shoulder.

"Don't be silly, sweetie!" he said. "I know I've been bitching about Barbara but I haven't had so much excitement since Kylie Minogue came out for Mardi Gras! *Of course* we want to continue it, or at least I do. Well, sans bloody Barbara of course. After her disgraceful behaviour, she's banned for life."

They all nodded enthusiastically and each one gave Alicia a warm smile. When it was Anders' turn to smile she could feel her heart thump through her cotton blouse.

She tried to hide her blush as she retrieved her book from her handbag. "Okay, in that case, I have just one new rule to add to the list."

Again they all looked at her, puzzled.

"Rule number seven: Everybody must show up promptly to each book club. I don't want any more real-life mysteries for a while."

They laughed as they opened *Murder on the Orient Express* and began to discuss…

Three hours later, as the club members gathered their books and bid their farewells out near the front gate, Perry pulled Alicia and Lynette back inside.

"Should I say something to Claire?" he asked and Lynette stared at him, a look of mild panic on her face.

Alicia glanced from her sister to Perry, not quite getting it. Then it dawned on her. "You mean about her fiancé?" He nodded. "No way! No, no, no! Not here," she hissed, "not like this, she'll be mortified. And she'll never want to see you again. Or any of us for that matter. She'll hate us!"

"What? For telling her the truth and saving her from a fate worse than marriage?" Perry snorted loudly. "Charlie's behaviour is putting her health in danger too, you know. I have to say something."

"You're one to talk," she spat and both Perry and Lynette looked at her confused. "Well, it takes two to tango, Perry. You ought to be ashamed of yourself."

"What are you on about?" asked Lynette.

"Perry and Charlie," she said.

"Perry and Charlie what?" asked Perry. He frowned. "You don't think that I... that Charlie and I...?" The frown turned to a look of horror. "I may be desperate these days, darls, but I don't play around with other people's fiancés, and certainly not pseudo straight ones who can't find their way out of the closet. What do you take me for? I have my standards, puh-lease!"

He sat down on the sofa with a humff and Lynette turned on her sister.

"Gee, Alicia, you've got this one all wrong. Perry hasn't been having an affair with Charlie. His flatmate, Jonathan, has."

"Jonathan?"

"Yes, Jonathan Grayson, the author. The one Charlie's been working on the manuscript with."

Alicia sat down with a clunk, too. "Oh my God," she said. "Sorry, Perry, I got it all wrong—"

"Got what all wrong?" asked Claire who had an uncanny ability to walk in at the most inopportune times. She had a silk Hermes scarf wrapped around her glossy black locks now, a clutch purse under one arm and a look of pitiful calm on her face. "Come on you lot, we're all out the front, waiting to say goodbye. What's the hold up?"

Alicia looked at her, unsure what to say, but she didn't have to say anything. Perry had already jumped up, taken

Claire's hands in his and was drawing her back down to the sofa.

"I have some grim news, my sweet, and I think it's about time you heard it."

She looked at him blankly, then up at Alicia and Lynette. They both tried to give her a reassuring smile, but they had a hunch nothing was going to help this news go down any easier. Perry gripped her hands tighter and forced her to look back at him.

"It's about your fiancé."

"Charlie? What about him?"

He took a deep breath. "I say this as a friend, nothing more." Another deep breath. "He's not who you think he is."

She blinked several times then laughed. "Oooh, sounds like another Christie plot. Don't tell me, he's CIA, a *spy*."

Perry shook his head sadly. "Oh if only he was. It's much worse than that, or at least it is for you, I'm afraid." He paused again then said very simply, "He's gay."

At first Claire didn't seem to register what Perry had said, still watching him as though happily waiting for more. Then it must have hit her like a slap across the face because she jumped up and held a hand to her cheek, her eyes flashing with anger.

"What did you just say?"

"I'm sorry, Claire, but I know for a fact that Charlie is gay."

Her jaw dropped. "You are *unbelievable*," she snapped. "First you try and turn Anders—the way you've been flirting with him is outrageous! Now Charlie? Will you stop at no one?" She placed the hand on her hip. "Not everyone bats for your side you know? Some men love women I'll have you know!"

Perry sighed. "I do not doubt that he loves you, Claire, but he loves my flatmate too, I'm afraid, or at least he does whenever he gets a chance." He winced, hadn't meant to sound so crass. "I'm only telling you this because you have a right to know. Your fiancé is a fraud."

He sat back in his chair and sighed again. Lynette stepped towards Claire.

"I'm so sorry, Claire, but he's right, or at least, half right. Charlie is obviously bisexual, but maybe you already knew that?"

"How dare you?" she said, now turning on Lynette. "Charlie is my fiancé. My *fiancé.*" She stopped, gulped hard. "He's my soul mate, we're perfect for each other. Perfect..."

She backed towards the door as if about to flee, so Alicia stepped in this time and held her arm, pulling her back in. "Hear Perry out, Claire. You might not want to hear this, but it's vital that you do."

The anger in her eyes was strong, but there was a glimmer of doubt there, too, and the doubt eventually won out. She stepped back into the room and took a seat across from Perry, her hands neatly entwined in her lap, her beautiful feline eyes not meeting anyone's. Alicia gave Perry the nod. He cleared his throat and began.

"When I first met you, Claire, at the Finlay house for that first Book Club get-together, you quoted your fiancé, Charlie. It was a quote I'd heard from another Charlie only recently: 'You can be the rose between two thorns'."

"So?" she scoffed, staring at the ceiling now. "There must be loads of Charlies who use the same quotes, this is ridiculous."

"Let him finish," whispered Alicia and Claire glanced at her and away.

"Then, later that day, you said your Charlie worked in publishing, and well, that's when I began to wonder. You see, the Charlie I know, the one who uses that exact quote, he works in publishing, too." He held up a hand before she could say anything. "The Charlie I know has been seeing my flatmate, a budding novelist called Jonathan Grayson. They've been lovers for a few months now." He stopped and let the news settle in while he watched her for signs of distress. Claire did not flinch, her expression now vacant.

"I hoped I was wrong, Claire, honestly I did. I'd only met my flatmate's handsome Eurasion lover once, when he said that quote jokingly as he was running out my front door very early one morning. He was talking about a meeting between himself, Jonathan and a book editor called Miller. Ring a bell?"

A look of comprehension crossed Claire's brow but she still couldn't meet his eyes, so he continued. "I met Charlie just one other time, Claire. At your boutique, the evening you introduced us all to your fiancé. And he recognised me, too, of that I am certain. He broke up with Jonathan that same night, just before my flatmate was due to fly to England to check out cover designs for his new book. He didn't explain why. He didn't have to, at least not to me. But Jonno's cut up. He didn't know, either. He fooled you both."

Finally, unable to hold it together any longer, Claire burst into tears and both Alicia and Lynette ran to her, trying to comfort, knowing it would never be enough. Perry produced a box of tissues but Claire was already reaching into her handbag for a cotton handkerchief. It was fringed with lace and monogrammed with her initials.

At this point Missy and Anders strode in, clearly impatient with waiting out front, but before they could say anything Lynette had jumped up and was shooing them back outside, leaving Alicia and Perry to sooth the distressed woman.

"My life was so perfect," she said between sobs. "I had my beautiful boutique, my beautiful boy. My mother even approved of him, and she doesn't approve of *anyone*. We were going to buy an apartment in Elizabeth Bay, one of those beautiful art deco places, you know the ones?"

They both nodded and she continued staring at them wistfully.

"I first met him at the shop, you know. He came in looking for a fedora and I thought he was the bees knees. He didn't flirt with me like so many men do… God, how could I not have seen it?"

Alicia shook her head. "Just because he doesn't flirt and dresses well, doesn't mean he has to be gay," she said but Perry rolled his eyes at her, not quite agreeing.

"He was just so polite and chivalrous and…"

"And all the things we women expect from a man because we read too much bloody fiction," Alicia said. "He looked like the man of your dreams, Claire. But he wasn't. He's not."

Claire nodded and, after a few minutes, blew her nose delicately and wiped the tears from her eyes. "You know, I ought to thank you, Perry." She gave him a sideways glare. "I suspected something, of course. How could I not? I just wasn't ready to face it, yet. That's all." She sniffed. "All those late nights at work 'correcting proofs', all those long dinners 'discussing the marketing campaign'. Ha! I did suspect, of course I suspected…" She gulped hard. "But it's hard to accept an affair with another woman… let alone a man. It's just… it's *disgusting*." She stopped and looked at Perry, mortified. "I'm sorry, I don't mean that you, that being gay is disgusting… I… I just mean that the betrayal is so much worse."

He squeezed her hand. "Of course it is, sweetie. I understand that. He lied to you, he lied to Jonathan, and he lied to himself. I'm not sure which one is worse but he's not worth these tears, Claire, you do know that?"

She sniffed again, dabbing at her nose gently with her hanky. She nodded. Then, oddly, she laughed, a kind of giggly girlie laugh. "Missy was right," she said when she'd recovered. "Four years is a *ridiculously* long time to be engaged. I should've twigged after two!" She giggled again. "She knows more about human nature than we give her credit for, that woman."

Of this they could all agree.

"You going to be okay?" Alicia asked as she helped her to her feet.

"Oh yes," said Claire, placing her hanky in her bag and straightening the scarf on her head. "No mere mortal is going to destroy me. Not even Charlie what's-his-name!"

And with that she strode out of the room, head held high, her future no longer on hold, waiting for a man she could never have. Claire's life was back in her own hands again, and there was a certain freedom in that, at least there was for Claire Hargreaves.

Alicia watched her go and then turned to give Perry a hug. "Good work," she said. "That was brave."

"And apologies, perhaps?" he said, pouting.

She laughed. "And yes I am very, very sorry for suspecting you of something so hideous. Looks like Charlie Szeto and Barbara Parlour would make a good match. They're both experts at fooling everyone around them."

"Not quite everyone," he said, locking his elbow through hers and leading her back outside. "Thank God for you and me, my darling. The world would be in such a muddle without us."

~~~~~~~~

Later that night as they made their way to bed, Lynette stopped Alicia on the stairs and asked, "Are you okay? You've had such a huge couple of weeks. And I'm not just talking about Barbara Parlour."

Alicia nodded. "I'm fine, thanks, Lynny. Exhausted but so glad it's all over. Barbara might be vile, but I'm also glad she's still alive, if only for Holly's sake. As for Charlie Szeto—good riddance!" She sighed. "It's horrible what's happened to Claire but, like she said, she'll survive and she'll be stronger for it, too."

"And what about the dishy doc?" Lynette raised her eyebrows a few times, teasingly.

"What about him?"
~~~~~~~~

"Well, what's happening, woman? It's pretty bloody obvious the guy likes you. Are you finally going to connect, or you going to keep playing coy until you're middle-aged?"

Alicia laughed. "I honestly don't know what's happening with Anders," she said. "I'm open to it and I've told him that. I think it's another case of not rushing things, seeing what happens down the track. He's coming out of a pretty horrible marriage breakdown."

She hadn't told Lynette all the ugly details. It was hard keeping secrets from her sister but Anders had begged her to keep it private, so she had honoured that.

Luckily, her sister wasn't as curious as her and simply said, "Fair enough. Oh, one other thing, I was thinking of getting started on the next book for Book Club." She produced a beat-up, paperback copy of *Cat Among the Pigeons*, Missy's choice this time. "Found this on our book shelf. Forgot we even had a copy. You want first dibs or can I get cracking on it?"

Alicia ran a hand through her shaggy blond hair and yawned. "You go right ahead, Lynette. I might give mysteries a miss tonight. I think my exhausted *'grey cells'* could do with a rest."

"Well, sweet dreams," Lynette said, padding off towards her bedroom.

"But let me know as soon as you're done," Alicia called out to her. "Tomorrow's another day, after all."

They both laughed as they bid each other good night.

~~ the end ~~

ACKNOWLEDGEMENTS

Special thanks to Sophie Hamley, who first took a punt on
me and encouraged me to fly.

Thanks to Elaine Rivers, the best Beta reader a writer could
wish for. She is full of positivity and insight,
and doesn't miss a beat.

And finally, thanks, as always, to Christian who encourages
and enables my creativity, even when the coffers are low
and the kids are chaotic.

ALSO BY THE AUTHOR

Killer Twist (Ghostwriter Mystery 1)

KILLER TWIST is the first stand-alone mystery in the popular 'amateur women sleuths' series featuring feisty ghostwriter Roxy Parker.

"A fun read with a well defined protagonist, easy style, lots of local flavour."
Parents' Little Black Book @ Amazon

"Roxy Parker is a compelling character and I couldn't help but adore her. A great cozy. I enjoyed it immensely and will be ordering the second."
Rhonda @Amazon

After the Ferry: A Gripping Psychological Novel

IT'S the 1990s, pre-mobile phones, and a young traveller must make a terrifying choice: Will she jump ship with a seductive stranger? Or stay cocooned on the Greek ferry with friends and miss what could be the love of her life?

"A great read…suspenseful and very well written. I highly recommend this book."
Heather, Booksprout

calarmer.com